www.andymcnab.co.uk
www.rbooks.co.uk

Also by Andy McNab:

BOY SOLDIER (with Robert Rigby)

Boy Soldier

Payback

Avenger

Meltdown

For adults:

Bravo Two Zero

Immediate Action

Seven Troop

Spoken from the Front

Aggressor

Brute Force

Crisis Four

Crossfire

Dark Winter

Deep Black

Firewall

Last Light

Liberation Day

Recoil

Remote Control

SAS covert ops commander
ANDY McNAB

DOUBLEDAY

DROPZONE
A DOUBLEDAY BOOK
Hardback: 978 0 385 61710 9
Trade paperback: 978 0 385 61697 3

Published in Great Britain by Doubleday,
an imprint of Random House Children's Books
A Random House Group Company

This edition published 2010

1 3 5 7 9 10 8 6 4 2

The Random House Group Limited supports the Forest Stewardship
Council (FSC), the leading international forest certification organization.
All our titles that are printed on Greenpeace-approved FSC-certified paper
carry the FSC logo. Our paper procurement policy can be found at
www.rbooks.co.uk/environment.

Mixed Sources
Product group from well-managed
forests and other controlled sources
www.fsc.org Cert no. TT-COC-2139
© 1996 Forest Stewardship Council
FSC

Set in DIN

RANDOM HOUSE CHILDREN'S BOOKS
61–63 Uxbridge Road, London W5 5SA

www.**kids**at**randomhouse**.co.uk
www.**rbooks**.co.uk

Addresses for companies within The Random House Group Limited can be
found at: www.randomhouse.co.uk/offices.htm

THE RANDOM HOUSE GROUP Limited Reg. No. 954009

A CIP catalogue record for this book is available from the British Library.

Printed in the UK by CPI Mackays, Chatham, ME5 8TD

GLOSSARY

AAD	Automatic Activation Device: senses rate of descent and altitude – mechanically activates reserve parachute if a skydiver passes below a set altitude at a high rate of descent.
A/C	Aircraft.
Accuracy	Also known as 'precision landing'. Competition discipline in which the skydiver tries to land on a target three centimetres in diameter.
AFF	Accelerated Freefall training, comprising freefall jumps of forty seconds or longer, accompanied by a qualified jumpmaster.
AGL	Above Ground Level. Altitudes are in reference either to Ground Level or Sea Level (MSL). Skydivers always use AGL when referring to altitude.
Airspeed	Speed of a flying object through the air.
Altimeter	Device indicating altitude.
Base	Core around which a formation skydive is built. Can be a single person or a group.
Body position	Freefall body posture.
Boogie	Gathering of skydivers.
Bounce	To land at unsurvivable speed. Also to frap, or go in.
Box man	A neutral, face-to-earth body position in which the arms form right angles at shoulder and elbow, and the legs are spread at about forty-five degrees from the long axis and bent forty-five degrees at the knees. Generally considered the ideal position for formation skydiving.
Brakes	The brake lines of the canopy are also steering lines. Used together, they slow the parachute. Used independently, they result in a turn.
Break off	To cease formation skydiving by tracking away from the formation prior to deploying the canopy.

Burble	An area of low air pressure above a descending skydiver caused either by them in freefall or by their canopy in flight.
Call	Time remaining until you are to board the aircraft or jump out of it.
Canopy	Another name for parachute.
Crabbing	Canopy flown at an angle sideways to the ambient wind, resulting in a path across the ground that is sideways as well as forwards.
Creep	Practising formation skydiving sequences while lying on a creeper.
Creeper	A board with wheels on which a skydiver lies to simulate freefall manoeuvres.
Cut away	To release the main parachute. Standard emergency procedure prior to deploying the reserve.
Dirt dive	Skydive rehearsed on the ground.
Drogue	In a tandem jump, a drogue parachute is released shortly after exiting the aircraft to reduce the speed of descent. It is later used to deploy the main canopy.
Dropzone/DZ	Skydiving landing zone.
Exit weight	Total weight of jumper, equipment and clothing.
Fall rate	Speed at which a skydiver falls. Matching fall rate is essential to successful formation skydiving. This is done with jumpsuits, weights and body position.
Flare	To pull down the brakes of the canopy, thus increasing the angle of attack and reducing the descent rate.
Floater	Skydivers who leave the plane before the base are called floaters since they must use a slow fall rate to get up to the base. Floating also refers to an exit position outside the plane.
Formation	1) A freefall skydiving formation of more than one jumper. 2) A flight of more than one jump plane.
Freestyle	Acrobatic individual skydiving.

FS	Formation Skydiving. Skydivers attempt to go through a predetermined sequence of freefall formations.
GPS	Global Positioning System.
Grippers	Handholds built onto formation skydiving jumpsuits to make the suits easier to hold onto.
Hand deploy	To activate a canopy manually by deploying the pilot chute as opposed to pulling a ripcord.
Harness/ container	Webbing/fabric holding main and reserve canopies to the skydiver.
Heading	Direction in which the aircraft, skydiver or parachute is facing.
Hook knife	Small knife carried in jumpsuit or on rig to cut lines or webbing.
Jump run	Flight path taken by the jump plane.
Jumpsuit	An overall designed for skydiving.
Main	The primary canopy.
PLF	Parachute Landing Fall. A technique used to minimize injury during rough landings, a PLF distributes the landing shock along feet, calves, thighs, hips and shoulders.
Reserve	Auxiliary parachute carried on every intentional parachute jump.
Rig	Slang for the entire canopy, including main and reserve canopies and the harness/container.
Rigger	Someone who is qualified to pack and check the rig.
Ripcord	Deployment system on all reserves and most student parachutes. The ripcord is a piece of cable with a handle at one end and a pin at the other. When pulled, the pin comes out of the closing loop holding the container shut, and the pilot chute is released.
RSL	Reserve Static Line. A backup device for automatically deploying the reserve if the skydiver cuts away. Only effective in malfunctions where the main canopy is at least partially deployed.
RV	Rendezvous.

Skygod	Skydiver whose ego has grown faster than his ability.
Stall	When the angle of attack becomes too high to sustain lift.
Steering lines	The lines that run from the steering toggles to the trailing edge of the canopy.
Steering toggles	Handles attached to the ends of the steering lines.
Swoop	**1)** To dive down to a formation or individual in freefall. **2)** To aggressively approach the landing area in order to produce a long, flat flare and exciting landing.
Tandem	Two skydivers share a rig, one of whom is in a separate harness that attaches to the front of the other harness.
Terminal velocity	The speed at which drag matches gravity, resulting in a constant fall rate. Generally terminal velocity for formation skydiving is 120–135 mph.
Track	Body position that creates a high forward speed. Used to approach or veer away from other skydivers in freefall.
Wave off	Before deployment a skydiver makes a clearly defined arm motion to indicate to others nearby that he is about to open his canopy.
Wing loading	The weight a canopy can carry in relation to its surface area.
Wuffo	Slang for a person who doesn't jump.

CHARACTERS

Ethan

Driven by a fierce determination to make something of his life, Ethan will push himself to the limit, face his fears head on and stand by his friends no matter what. Skydiving is just the opportunity he's been looking for, and he doesn't want to be simply good, he's out to be the best. Period.

Johnny

Quick with the witty comments and fast in the air, he's a living, breathing definition of 'adrenaline junkie'. But beneath the smart-arse persona lies a seriously capable operator who doesn't know the meaning of the word quit. His only problem is that he likes to go it alone, and that doesn't always work well with a team.

Luke

The one the rest of the team depend on to make sure everything is safe and sorted. He's quiet, methodical, and all about the detail. When it comes to skydiving, if Luke doesn't know it, it's not worth knowing.

Kat

Pretty, athletic and impulsive, she loves being that rare thing among her peers – a girl who skydives. She does it because she knows she's good at it and because it makes her sexy as hell.

Natalya

A serious girl with a mysterious past buried deep somewhere in eastern Europe. No one quite knows where she came from or how she ended up skydiving in the UK.

Sam

A world-class skydiver, skilled undercover operator and exceptional soldier, Sam is tough, serious and a natural leader. He has a long history with the SAS – having led operations across the globe – and he hasn't exactly retired. He's responsible for bringing the team together in the first place. His word is law. And he's someone you really don't want to cross.

Skydiving

You jump from a plane at 12,000 feet, reach speeds of over 120 mph, then glide in under your canopy, gazing at the most amazing view of the earth you'll ever see. Adrenaline never tasted this good.
Warning: **dangerously addictive.**

BASE jumping

You don't jump from a plane, but from a fixed object closer to the ground. BASE stands for Building, Antenna, Span (bridge or arch), Earth. Unlike skydiving, a BASE jumper rarely reaches terminal velocity (120 mph).
Warning: **this is the closest you can get to falling to your death without dying.**

Prologue

'What do you mean Ryan's gone? Explain.'

Gabe's voice was hard and businesslike, but then when was he anything else? On the other end of the line, phone against his ear, Sam leaned back in his chair. Outside his window the moon stared back like a bullet hole in a bed sheet.

'He's not been seen at FreeFall for two weeks,' he said. 'He's missed God knows how many jumps. It's not like him at all and that's what worries me. Even if he does come back . . .' Sam let his voice trail off in frustration. He'd invested so much time and effort in the whole project and Ryan's unexplained disappearance had brought it to a dead stop.

'And you've no idea where he is, where he's gone?'

'No,' said Sam, shaking his head, despite being alone in his office. 'The kid's a ghost. That's why we picked him, remember?'

Gabe fell silent.

Sam waited patiently.

Then came the reply. 'Find a replacement.'

Sam laughed, couldn't help it. 'You really think it's that simple?'

'No,' said Gabe. 'I don't.'

And Sam believed him.

'Look,' said Gabe, his voice almost losing its edge, 'I know you can't just walk down a high street and pick someone out of a crowd, but we need five in this team for the whole thing to work, not four.'

'I know,' said Sam.

Ryan had been the last; he'd have brought the team to the magic five they were looking for. If he'd made the grade with his skydiving then he'd have been told the truth about the team – and invited to join. Sam was sure Ryan would've jumped at the chance. He'd seemed perfect: independent, bright, driven, a natural skydiver, and with no family ties to speak of. So why the hell had he just vanished?

Sam was pissed off. Ryan's disappearance meant he'd got it wrong. And Sam never got things wrong.

'Did I say something funny?'

'I doubt it,' said Sam. Gabe had lots of qualities, he thought, but a sense of humour wasn't one of them.

'Then do it,' Gabe continued. 'Anyway, we had our eyes on two possibles originally. What about the other?'

2

'I never had my eyes on two,' said Sam. 'You did. I found Ryan. You found Jake.'

'So focus on Jake,' said Gabe, like he wasn't expecting an argument.

'You've read my report?'

'Of course I've read it,' replied Gabe, sounding more than a little irritated. 'And he's ticking the boxes.'

'But not necessarily the right ones,' Sam cut back. 'Jake's too interested in himself. There's no way I'm bringing him onto the team until I'm absolutely sure. You know that. And it's my word on this – that's the agreement.'

'You saying I'm a bad judge of character?'

'You picked me,' said Sam, and the smile that flickered across his face was anything but warm.

For a moment, neither man spoke.

Sam broke the silence. 'So what about Ryan?'

'If he's gone, he's gone,' came the reply. 'Unsuitable. We're better off knowing now than halfway through an operation. I'll try and trace him, find out what happened. But he's no longer your concern. Anything else?'

Sam knew the conversation was over. 'No,' he said.

'Good,' said the voice. 'Keep me posted on the team – and on Jake.'

The phone went dead. No goodbyes, no farewells, just silence.

Sam replaced the receiver and leaned forwards, resting his arms on his desk. In the gloom of his office, lit as it was by only a simple desk lamp, Sam stood up and walked over to a filing cabinet. The thing looked tired and beaten, like it had been dropped just a few too many times off the back of a truck. He slid open the second drawer, pulled out a thick folder and flicked through it.

From the pages of the files inside, the photographs of four faces stared out: two male, two female. Of the males, one was serious, collected, had eyes that looked like they could spot a flea on a rat's arse at a couple of miles. The other had a wildness about him, like he was ready to jump out of the photo, steal your girlfriend and ride off into the sunset. The girls were just as different. One had haunted eyes in a pale face that showed nothing but determination. The other looked like she wanted to take on the world in a bar fight, and come out not just the winner but with her makeup intact and not a hair out of place.

Sam picked up another two files. Jake and the missing Ryan stared up at him. But it wasn't Ryan's disappearance that bothered Sam; it was what he'd do if Jake didn't make the grade. And, deep down, Sam had a hunch he wouldn't. Not just because Jake's attitude was all wrong, but because if a mission went tits up and the team were facing a total shit storm, Sam's gut instinct told him that Jake would bottle it. He was prepared to give Jake the training, but if he didn't shape up there was no way in hell Sam was going to put the team at risk.

After a few moments, Sam replaced the files in the cabinet and walked to his office door. Reaching out, he flicked the room to darkness, then slipped away into the night. But one thought haunted him: when Jake screwed up, just how the hell was he going to find anyone else?

1

The yell from above shattered the night like a brick through a window.

Ethan jarred to a halt, earphones halfway to his head. He'd been out for another late-night walk to clear his mind. It hadn't worked.

Looking up, he saw someone falling from the roof of the block of flats he called home; a silhouette racing towards him, getting bigger, closer, on target for a direct hit he knew would kill him.

His breath caught in his throat.

His voice didn't.

'Shit . . .'

Keeping his eyes pinned on the figure, Ethan quickly

pulled himself out of its way, turning back up the street to a vandalized bus shelter that was tagged to hell.

Suddenly another sound filled the darkness, like bed sheets flapping in the wind, followed by a whoop and a shout of 'Yeah – nailed it!' and the silhouette exploded in the sky, expanding from a black smudge to a black oblong. Its descent slowed dramatically. It drifted away from Ethan, riding wind and moonlight.

Stunned and staring, he watched as the shape floated down just ahead of him, a human figure dangling underneath what he now guessed was a parachute. It landed gently, silently.

Ethan couldn't believe it: some idiot had just parachuted from the top of the block of flats – *his* block of flats. He watched as the figure rapidly gathered in the parachute to nothing, bundling it up as though rolling the night into a ball, then jogged towards him.

A van in the road next to him sparked to life. Another figure loomed out of the darkness, emerging from the far side of the vehicle, video camera in hand. As the van door swung open, music blared out into the night, a barrage of heavy guitar and drums.

The idiot with the parachute stopped in front of Ethan. Ethan recognized him from the year above at school: he had been in the upper sixth; Ethan was in the lower. His hair was long, blond, wild; Ethan's was night-time black, and sprang from his head like a frozen explosion. He had given up trying to do something with it years ago. He almost felt the same way about his life, but something kept him looking for the right thing to do with it. He wanted a purpose – he just hadn't found it yet.

'Totally awesome, Johnny!' yelled the van driver, pointing the video camera at the guy with the parachute standing next to Ethan. Ethan turned and found himself providing an involuntary wave for the movie. Idiot.

The parachutist Ethan now knew as Johnny tapped him on the shoulder and said, 'Pen?'

Ethan shook his head.

Johnny ran over to the van, reached inside, came back. He grabbed Ethan's hand and wrote on it.

'Check this in about an hour,' he said, indicating the scribble on Ethan's palm. 'You're famous!'

Ethan stared at his hand and the MySpace address now scrawled on it.

It was a stupid question, but Ethan couldn't help himself: 'Don't people usually jump out of planes rather than off buildings?'

Johnny grinned. 'This is BASE jumping. You do skydiving first, then this – same deal, less room for error.'

'More chance of death,' said Ethan. 'Why do you do it?'

Johnny leaned a smile in close. 'Life's too short not to,' he said.

Then, pulling the parachute in with him, he jumped into the van next to the driver.

Doors slammed, and the road swallowed the van.

Quiet. It was all suddenly so quiet.

Ethan stood there for a moment, staring at the space where the van had been, watching flashbacks in his mind of what he'd just witnessed. The adrenaline still surged through him; he could feel it like pinpricks in his fingers. And he hadn't even been the one doing the jump. He tried to imagine what it had felt like for Johnny.

Just when he was wondering what to do with his life, searching for a purpose, some nutball had jumped off his roof. For some reason Ethan couldn't explain, it changed everything.

Staring at the web address on his hand, he headed home.

2

'Ethan?'

He heard his sister, Jo, calling him as he reached his bedroom door.

He turned back up the hall and went into the kitchen. Like the rest of the flat, it was small and functional. If a surface could be used, it was. Shelves sagged under the weight of tins jostling for position. Squeezed in here and there were photos of Ethan and Jo and their mum. Dad wasn't anywhere. The only thing attached to the wall that wasn't a shelf or a photo was one of Jo's paintings. Ethan didn't understand it, or even like it that much, but he admired it. Jo had always been into her art and knew it was what she wanted to do with her life. He envied that. After school, Ethan's future was confused. He hadn't a clue what to do with it. And that scared him a little. He often wished he had something that interested him in the same way art did Jo. But nothing had ever really grabbed him and refused to let go.

The earlier shots of Jo showed a happy girl with flyaway hair. The later ones showed a girl dressed in black, hiding behind make-up. Ethan smiled – his sister's approach to fashion had always been interesting. She was as much a piece of art as the stuff she painted.

Ethan looked at the pictures of his mum. She mostly looked tired but happy, though nowadays she looked just tired, he thought. And he knew whose fault that was. They all did: two kids, two jobs and an arse for a husband – it was a killer. Ethan felt the anger rise in him as a picture of his dad snagged in his mind. If there was one reason to find a purpose in life, then it was to show that bastard that nothing he could say or do would ever affect Ethan again.

Jo was by the fridge, hiding behind her long black fringe. 'You're home, then,' she said. 'Hungry?'

Ethan nodded. 'Dad still out? Shame he comes back, if you ask me.'

Jo took a bowl of pasta out of the fridge, put it in the microwave and turned the dial to heat it for two minutes. 'Mum made this for us,' she said. 'She asked where you were. I couldn't tell her because I didn't know.'

Ethan tried to ignore her disapproving look. 'I meant to leave a note,' he said.

Jo sighed. 'She's worried about you.'

'Oh,' was all Ethan could manage, the guilt nagging at him again. The last time he'd seen his mum had been two days ago; somehow their paths hadn't crossed – him getting home late after his last exam, her heading out for the night shift.

The microwave pinged. Jo got out a bowl of steaming pasta and handed it to him, then put in another bowl for herself.

She turned back to him. 'She thinks you're too much like Dad – you know that, don't you?'

The words stung Ethan. 'He's a waster, Jo,' he said, spitting bitterness with every word. 'All he does is drink money away – or lose it at the bookies.'

'Think I don't know that?' said Jo. 'She's worried you're going the same way.'

Just talking about his dad made Ethan's blood boil. He found it hard to stay calm. 'Look,' he said, 'just because I'm not sure what I'm doing with my life doesn't mean I'm going to end up like him. I'm not going to be a jobless alcoholic. I'll have my A-levels. Dad's got nothing.'

Jo didn't answer. The microwave pinged. She took out her pasta.

'Thanks for your support,' said Ethan. 'Really.'

Jo shrugged and started to eat.

Ethan stood there in silence. He hated his dad; always had. He was a bully. And now Ethan was seventeen his dad had started to really push him around. Ethan had nearly lost it with him more than once, but his mum had always stepped in, calmed things down.

'Where did you go, anyway?' asked Jo.

'Out,' said Ethan. 'Trying to clear my head. Everyone I know seems to have a plan for what they're doing, where they're going, but I . . .' His voice trailed off. Then he said, 'I keep thinking about the Royal Marines.'

'Dad would hate that,' said Jo.

Ethan smiled. 'Exactly.'

'Look, I know you're not like Dad. But Mum worries, Ethan, you know that.'

'I know. And I promise I'll never be like him. Ever.'

'OK,' said Jo. She patted him on the arm and headed for her bedroom.

Ethan went to his room. It was pretty bare except for a few posters from *Kerrang!*, the computer on the desk in the corner, and his bed. Clothes and magazines littered the floor like rubbish washed up on a beach.

He kicked a space between some magazines and put the pasta down on the worn carpet. Then he flicked on his computer. It was old and took a while to warm up, but soon the screen flared blue and he logged on.

The myspace page loaded and Ethan found himself staring at Johnny's face. He clicked the MOST RECENT icon. The screen filled with a shaky image – a skyline he recognized as the one outside his window. Ethan realized this must've been what the bloke in the van had been filming: Johnny BASE jumping from the roof above his flat. The image blurred in a rush as a whoop and a yell burst from his speakers: the sound of Johnny leaping into nothing. The image changed again, slowed, and Ethan watched the view float by as Johnny glided to the ground in front of the flats.

In the next scene, Ethan saw himself standing next to Johnny, shock on his face, waving.

Flicking through Johnny's myspace pages, Ethan surfed numerous films taken by Johnny and his friends. In all of them, Johnny was grinning and laughing as he jumped off things, or out of planes. Ethan lost track of time, clicking on picture after picture, movie after movie. And he saw something in Johnny's face that he wanted for himself. Johnny looked so alive, like every minute mattered, counted for something. Ethan's life had never really felt like that. It was almost as though he'd spent it in a waiting room with no idea what he was actually waiting *for*. But perhaps it was time to try and change that.

He went back to his pasta. It was cold but he ate it anyway. Mum's food always tasted good, no matter what it was.

As Ethan finished off the pasta, he clicked a link from Johnny's site. The screen jumped to an image of blue sky filled with skydivers. Underneath it were the words FREEFALL SKYDIVING CENTRE, followed by an address – it was the old army base just out of town. Ethan clicked through the site, drawn in by more images of people leaping from planes, faces alight with excitement.

Something caught his eye. It was a job ad: *Help needed for summer season. Bad pay, insane customers, interesting hours. Discounted lessons available.*

It was late, but Ethan phoned anyway, and left a message. He put down the phone and sat back in his chair. Something about what he'd just done fizzed through him. He didn't know why but it seemed important, like he'd made a move that mattered, changed something. OK, so it was just a job, but what else was he going to do with his summer?

3

'Stand over there and smile at the birdie.'

The security guard at the entrance to the old army base was pointing at an X on the wall, bullet-to-the-brain high. Ethan did as he was told and walked over to it, resting his head against the X and turning to face a webcam. He smiled at the stuffed parrot sitting on top of it.

The security guard took Ethan's picture, and a few moments later handed him his pass. It was a terrible photo, but then Ethan never liked pictures of himself.

'The jump centre's first left at the mini-roundabout,' said the security guard. 'Follow the road round, take the second right. If you get lost, look for people falling out of the sky and listen for the screams.'

Ethan didn't know whether to smile or not, so he just nodded and headed back to his bike. He still couldn't believe he'd got an interview for the job at FreeFall. Someone called Sam had phoned and told him to come in as soon as possible, preferably that day. So Ethan had done just that, gobbling his breakfast and racing out into the morning.

He jumped back on his bike, clicking through the gears as he followed the guard's instructions. The guy was right – people were literally falling from the sky.

Ethan watched as parachutes exploded into life above him. Reds and yellows and blues studded the sky as skydivers drifted downwards. Some people, riding parachutes no bigger than large kites, swooped down to earth, spiralling fast, banking hard, slamming through the air at an impossible speed. Others, with much larger chutes, glided along, gentle as eagles. Ethan noticed how some chutes were carrying two people strapped together. All those arms and legs made them look like huge black spiders.

As he stared, Ethan wondered what it felt like to jump out of a plane. He remembered the BASE jumper, Johnny, and how his eyes had seemed wildly alive. As parachutes floated down, he imagined being up there himself, leaping from a plane, plummeting to earth.

His stomach somersaulted. Would he do it? Hell, yeah – you bet he would.

He'd never be able to afford it, though.

And with that thought suddenly dulling everything, Ethan pedalled on.

* * *

15

Leaving his bike in the car park, Ethan walked past a cabin that contained both the reception and shop, and found himself on an area of tarmac between some old aircraft hangars and a large green field where the skydivers were landing. He turned to watch a few more come in, the hangars now behind him, then turned back to get his bearings. The place was Saturday-morning busy. Everywhere he looked, people were either walking with nervous purpose and even more nervous smiles, or gazing anxiously up into the sky as skydivers continued to fall out of it. Ethan made his way through the crowds towards a building to the right of the hangars with the word CAFÉ written on the door. Beyond it he spotted a number of skydivers on a patch of grass. They were wrestling with their parachutes – laying them out on the grass, sorting and untangling the lines, then packing them into what looked like daysacks.

As Ethan pushed on through, a motorbike pulled up in front of him. The rider pulled off his helmet, grinned at Ethan and slid off the bike.

It was Johnny.

Ethan waved and nodded a smile.

Johnny propped up his bike and came over. 'Knew I'd see you at the DZ,' he said.

'DZ?' asked Ethan.

'The dropzone,' said Johnny. 'If you want the full definition, then it's a column of airspace around a central point on the ground where you land when skydiving.' He winked. 'Landing area to you and me.'

'Right,' said Ethan, and turned to watch as a skydiver flew in.

'Looks easy from the ground,' said Johnny. 'Doing it at a hundred and twenty mph is a little more difficult.'

He quickly pulled off his biking overalls. Underneath he was wearing some kind of boiler suit, albeit one that looked a lot more cool than something you'd wear to fix your car. It was black and red, with slim silver pads stitched at elbow and knee, stretching up and down the outside of each arm and leg. Johnny turned to a bag strapped on the back of his bike, and pulled out a black helmet, visor down, and what looked like an enormous watch.

'I checked out your MySpace page,' said Ethan. 'It was awesome.'

Now there was a word he never used, and it sat in his mouth like a sour gobstopper.

Johnny grinned. 'Of course it was – it's about me! Here to have a go yourself?'

Ethan shook his head, amazed at Johnny's impressive self-confidence. 'I'd love to, but I'm here about the job,' he said. 'You know where Sam is?'

'Through that door,' said Johnny, pointing at a flat-roofed building attached to the side of the old hangar. 'Just follow the signs for the office. You'll find it easily enough.'

'Cheers,' said Ethan, and made to walk away, but Johnny called after him. He turned to see Johnny pointing upwards as a skydiver howled past, terrifyingly close to the ground.

'It's only a matter of time, you know,' Johnny said.

Ethan watched the skydiver land almost silently, then looked back at Johnny, who grinned.

'Life's too short not to,' he told Ethan.

* * *

Following Johnny's instructions, Ethan headed for the door. It slid open across a worn carpet with a half-moon scratched into it. The room was basic and a little shabby, Ethan thought as he stepped inside, but it was unbelievably well ordered. A pair of filing cabinets stood against one wall, a well-stocked bookcase against another. A TV was fixed to one wall, streaming Sky News. The other walls were covered with skydiving pictures and photographs rather than wall-paper. Some of them were military: soldiers in places Ethan had only ever seen on posters in the windows of adventure travel shops.

But Ethan only noticed these details later, because in front of him, sitting at a large, organized desk, was one of the most imposing men he had ever seen. His hair was shaved close to his head – slightly longer on top – and his sleeves were rolled up, revealing tattoos. His shoulders were broad, his face hard and stern. Small scars criss-crossed the skin around his left eye; a bigger one extended under his right ear and part way across his throat.

So this must be Sam, thought Ethan. *Holy shit*.

The man saw him, stood up and reached out with his right hand. Ethan took it and found it was like being held by a vice lined with sandpaper; the skin was rough and calloused, the grip ferociously strong.

'I'm Ethan Blake,' said Ethan. 'I'm here about—'

'The job?' said the man. 'Yes. Sit.'

Ethan sat on the only other chair in the room.

'CV?'

Ethan handed it over.

'Experience?'

Ethan remembered what the career adviser at school had said – something about using buzz words, key phrases that employers pick up on, that make you stand out above the rest.

'I've got my food hygiene certificate,' he said, trying to sound confident. 'And I've worked in a number of high street retailers. Lots of customer-facing work. I was promoted to—'

The man cut in: 'Why aren't you working there now?'

Ethan spluttered an answer – something about needing a change, wanting to do something different. It wasn't the whole truth, just some of it. He didn't think now was the time to admit that the jobs had bored him to tears.

The man was silent for a moment and Ethan realized he still hadn't introduced himself. Perhaps it wasn't Sam? It could be anyone. Who was he talking to?

'Why do you want this job?'

Ethan was silent for a moment, thinking.

'This is a skydiving centre,' the man went on. 'People only come here if they've got a sense of purpose, even if that purpose is simply to jump. I don't do layabouts or slackers. You want to waste your time, then you leave right now. So, do you have a purpose, Ethan? Well?'

For a few seconds Ethan didn't know what to say. Then a picture of his dad lying passed out on the sofa flashed into his mind – along with a reason for being there. It made total sense. 'I don't want to waste my summer,' he said at last, almost with relief, as though hearing the words made him realize just how true they were. 'And I'm thinking of joining the Royal Marines. I figured working here I'd meet some interesting people, learn some relevant skills . . .'

The man wrote something down, then looked up again. Ethan could feel his eyes drilling into him like they were searching for something. 'Where did you find out about the job?'

'Your website.'

The man raised an eyebrow. 'You skydive?'

Ethan shook his head. 'No. I bumped into someone who does. His MySpace site had a link.'

'Johnny?'

Ethan nodded.

'Hmmm . . .'

Silence.

'When can you start?'

Ethan looked up, surprised. 'Pardon?'

'Ignoring the fact that the deadline for applications expired a week ago,' said the man, 'when can you start? I need someone immediately.'

Ethan felt a smile spreading across his face. He opened his mouth to speak, but was cut off.

'You busy today?'

'No,' said Ethan.

'You are now,' the man told him. He stood up and offered Ethan his hand once again. 'I'm Sam,' he said. 'I run FreeFall. Welcome aboard.'

Unable to find anything to say, Ethan grinned and shook Sam's hand. Once again he noticed the strength of the grip. But there was something else that struck him. It was the way Sam had said, 'Welcome aboard.' It was as though he really meant it, like it was one of the most important things he could say to anyone.

'Wait in the café and I'll sort out the paperwork,' said Sam.

At last Ethan managed a 'Thanks, that's great.'

Sam turned. He wasn't smiling. 'Survive your first week, and I'll believe you.'

Sam wasted no time in getting Ethan known around the centre, introducing him to far too many people for Ethan to remember all their faces, never mind their names. The job, Sam explained, required Ethan to be available across the centre to help out whenever and wherever necessary. And no sooner had he learned the ropes in one area than he was whisked off to another. By the end of the day Ethan had taken bookings, sorted out DVDs of people's first skydives and static line jumps, guided groups from the hangars to the DZ, watched the training for a tandem skydive, manned the tills in the shop, sold a couple of skydiving rigs, called groups to their jump over the tannoy system, and washed dishes for Nancy, who ran the café. Everyone had been friendly from the off, particularly Nancy, who was plump, but wore it proudly, like it was an advert for her food.

It was soon early evening and Ethan was sweeping the yard area in front of the hangar when Sam came over. He stood, arms folded, looking at Ethan.

'Well?'

Ethan stopped sweeping. 'It's cool,' he said, and meant it. 'It's an amazing place. Thanks for giving me the job.'

'Don't get all Hollywood on me,' said Sam. 'No one else applied. I'll see you tomorrow. Eight o'clock.'

* * *

That night Ethan drifted off to sleep with his mind full of the dozens of faces, young and old, he'd seen happily throwing themselves out of planes.

Whatever it was about skydiving, about Sam's freefall centre – *about Sam* – that made them do it, he wanted some of it for himself.

He spent the next six hours and eight minutes dreaming of falling through the sky.

4

'It's for my birthday,' said the middle-aged man at the counter. Ethan was taking bookings at the FreeFall reception. It was early in the morning and people were flooding in to head off into the sky. He wished he was one of them.

Ethan had had a busy few days since taking the job and, with the week drawing to a close, was only now beginning to settle into the place, get a feel for how to do things – and for how to *not* sound like a total tit when anyone asked him what skydiving was all about. He could now tell people what happened, what the training involved, what the equipment was. Even his mum and his sister had been impressed – not just because he had a decent summer job, but because it was something out of the ordinary; something he really enjoyed.

Ethan looked up and saw that the man's smile refused to let go of his face. There were three other younger men standing behind him. The guy gestured to them. 'They thought it'd be fun to throw their dad out of a plane for his sixtieth.'

Ethan smiled as the man handed over a voucher for a tandem skydive, then turned back to his family. As Ethan logged the details into the computer, he listened to the guy chatting with his sons and a well-dressed woman – presumably his wife. They were all laughing and joking, as if jumping out of a plane to celebrate a birthday was a normal thing to do.

He typed in the man's occupation. And paused. 'You're a vicar?'

The man nodded.

During his first few crazy days at FreeFall, Ethan had seen plenty of people from all walks of life sign up to jump out of a plane, but never a man of God.

The vicar winked at him. 'At least I know where I'm headed if something goes wrong.'

It was lunch time before Ethan had a break. He sat down on a tired picnic bench and pulled a magazine he'd found in the FreeFall shop out of his pocket. The cover showed a skydiver upside down and smiling.

He flicked through, staring, between mouthfuls of bacon and bread, at the pictures. OK, so he didn't really understand everything that was in the mag, but he was still fascinated by it. And with all the time he'd spent at FreeFall, he was beginning to wonder whether he could ever find the money to have a go himself.

'I've still not made the front cover,' came a voice from behind Ethan. He looked round to see Johnny pulling up a chair. He was in his skydiving suit and carrying what looked like a small surfboard.

'Bit far from the sea, aren't you?' said Ethan.

'I do freestyle,' said Johnny. 'And let me tell you, surfing through the air on this thing beats doing it on the sea.'

'I'll take your word for it.'

Behind Johnny, Ethan saw the minibus pull up, fill up and drive off, taking another group down to the plane that waited just out of sight on the runway.

'I need to get some binoculars,' he said as the minibus disappeared. 'I want to see what it's like when people actually leave the plane.'

'Only way to really see that is to do it,' said Johnny. 'How's the job?'

'Busy,' said Ethan, lifting a can of drink to his mouth and taking a swig. 'But fun. This morning I had a vicar in to do a tandem. Nuts or what?'

Johnny reached over and ripped a chunk off Ethan's sandwich. 'Takes all sorts,' he said, stuffing the sandwich into his mouth. 'Speaking of which, what do you do when you're not here – other than the joy that is school work and exam revision?'

'Sod all,' said Ethan. 'You've seen where I live. Jumping off the roof seems like a good idea more often than you'd think.'

Johnny laughed. 'That bad?'

'Worse.'

Johnny didn't press him, but Ethan continued – he

25

couldn't help himself. 'Jo, my sister, she's all right, and Mum's your typical mum.'

Johnny raised an eyebrow.

'You know . . . Can't help feeding you or commenting on what you're wearing.'

Johnny nodded a knowing smile.

'But my dad's a tosser.' Ethan's voice was angry. 'The sooner I leave home the better, to be honest. Either that or I kill him.'

He fell silent for a moment. The last thing he wanted to do was talk about his dad; have him ruin what he was doing now, here, away from the flat. Wasn't that part of the reason he had come to FreeFall anyway? To get away from his dad – to be somewhere he couldn't be affected by him? So he focused on finishing what was left of his lunch – which wasn't much, thanks to Johnny.

The sound of the plane taking off thrummed through the air. Ethan turned with Johnny to watch it go airborne.

Johnny leaned back in his chair. 'Got any plans?'

'How do you mean?' said Ethan.

'You know, travelling or uni or whatever.'

Ethan shook his head. 'Finishing my A-levels will keep Mum happy, and after that, well, I've thought about the Royal Marines.'

'Seriously?'

'Yeah,' said Ethan. 'I just can't stand the idea of an ordinary life in a shop or an office. And I don't want to end up like my dad. He's the best reason you could ever meet for mindless violence. Steals from Mum . . . never has a job for more than a few months . . . drinks.'

'Nice,' said Johnny.

'What about you?' asked Ethan. 'You're no longer at school now, so what next?'

'I forget the plans and just get on with living. It's more fun that way.'

Ethan shrugged. 'Maybe for you. But I wouldn't mind at least having some idea of where I'm going.'

Johnny laughed. 'I figured there was another reason Sam hired you.'

'Why's that then?'

'He just thinks people should have a purpose,' said Johnny. 'Or be given one.'

'He's quite a scary bloke,' said Ethan, thinking back to his interview. 'Seems nice enough, but he looks bloody hard.'

'Ex forces,' said Johnny. 'And if you let on you're thinking of joining up, he'll have you doing push-ups and bleep tests before you know it!'

'Really?' said Ethan.

Johnny nodded, his face almost serious. 'And he's a world-class skydiver.'

'Does he teach you?'

'Me and a few others,' said Johnny. 'He wants us to be the best skydiving team there is. He works us hard, doesn't stand for any messing around, but there's no one better.'

Ethan looked up, trying to see if the plane was over the DZ yet.

'Listen out for a drop in the sound of the plane's engines,' said Johnny, following Ethan's line of sight. 'That means it's slowing down so people can jump.'

Immediately after he spoke, Ethan heard the change in

27

the sound of the plane. A few seconds later, tiny dots dropped into the sky like erratic flies. Straining his eyes, he followed the dots as they grew larger. He soon realized that one of them was actually made up of a number of dots; a group doing a formation dive. The dot exploded. Parachutes burst into life and drifted down like confetti.

'Check these guys out,' said Johnny as the four skydivers from the formation came in above them. 'They're swooping.'

Ethan didn't have a chance to ask what swooping was: in quick succession, the skydivers turned into the DZ at an impossible speed. He watched as they sped through the air, only inches from the ground, then pulled into a perfect landing.

As they touched down, he noticed their parachutes; they were the smallest he'd seen – more like power kites.

'Cool, eh?' said Johnny, grinning. 'A swoop's a high-speed landing. The control you need is amazing. It's unbelievably difficult. Which is why I'm the best.'

Ethan ignored Johnny's comment and said, 'Those para-chutes – they just don't look big enough.'

'They're Raiders,' said Johnny. 'Small, fast and scary. And the word's canopy, not parachute. If you're gonna work here, you may as well sound like you know what you're talking about.'

'You tried one?'

Johnny shook his head. 'Sam's got some on order for us though – me and the rest of the team, that is. Want a go?'

Ethan saw the challenge on Johnny's face. 'Yeah, no worries,' he said. 'I reckon it's easy. It's just people like you want to make the rest of us think it's difficult so you look cool.'

'But anyone *can* skydive,' said Johnny, and Ethan saw a wild spark in his eyes. 'And it *is* easy. Just look around you!'

Ethan did just that. Like every other day he'd been at FreeFall, he was amazed at the variety of people who had all signed up to jump: pensioners, teenagers, mothers . . . even vicars.

'Statistically it's safer than driving or crossing a road,' Johnny told him. 'You're more likely to get hit by a meteorite than be killed skydiving.'

Ethan rested his can on the table and looked directly at Johnny, who shrugged.

'OK, so some of that may not be strictly true.'

'That *is* a surprise.'

'But you've just got to try it!' said Johnny, and Ethan saw that wildness fire up again. 'It's the most awesome thing ever. It could make you almost as cool as me! It's a life-changing thing!'

'Yeah,' said Ethan, getting up from the table to head back inside, 'and so's the money I'd need to do it.'

At the end of the day Ethan was just making for his bike when a voice called, 'Ethan? Got a minute?'

He turned to find Sam striding towards him.

'How's your first week been?'

Ethan started to reply and found he couldn't stop. All he could do was spill out everything he'd done that week – how much he'd enjoyed it, the people he'd met, how he was still amazed by the whole skydiving scene, loved watching people jumping, coming in to land, their faces carrying the biggest smiles. He couldn't remember being so enthusiastic about anything in his life. It felt good.

'Here,' said Sam, handing Ethan some forms. 'A banking form so I can pay you direct into your account. The others are parental and health forms.'

'What for?' asked Ethan, and read the answer on the forms as Sam spoke.

'Perk of the job. You get a free tandem skydive. With me.'

Ethan wasn't given a chance to respond; Sam was gone.

Walking to his bike, he slipped the forms into a pocket. He couldn't wait to get his mum to sign them.

No sooner had Ethan pushed through the front door of the flat than Jo stopped him in the hall.

'Dad's here,' she told him.

'So?' said Ethan. 'Where's Mum? I've got some forms for her to sign.' He could hear the TV blaring in the lounge. A loud burp rode over it, followed by a guttural laugh.

'He's drunk.' Ethan could see the warning in Jo's eyes.

'You're not telling me everything, are you?' he said, forgetting about the forms in a second. 'What's he done?'

Jo hesitated, then said, 'It's Mum, but she's OK. He just shook her up a bit. He didn't hit her. She's going out to work in a minute.'

Ethan turned and walked down the hall.

'Ethan,' Jo called after him. 'Don't—'

But he was already in the lounge, kicking over the half-empty lager can that was propping the door open.

He found his dad sprawled on the sofa like a beached whale. The reek of alcohol stung his nose; on the floor a half-eaten kebab rested on greasy paper next to a pile of empty lager cans.

For a few moments Ethan stood there, watching his dad's fat, pale belly rising and falling, bursting through the buttons of his shirt.

Then his dad turned and looked up at him. 'What do you want?'

'What did you do to Mum?' Ethan's voice was cold, hard.

'I just got her to shut up, that's all. Don't worry, son. I didn't hurt the precious little thing.'

Ethan hated the way his dad called him 'son'. He didn't want to be reminded. He stood there clenching his fists. He could feel his nails biting into his skin. His dad went back to watching the TV, cracking open another lager.

Ethan walked over to the TV and turned it off.

'What the hell are you doing?' his dad shouted, dragging himself up out of the sofa. 'I was watching that!' He swayed slightly and took a deep pull from the lager can.

'I want you out,' said Ethan. 'We all do. Take what you want and fuck off.'

His dad leaned closer and Ethan gagged at his breath. It smelled like a pub carpet. 'You orderin' me around?' he demanded. 'Who are you to order me, eh? I'm your dad, get it?'

He tried to shove Ethan out of the way, heading for the TV, but Ethan stood his ground.

'You've gone too far,' he said. 'Hitting Mum, that's too much. I want you out.'

'I didn't hit her. I just shook her a bit, that's all.'

'I don't care,' said Ethan. 'I don't want you laying a hand on her. Just go.'

'My flat, my rules,' said his dad. 'Just who the hell do you think you are? Think you're something special, is that it? You're a nothing, Ethan, worse than nothing. Now get out of my way.'

As his dad reached to turn on the TV, Ethan grabbed the greasy collar of his shirt and threw him back onto the sofa.

He landed awkwardly, and roared, 'Right, you little bastard! Now you're gonna get it!'

Ethan didn't move. He was ready for this, had been for years. He clenched his fists.

But then they both heard the scream from the doorway, and turned to see Mum and Jo.

'Stop it! The pair of you! Just stop it!' snapped Mum.

'Mum,' said Ethan. 'He—'

'I'm not interested,' she said, tears welling up in her eyes. 'Don't be like him, Ethan. Don't let him win.'

Ethan's dad leaned closer, and laughed. 'Yeah, Ethan, do what your mammy says, there's a good little boy.'

Ethan lifted a hand to shove him backwards, but Jo rushed in between them.

'It won't help,' she said. 'Just leave him be.'

His dad laughed, moved past Jo to switch the TV on again, then slumped back onto the sofa.

Ethan shook his head and walked out of the room. As he passed his mother, she reached out for him, crying now, but he was too wound up to stay in the flat.

'You're going to have to throw him out one day, Mum,' he told her, making for the front door. 'Count on it.'

Then he was outside, the door shut behind him.

He took a moment to calm down, then walked on. As he

did so, he felt something in his pocket and pulled out the forms Sam had given him – the ones he'd wanted his mum to sign so he could do a tandem jump. Too late now. He wasn't about to go back to the flat for a while, so he'd have to try and catch her in the morning.

Looking at the forms brought Ethan back to himself, made him remember what he was doing with his life now. He wasn't going to let his dad ruin what he had at FreeFall. So he focused on that, and the fact that soon he might be jumping out of a plane himself. His mind instantly filled with all the faces of the skydivers – the wild look in Johnny's eyes – and the thought that he might soon look the same.

The thought sent excitement coursing through him, adrenaline flooding his system, making his stomach turn a somersault. It wasn't the first time.

It wouldn't be the last.

5

The morning was coming to a close and the sky, which had been clear, was now clouding over. Ethan was helping to move some tandem skydiving rigs into the hangar. They were heavier and more bulky than a normal rig, and with one on his back and one in his arms, he was moving a little awkwardly.

Unable to use his hands thanks to the weight he was carrying in front of him, Ethan turned round to push backwards through the hangar door. But on his way through he backed right into a girl in skydiving kit coming the other way.

'Hey! Watch it!' she yelled, jumping out of Ethan's path. Ethan had too much momentum to stop, and her abrupt shout made him jump and lose his balance. Before he knew it, he'd stumbled through the door, tripped over his own feet and landed on the floor, sprawling like a beetle on its back, legs and arms flailing.

He looked up. The owner of the voice looked down. She was laughing and she was gorgeous.

'Hi,' said Ethan, none too impressed with himself for behaving like a complete idiot in front of this girl. She looked as if she was about his own age.

'Here,' she said, reaching out a hand and hauling him to his feet with surprising strength.

'Cheers,' he said.

'No worries,' the girl replied. 'You just owe me one, that's all.' She smiled. 'I'm Kat. I'm guessing you're Ethan, right? Sam's new squaddie?'

'I'm not in the forces,' said Ethan, but Kat grinned and cut him off.

'It's what we call anyone Sam brings in new to the centre,' she told him. 'It's because he generally has you running around for the first few weeks doing everything he says, like he's forgotten he's not actually in the army any more. Has he got you doing press-ups yet?'

Ethan didn't quite know how to answer that.

'Joke!' said Kat, and laughed.

The sound of her laughter bounced around the hangar. Ethan stared. His first guess had been right: definitely his age. She was slightly shorter than him – he guessed about five foot eight – and wore her long blonde hair pulled back in a tight and perfect ponytail. She was dressed in exactly the same outfit he'd seen Johnny wearing when he was jumping. But it looked better on her. A lot better.

'Don't speak much, do you?' said Kat, pulling her hair out of the ponytail and shaking it loose.

'No, er, sorry,' said Ethan, trying not to stare, which was pretty difficult. He smiled. 'You just jumped?'

Kat nodded. 'Practising some four-way formation stuff with the team.'

'You jump with Johnny?' asked Ethan, guessing that they were in the same outfits for a reason.

'Yeah,' Kat said. 'You know him?'

Ethan nodded. 'He did a BASE jump off the block of flats where I live. He's kind of the reason I've ended up working here, I guess.'

Kat smiled. 'Always likes to make an impression, does Johnny, good or bad. You up for a coffee?'

'Can't,' said Ethan as he quickly jogged over to put the rigs down in the place Sam had shown him. He grabbed his bag. 'But I'm going to be helping Nancy out for the rest of the day so I'll walk over to the café with you.'

'Cool,' said Kat, pulling the hangar door open. 'After you.'

'Thanks,' said Ethan.

'I wasn't being polite,' Kat explained. 'It's just safer if you go first.'

Ethan saw a teasing smile flicker across her face.

'Cloud's coming in,' she said, looking up at the sky outside. 'No one's gonna be jumping for a while. Which means you and Nancy will be busy.'

'Busy's better than bored,' said Ethan as they headed for the café. 'Way better.'

'Fair point,' said Kat. 'So when are you going to jump? You

can't really work here and be taken seriously if you're only a spectator, can you?'

Ethan reached into his bag and pulled out the forms Sam had given him a couple of days earlier. He hadn't been able to catch up with his mum since the run-in with his dad.

'Sam gave me these,' he said, showing Kat the crumpled forms. 'Just haven't had a chance to talk to my mum and get them signed.'

'You're not putting it off, are you?'

Ethan shook his head, slipping the forms back into his pocket. 'No way,' he said. 'Not when it's free. I couldn't afford to do it otherwise.'

'So Sam's doing the jump with you, is he?'

Ethan nodded. 'It's not like I had any choice in it. He just gave me the forms, told me I was doing a tandem with him, and walked off.'

Kat laughed out loud. 'You must've made an impression,' she said. 'He doesn't do that for just anyone. Anyway, you'll love it, trust me. It's just one of those things you have to do before you die, simple as that.'

Before I die? thought Ethan. *Well, that puts it in perspective.*

'And if Nancy can do it, so can you.'

'Nancy?' said Ethan, stopping dead halfway through the doorway to the café. '*Nancy* did a jump?'

'Too right! You should've seen her face afterwards!'

'But, Nancy . . .' said Ethan. 'It just doesn't seem . . .'

Kat turned to him and leaned in conspiratorially. 'She reckons that that one jump has got her more action than she's ever had in her whole life! Apparently it's the perfect way to impress men!'

Ethan laughed and headed over to the counter, then turned at the sound of the café door bursting open behind him. A guy stood in the doorway, his hands raised in the air like he was some kind of returning dignitary. He was wearing the same outfit as Kat and Johnny; another team member, Ethan guessed.

'It's OK, everyone, I'm here,' the guy said, a smug smile slapped across his face. 'You can all relax.'

Ethan couldn't help but notice that no one in the café seemed in any way interested in whoever this idiot was.

'That's Jake,' said Kat as the figure turned, winked and strutted over. When he reached Kat, he rested his arm on her shoulder like he was doing her a favour. They were clearly an item – though Ethan noticed that she seemed to shrink a little, like a candle fighting to stay alight. Not that Jake noticed. All he seemed to care about was whether everyone else was watching him.

'Hey, babe,' said Jake loudly to Kat. 'Missed me? Course you have!'

Kat nodded and sort of smiled as Jake leaned over to kiss her cheek. 'This is Ethan,' she said, gesturing towards him.

The look Jake gave him wasn't exactly friendly.

'Oh, the new boy,' he said dismissively, addressing Kat as though Ethan didn't exist. 'Busy tonight?' he asked, moving in to nibble her ear.

She shook her head, pulled away from him a little, and shrugged.

'You are now,' said Jake. 'We're out tonight. Just you and me. I've got a table booked. I'll pick you up in the Porsche. It's gonna be amazing, trust me!' He leaned in for another kiss.

'You own a Porsche?' said Ethan, not quite believing what he'd heard. Jake looked no older than Johnny. How the hell could he own a Porsche?

Jake glanced at him, nodded, then turned back to Kat, pulling her close.

'Ethan's going to do a jump too – aren't you, Ethan?' said Kat, smiling. 'Sam's got him working all over the centre.' She gave a laugh, but it didn't sound quite as happy and full of life as the last time Ethan had heard it.

Jake released Kat, and this time he looked Ethan up and down like he was really checking him out. Then he shook his head. 'Great,' he said. 'That's all we need; another rookie in the sky.'

'I didn't know people were *born* skydiving,' Ethan retorted, before his brain kicked in to tell him to keep his mouth shut.

'You *what*?' said Jake.

He shrugged. 'We've all got to start somewhere, haven't we? I mean, I know it's hard to believe, but I guess even you had to do a first jump once upon a time.'

Ethan saw Jake's eyes narrow as he came closer, until there were just inches between them. 'You haven't even jumped yet. What would you know about anything?' he said icily.

Ethan suddenly felt very sure that he and Jake hadn't just got off on the wrong foot, but were about to use those feet to kick each other round the café – but then Johnny strolled in and put his arm round Kat.

'I see you've met some of the team,' he said easily, grinning at Ethan. 'Natalya's disappeared again, but she does that. And Luke's around somewhere. Probably ironing the creases in his forehead.'

Kat laughed; Jake didn't. But Johnny had drawn his attention away from Ethan and now he grabbed Kat again, dislodging Johnny's arm.

Ethan smiled at Johnny. 'I'm doing a tandem,' he said, and just saying it felt completely amazing, like he'd taken a sudden and definite step into something that was completely different from the rest of his life. 'Sam's taking me. Perk of the job apparently.'

Jake shook his head, but Johnny buzzed at this. 'That's awesome!' he said. 'You'll love it! When's the jump?'

Ethan shrugged. 'Need to get the forms signed first, then I guess it's just down to Sam. Does he always take new staff up for free?'

Jake frowned. 'Sam's losing it,' he said. 'I mean, it makes sense to take people like us up, but he can't go around giving just anyone a free jump, can he? What's wrong with him? Age getting to him? Gulf War Syndrome finally kicking in?'

'I'm not complaining,' said Ethan. 'I can't wait, to be honest.' Then he turned and looked at Jake. 'It's not like you have to be superhuman, is it? Even Nancy's done it.'

Jake opened his mouth to speak, but before he could say anything Kat pulled him away, turning back to wink at Ethan. 'Well, you certainly know how to make friends and influence people, don't you?' she said softly before following Jake out of the café.

Ethan looked over at Johnny, who laughed and slapped him on the shoulder. 'Don't worry about Jake,' he said. 'He can't help being a total dick.'

Ethan laughed. 'So what's with him and Kat then?' he asked, thinking that they just didn't seem right together. 'And what's with the attitude and the need to mention the Porsche?'

'Jake's deluded,' Johnny told him. 'Bit of a tosser in most ways really. Thinks he owns everything he can see, including people. And he loves everyone to know just how rich he is.'

'And he and Kat . . . ?'

Johnny shook his head. 'They've a history, that's all. Doesn't make sense to anyone, least of all me.'

'Why's that?'

Johnny grinned, his eyes glinting. 'What, with me around? How does he even get a look in?'

Ethan was about to reply when Nancy called over from the serving hatch. She was running low on chips – would he be a love and nip round the back to get some out of the freezer.

Ethan made his way outside. Johnny followed, jumped on his motorbike, pulled on his helmet and kicked the engine into life.

'See you tomorrow?' said Ethan.

Johnny nodded, then spun his bike round and floored it.

Ethan watched as Johnny wheelied out of the centre, one-handed. He shook his head and smiled. Something told him that if he had a bike, he'd probably do just the same – or at least try it and fall off.

Overhead, the clouds started to break and the sky cleared. Ethan breathed in deeply. He felt happy, but it was more than that. Now that he was doing a tandem skydive he felt like he belonged. He had a reason to be there at FreeFall; a purpose.

And Sam had given it to him.

6

'Honestly, Mum, I'll be fine. It's totally safe.'

It was early the following morning and Ethan was doing his best to persuade his mum to sign the forms for Sam. He'd managed to get up in time to catch her before she headed out to work. Dad was nowhere to be seen. He'd probably dossed at one of his mates' places after drinking himself into a stupor.

'Totally safe?' Ethan's mum was looking at him dubiously.

Ethan nodded. 'Absolutely,' he said. 'Totally.'

'But if anything happened to you . . .'

'It won't, Mum, really it won't,' said Ethan. 'Sam's an amazing skydiver. Ex forces. He knows what he's doing.'

He watched as his mum looked at the forms again.

Nowadays the tiredness seemed etched into her face permanently, like it would never leave. He simply couldn't understand why she didn't just kick his dad out once and for all. Having him around was wearing her away little by little.

At last she reached for a pen and signed the forms. 'Does your dad need to see these?'

'No,' said Ethan, and took them – scanning them quickly to make sure that his mum had signed in the right places. He didn't want Sam to find any mistakes: this was too important. Then he folded them up, slipped them in an envelope and pushed it deep into his bag.

As he turned to leave for work, his mum gently held his arm and looked up at him.

'I'll see you later,' said Ethan, turning to go, but he wasn't quick enough to escape a kiss. 'Mum!' he moaned jokingly.

She smiled, and for a brief moment Ethan saw a flicker of the person she used to be. He grinned back, waved, and was gone.

It was still early and FreeFall was quiet. Sam hadn't even arrived to open up yet, so Ethan took a walk. It was a crisp morning, and as he strolled out onto the DZ, his feet left faint scuff marks in the dew on the grass, like finger smudges on a wet window. It was strange being out here alone, wandering around a place he was used to seeing filled with people, all chatting noisily, rushing around with whoops of amazement.

He stretched and breathed in the morning. Yep, there really was something about this place – something that felt right. It was like he was discovering something about himself.

The roar of an engine broke into the moment. Ethan turned.

Sam had arrived. His Land Rover Defender 110 King Cab rolled to a halt beside the office. It was the very definition of the word 'beast', Ethan thought. He couldn't work out how something so huge could actually be road legal. The tyres looked ready to chew up and spit out a mountain, and the suspension had been jacked up to an impossible height. Aluminium checker-plate covered the bonnet, the wings, the bottom of the doors and various other bits Ethan didn't know the names for. A winch sat out front. Inside was a world of dials and gauges. And it was black.

It looked, thought Ethan, pure evil.

Sam clambered out, waved a salute to him.

Ethan jogged over, pulling the envelope containing the forms out of his bag on his way. 'All signed,' he said, and handed it to Sam.

He felt he should have said more, because it felt like an important moment, but no words came, and for a second he just stood there, feeling a little awkward.

Sam took the envelope, checked the forms and nodded. 'Good,' he said, and looked back at Ethan, a rare smile on his face. 'How do you feel?'

'Like I want to get up there and do it now,' said Ethan. 'I can't bloody wait.'

'Right answer,' said Sam, walking round to the back of the Defender and pulling down the tailgate.

Ethan followed and asked when he would be jumping. Sam pulled a huge rucksack from the back of the Defender, then slammed the tailgate shut. 'Soon as possible,' he said. 'Over the next couple of days, if the weather holds out.'

'Really? That soon?'

Sam nodded. 'No point hanging around. Once you've set your mind on doing something, best to get it done. Right?' And slapping his hand on Ethan's shoulder, he headed off to his office.

As Ethan set off after him to get his work assignment for the day, he looked up at the sky. He was going to do a tandem skydive. There was no turning back now, not with someone like Sam. And he couldn't stop grinning, no matter how much his cheeks ached.

Lunch time came round so quickly Ethan almost forgot to grab a bite to eat. It was a good day for jumping, and FreeFall was heaving with people excited and nervous about taking their very own leap into the unknown.

Like a flock of geese, another group of tandems were coming in to land. The air was filled with the sound of cheering families and friends, cameras clicking, whoops, applause.

Ethan heard his name and turned. He saw Johnny standing some way from the DZ on an open area of grass. He was with Kat, Jake, and two others Ethan hadn't seen before. Natalya and Luke, he assumed, remembering the names of the other two members of the team. Sam was standing slightly apart from them, supervising.

Luke seemed to be a couple of years older than Johnny – probably twenty or so. Natalya was about the same age as Ethan. Her skin was pale, and she had rich red hair.

Johnny waved at Ethan, then pointed up at the sky. He

shouted again and Ethan caught three words: *jumping*; *five*; *formation*.

Ethan gave a thumbs-up and watched as the team got themselves into a circle. He knew they were practising their formations on the ground before jumping. He'd seen other groups do it, but never Johnny's team. They started spinning themselves into different shapes. Sam was directing them, observing, correcting. Johnny was strolling around the group; Ethan noticed that his helmet had a camera strapped to it.

Then the group burst out of their formation and jogged off to the minibus that would take them to the plane. As they clambered in, Johnny turned and gave Ethan an exaggerated salute, like a pilot heading off on some death-defying mission. Very tally-ho.

Ethan laughed. God, he wanted to go with them and jump!

The minibus revved and drove off, a plume of grey smoke spluttering from an exhaust that was held on by an old wire coat hanger.

Sam came straight over to Ethan. 'You'll need these,' he said. 'Binos.'

He handed Ethan a pair of binoculars that looked almost as mean as his Defender. They were covered in a rubberized skin which had clearly saved them more than once from getting smashed up.

The sound of the plane's engine ripped through the air and Ethan followed it as it took off. He put the binoculars up to his eyes. Their clarity and magnification was unbelievable. He zoomed in, and could see the pilot in the cockpit. Soon, though, there was little point following the plane. Best to wait for that drop in the sound of the engine, like Johnny had told him, then spot it again and watch for the sky to fill with black dots.

'Still want to do it?' asked Sam.

'Can't wait,' said Ethan, and nodded at the plane. 'How long have they been jumping?'

The question he really wanted to ask was how long would it take for him to be as good as they were, and how much would it cost, but he didn't want to sound too cocky.

'Luke's the most experienced,' said Sam. 'He's been jumping for three years. The rest just under two. What's more important though,' he went on, 'is the number of jumps. The more air time you get, the better the skydiver you become. Some people are better at it though . . . natural.'

'Like Johnny?' said Ethan.

'Like all of them,' said Sam. 'That's why I chose them for my formation team.'

'Must be amazing up there.'

'Trust me, it is.' Sam turned to Ethan with a faint smile. 'You spotted the plane yet?'

Ethan listened. The thrum of the engines was still audible. He looked up, and Sam did the same – just as the sound dropped a little.

Ethan put the binoculars to his eyes and stared skyward.

Nothing.

The sky was clear.

Then he found the plane; it was clearly visible. *That's 12,000 feet away*, thought Ethan, remembering some of the stuff he'd picked up already since working at FreeFall. *And that's a hell of a long way to fall . . .*

Skydivers filled his vision, spilling from the plane. He caught sight of a group speeding through the air. They drew together in one formation, then moved smoothly into another. Ethan tracked them, straining his eyes through the binoculars to see what they were doing. He imagined doing it himself, racing towards the earth with Johnny and the rest, pulling moves like a pro.

The formation burst, and the black dots split off from each other – *zip-zip-zip-zip-zip* . . .

'What do you think?' asked Sam. 'Any good?'

'Looked fine to me,' said Ethan, still gazing through the binoculars. 'At least, I think it did.'

'Were the formations stable? Did anyone break off too early?'

Ethan replayed in his mind what he'd seen. 'No, it was all good. Looked amazing.' He paused and lowered the binoculars to glance at Sam. 'Wouldn't mind doing it myself.'

Sam looked at Ethan as canopies burst into colour above. 'Good,' he said. 'That's just the right attitude. Shows me that you're not just thinking about the tandem. You're thinking beyond it, to the next level. Just what I'm after.'

Ethan was just wondering what on earth Sam meant by that final sentence when he spotted something strange. He quickly raised the binoculars again.

While everyone else was now gliding in, doing turns, one skydiver was plummeting towards the ground, canopy pulled but flapping uselessly above, like a bedraggled windsock. And the ground wasn't exactly getting further away.

Ethan lowered the binoculars and pointed. 'Sam?'

Sam was already looking, his eyes narrow, his face hard.

'That can't be right,' murmured Ethan.

'It's not,' Sam replied.

Ethan held his breath. He couldn't drag his eyes away from the falling skydiver. Morbid curiosity had him by the throat and was forcing him to watch: this was someone with seconds to live.

'He's going to be under a thousand any second,' said Sam. 'Why hasn't he cut away? If his AAD pings his reserve, it'll get tangled with his main canopy! What's he thinking?'

Ethan had no idea what Sam was talking about. But then, as if on cue, a crack sounded through the air, and he saw the skydiver's twisted canopy snap free and drift off like a deflated balloon: the skydiver had at last cut his main canopy away. Momentarily he was in freefall again, but then he was pulled back hard by a smaller canopy, which burst open above him, pulling him into a slow descent just a few seconds short of death.

Sam put out his hand. 'Binos, Ethan. Now.'

Ethan handed them over, then looked at the figure as it drifted safely to the ground.

Sam put the binoculars to his eyes, then growled, 'Jake . . .'

7

Ethan didn't even bother trying to keep up with Sam, who had turned and raced off towards his office. The man could seriously shift.

A hundred metres away from the DZ, the skydiver Ethan now knew to be Jake drifted down onto the long grass. Moments later, the other skydivers came in to land, but Ethan didn't have time to wait for them; he was due in the café and Nancy would be waiting. He wanted to see what had happened to Jake, to talk to Johnny and the rest about it, but seeing the mood Sam was now in, he didn't fancy making it worse by not being where he was paid to be. It wasn't long before Johnny and the rest of the team found him in the café.

'Hey, Eth!' said Johnny, strolling over to the counter. 'Did you watch the jump? Did Sam say anything? What were the formations like? I've got it all on camera, but you saw it. Any good?'

'It was great!' Ethan told him. 'I thought filming was just for people doing their first jumps and stuff, a souvenir of the moment.'

'It's how the formations are judged,' said Johnny as the rest of the team came over. 'Gives the judges something to look at. So my job is to make sure I get the best shots and the best angles to make these guys look better than they really are. It is, essentially, all down to me.'

'Bigging yourself up again?' asked Kat. 'Hi, Ethan.'

Ethan smiled. 'Great jump. I caught most of it through Sam's binos.'

Johnny turned round to the team, introducing Ethan to the two members he hadn't met.

First was Luke, who reached out his hand with a smile. 'Johnny says you're doing a tandem with Sam,' he said. 'Make sure he checks the clips are nice and tight, right?'

'You're having a laugh, aren't you?' said Johnny.

'No, just being cautious.' Luke's face was serious. 'Even Sam could forget something. You never know.'

'Luke's into the detail,' said Johnny, winking at Ethan. 'Uses a spirit level to make sure he's standing up straight in the morning, don't you, Luke?'

Luke shrugged. 'Devil's in the detail, Johnny.'

'Ooooh, spiritual,' said Johnny, then turned to the other girl in the group. 'This is Natalya.'

'Nice to meet you, Ethan,' she said quietly, and held out her hand.

Ethan noticed her accent immediately. His best guess was Russian, but that was only because he'd watched too many Bond movies. It was certainly eastern European. And she wasn't wearing any make-up – unlike Kat, who was wearing just enough to say *Notice me.* Ethan guessed that Natalya wasn't the kind of person who worked at being noticed by anyone.

'And you,' he replied, and took her hand. She gave a firm handshake – it was only when he let go that he was struck by how formal it seemed. The rest of the gang were relaxed with him from the off, but this was like meeting someone at a job interview or a wedding or something.

'Natalya's the serious one in the team,' said Johnny. 'So don't worry too much about her inability to smile. I consider it my life's mission to make her laugh.'

Natalya turned to look at Johnny. 'How very thoughtful of you, Johnny,' she said. 'And I do smile, just not all the time like you.'

'I'm all heart,' said Johnny. 'Well, all heart and knock-knock gags.'

'Without me, Johnny's life has no purpose, you see?' she told Ethan.

Ethan wasn't sure, but he thought he spotted the hint of a smile crease the corners of her eyes.

'Whatever you do,' said Johnny, stepping forward to whisper in Ethan's ear, his eyes trained on Natalya, 'don't call her Nat. She gets angry. And you wouldn't like to see her angry – would he, Nat?'

Natalya's face was stern, and Ethan decided to take Johnny's advice. For all he knew, she could be a Russian spy, and he figured upsetting one of those wasn't a good idea. He looked at the others and asked, 'You guys hungry?'

Everyone nodded, ordered, and a few minutes later Ethan returned with a loaded tray. Serving Luke first, he couldn't help but watch as he opened a tomato sauce sachet, emptied it, then took the ripped corner and pushed it back inside.

Johnny grinned. 'Luke?'

Luke looked up.

'How are your chips?'

'They're fine,' said Luke, biting into one. 'Why?'

'Oh, I just wondered, you know, if they were sufficiently straight for you, that's all. I can go and get a ruler from Sam's office for you if you want, just to make sure.'

Luke ignored Johnny – Ethan could see it was something he was well used to – and simply carried on eating.

'I'm surprised you know what a ruler is, Johnny,' said Kat, over the top of her mug. 'Kind of implies you've had time for things in your life other than perfecting the skill of being a flash git.'

Ethan stood and watched as the group joked around.

'I'm not flash,' said Johnny, faking emotional hurt. 'I'm just very, very good, that's all. And if I hide my talent, how are you lot ever going to learn? You need something to aspire to. A target. And that's me.'

'With a mouth the size of yours,' said Luke, 'there's already a large enough target.'

Johnny burst out laughing; the others, including Ethan, joined in.

As the laughter subsided, Kat asked, 'Where's Jake?'

Natalya looked over. 'He landed way out from the DZ. Maybe he had to cut away.'

'Cut away?' asked Ethan, remembering Sam mentioning it as they'd watched.

'If your main canopy fails,' explained Kat, 'then you have to let it go so you can deploy your reserve.'

'Well, that's definitely what he did then,' said Ethan.

Everyone looked up.

'What happened?' asked Kat.

Ethan saw her face flicker with concern. Everyone else was looking at him. 'I was with Sam,' he said. 'I was watching you all come in: you pulled your canopies and everything was fine. Then I noticed someone just falling.'

'How do you mean?' asked Luke. 'Was something wrong with the canopy?'

'I don't know,' said Ethan, and he wasn't lying. All he could tell them is what he'd seen and what Sam had told him. 'Sam did wonder why the canopy hadn't been cut away sooner.'

Kat looked really worried now, he realized, and so did the rest of the team.

'I think he was just touching a thousand feet when he finally cut the main canopy away,' he went on, trying to remember exactly what he'd seen. 'Then a smaller canopy snapped out and caught air. Sam could tell it was Jake through the binos.'

'Below a thousand?' said Kat. 'But that's insane. No one would leave it that late.'

'He must've got too wrapped up in sorting out his main canopy,' said Johnny. 'Probably lost altitude awareness.'

54

'He's bloody lucky the AAD worked,' said Luke. 'If it hadn't . . .' He went quiet.

'Sam mentioned the AAD,' said Ethan. 'And something about it maybe getting tangled in the main canopy. Is the AAD an automatic device or something?'

'That's exactly what it is,' Luke told him. 'AAD stands for Automatic Activation Device. You don't have to wear one, but Sam insists we all do.'

'I don't blame him,' said Ethan. 'I don't think I'd want to jump without one, having just seen what happened to Jake.'

'Safety, safety, safety,' said Luke. 'Means if the jumper's had to cut away from his main canopy but can't pull his reserve for whatever reason, then he's still not completely in the shit. It deploys at seven hundred and fifty feet – just enough time to save your life. But it can go tits up if your main chute is still attached. Jake's lucky as hell.'

Johnny leaned back in his chair, then glanced at Luke. 'It's all true,' he confirmed. 'As I said, Luke's all about the detail. What he doesn't know isn't worth knowing.' Then he winked at Ethan. 'But there's something you don't know about Luke: he doesn't need a reserve – do you, mate?'

Ethan saw the look on Luke's face and just knew that whatever Johnny was about to say next, he'd heard it far too many times before.

'He just uses the force, don't you, Luke?'

Luke sighed. Heavily. 'Here we go again . . .'

Johnny picked up his now empty mug, placed it against his mouth, and spoke into it, his voice deep and resonating.

'I find your lack of faith disturbing . . .'

It was a perfect Darth Vader impression.

Kat giggled. Nat almost smiled. Ethan muffled a laugh.

Johnny continued, holding his knife in his hand like a light sabre. 'You underestimate the power of the dark side.'

Luke did his best to ignore Johnny and continued to eat his chips.

But Johnny wasn't giving up. He was on his feet now and breathing heavily into his mug. He waved his knife around. 'When I left you, I was but the learner. Now I am the master!'

Everyone laughed, including Luke. Even Natalya joined in.

'Not bad,' said Ethan. 'Pretty convincing impression. You should act.'

'His whole life's an act,' said Kat.

Her expression hardened suddenly, and Ethan turned to see that Jake had come in.

'Thanks for waiting for me, guys. Not.' He slammed the café door behind him and came over.

Kat was first to speak. 'What the hell happened, Jake? What went wrong?'

'Nothing happened, babe,' said Jake, sliding his arm around her waist. 'I had it all under control.'

He leaned in for a kiss, but Ethan saw Kat pull away.

'Bullshit, Jake, and you know it,' she said.

'Would I lie to you? Would I? Everything was fine. Don't you trust me?'

Kat pushed him away, looking annoyed and confused.

Natalya stepped in. 'Your canopy was dead, Jake,' she said, her voice sharp. 'You should have cut away, but you did not. Instead, you kept fighting it. Kat was right – this is bull-shit. You are always full of it.'

'Shut it, Nat,' snapped Jake. 'I lost altitude awareness,

that's all, thought I could sort out my main canopy. The AAD saved me, didn't it? That's what it's for, right? What's the problem?'

Ethan saw the look on Natalya's face; it could've burned through lead. He was beginning to think she wasn't the kind of person you wanted to piss off.

'You are dangerous, Jake,' she said, tight-lipped. 'I'm not sure I want to jump with you again. Kill yourself – I do not care. Kill one of us? That is different.'

'She's got a point,' said Johnny. 'You should've cut away at two thousand, pulled the reserve yourself. An AAD's only in case of emergency. It's too bloody risky to depend on it like that. You could have been killed. AADs aren't foolproof.'

Jake gave an awkward laugh and tried to look relaxed. 'I had it all under control. It was just an error of judgement, that's all.'

'It is errors of judgement that get us killed,' hissed Natalya. 'And you make too many of them, Jake.'

'Look,' said Jake, 'like I said, I got too focused on sorting out my canopy, forgot to check my altimeter, that's all. I'm here, aren't I?'

'You were about five seconds from impact,' said Luke, his voice calm. 'If your AAD had failed, or if your reserve had got tangled with your main canopy, we'd be scraping you off the ground now instead of sitting here arguing. What were you thinking?'

'How do you know what happened anyway?' asked Jake, scowling now. 'You were all still in the air.' Then he saw Ethan. He pushed away from Kat and came over, got in Ethan's face. 'You tell them all this, Rookie?'

'I saw you falling,' said Ethan. 'I was with Sam.'

'So you finked on me? You ran and told the big scary boss man?'

'Hang it,' said Johnny, getting up and coming across. 'Sam was *with* Ethan. Ethan didn't have to tell him anything. Sam saw it all. Ethan just told us your canopy grabbed air at under a thousand; we guessed the rest.'

'But nothing happened, did it?' said Jake, now turning to Johnny. 'And all this dick's done is stir things up – hey, Rookie?'

Ethan was about to respond when a voice shot across the café.

'Jake!'

Everyone fell silent.

Sam was standing in the archway leading from the café to the bar area.

'Hey, Sam!' Jake grinned. 'Everything's cool, man. Had it all under control. And the rush – you haven't skydived till you've flown that close to wiping out! It was just awesome!'

Sam came over. He towered over the gang, his shadow falling across Jake.

'My office. Now.'

Jake opened his mouth to reply.

'Now, Jake,' said Sam. '*Now.*'

And seeing the look on Sam's face – even though he wasn't the one being called into his office – Ethan felt sick.

When Jake had left with Sam, Johnny flicked a glance at the rest of the gang. 'Dead man walking,' he said flatly.

No one argued.

8

Ethan heard Jake before he saw him. The crack of Sam's office door slamming split the air.

Ethan turned, saw Jake storming towards him.

'Rookie!'

Kat stood up and tried to stop him, but he pushed her out of the way and walked straight up to Ethan.

Ethan didn't flinch. He'd never been one for backing down from anyone. It had got him knocked around a few times at school, but he didn't care. Running away wasn't part of his character.

Jake shoved Ethan in the chest. 'I'm going to make you pay for this, Rookie . . .'

Ethan said nothing, did nothing. He just stood there, waiting to see what Jake would do next.

'You hear me?' said Jake as Kat tried to pull him away. 'You did this. All you had to do was keep your stupid mouth shut – that's all! You prick!'

Johnny and Luke walked over and stood between Ethan and Jake.

'That's it,' said Johnny, looking straight at Jake. 'Outside. Calm down. Now.'

Jake turned on Johnny. 'Don't tell me what to do, you shit!' he screamed, and Ethan could see he was losing control.

Luke stepped in. 'Jake, just do what Johnny suggested. Go outside and calm it.' Then he looked at Ethan. 'You, walk away,' he said.

Ethan nodded and turned back towards the counter. He figured it made more sense to let this one lie than help things get out of hand. He wanted the job and he wanted the tandem, and he knew Sam wouldn't look kindly on a fight at FreeFall.

Johnny and Luke stood firmly in Jake's way and Kat finally managed to get him to leave the café, taking him by the arm and dragging him out.

Johnny looked at Ethan. 'Kat was right about you,' he said, a smile breaking through the seriousness of the moment. 'You really do know how to make friends and influence people, don't you?'

'But I didn't do anything,' protested Ethan. 'And what was all that about? What happened? What's Sam done?'

Johnny and Luke sat back down at the table. Natalya hadn't moved, but now she leaned forward and looked up.

'The only thing he can do,' she said. 'If someone makes a

stupid mistake like that out on the DZ, then they are grounded until they've learned better. With Jake, it should have happened sooner. I have never trusted him. He is too wild. Too obsessed with himself. Even more so than Johnny.'

'Oh, you hurt me with your words,' Johnny groaned.

'What do you mean, grounded?' said Ethan. 'Kept inside for a week and not allowed to see his friends? Sam's not your dad!'

'No, he's not,' said Luke, 'but what he says goes. Jake won't be allowed to jump for a few weeks.'

'You serious?'

'Sam is always serious about this kind of thing,' said Natalya. 'Being grounded will give Jake time to sort himself out, get his priorities straight. And it will keep him out of the air while he is still considered a liability.'

'Yeah,' Johnny confirmed. 'Sam will want to make sure Jake doesn't do anything so stupid again. He'll probably interview him before letting him jump too. Check he's clued up enough on safety to be in the air. Jake will have to gen up on that stuff or Sam'll kick him out for good.'

'There would be no complaints from me,' said Natalya. 'I still cannot work out what Kat sees in him. She could do much better.'

Johnny gave a wink. 'With someone like me, you mean?'

Natalya shot him one of her steely looks, but he just winked again and added a very large smile, all teeth.

'Here's Kat,' said Luke, looking over at the door.

Her face was pale. She walked over, sat down, said nothing.

Natalya leaned over, concern etched on her face. 'Kat?'

61

Nothing.

'Come on, Kat,' said Johnny. 'Is it bad, really bad, or a full-on shit storm?'

Kat leaned back in her chair, hands on her head. 'Sam's not only grounded Jake for three months,' she said, 'he's kicked him off the team. He's out. Permanently.'

At this, Ethan heard everyone swear. Everyone but Natalya. She simply sat back in her chair, folded her arms and shook her head. But her eyes never left Kat, and Ethan could see she was concerned for her friend.

'Great,' said Johnny, and Ethan was surprised to hear disappointment in his voice. 'Jake finally ruined it for all of us.'

'What if Sam changes his mind when he calms down?' said Ethan, and realized as the words left his mouth how crazy they sounded. He'd not worked for Sam that long, but it was already obvious that he was not the kind of person to go back on a decision.

'He won't,' said Luke, confirming Ethan's thoughts. 'When Sam draws a line under something, he makes it clear exactly where it is. You cross it and you're out. No appeal. Nothing. Sam's word is law.'

Ethan looked at Kat. She was just sitting there shaking her head.

'Jake didn't want to talk about it,' she said. 'Not even to me.' Then she turned to Ethan and he could see just how upset she was. 'Why didn't you just keep quiet? Why did you have to go and tell Sam about it?'

'I told you – I didn't,' said Ethan. 'Sam was there with me. He told me it was Jake. I didn't know what was happening.'

But Kat wasn't really listening. 'You've ruined everything,' she said, standing up and pushing her chair away. It skidded for a minute, caught a hole in the floor, flipped.

'Don't talk crap,' said Johnny. 'Jake did this to himself. You know he's a liability.'

'Whatever,' said Kat.

'It's true, Kat. He's more bothered about how he looks up there – whether I've got his good side on camera – than anything to do with safety. We've all thought it, so don't kid yourself.'

'Looking good?' said Kat, turning on Johnny. 'You of all people should know about that being a major priority!'

'I look good because up there I do everything by the letter,' said Johnny, sounding serious for once. 'I certainly don't put you guys at risk. Ever.'

Kat started to say something, but then just turned and walked out. The café door slammed behind her as she left.

'I thought that all went rather well,' said Johnny, grimacing. 'Pity we're now utterly screwed.'

'How's that then?' asked Ethan.

Johnny sighed, and Ethan looked over at Luke, who just shrugged. Everyone seemed very downbeat.

'Can't believe the same thing's happened again,' said Johnny. 'Do you think we'll ever make a full team?'

'It is not quite the same this time, though, is it?' said Natalya. 'Jake did not just disappear without trace.'

Ethan rested his tray on the table and stared at Natalya. 'What do you mean? Who disappeared?' He saw Johnny and Luke glance at her.

Johnny leaned forward, folded his hands, looked serious

(serious didn't really suit him, thought Ethan). 'It's nothing,' he said. 'We lost a member of our crew a few months back. Jake was trying out as the replacement.'

'So what happened to him?' asked Ethan. 'Why did he disappear?'

Natalya opened her mouth to speak, but Luke got in first.

'Nothing that mysterious,' he said. 'It just didn't work out. One day he was here, the next he wasn't.'

'And we've never heard anything from him since,' finished Johnny. He grinned. 'I think he was intimidated by my amazing talent.'

Something about Natalya's expression told Ethan he wasn't getting the whole story. She had a distant look, like she was staring through Johnny, rather than at him, but she didn't argue. And Ethan didn't see any point in prying further. Hell, if Jake was their second team member to go, they were allowed to be a bit pissed off and weird about it.

It was a few moments before anyone said anything more. The silence felt awkward, and Ethan didn't fancy being the one to spark a conversation, so he cleared and cleaned a couple of empty tables.

At last Natalya spoke. 'We will just have to deal with it,' she said. 'It is not the end of the world.'

'Not for you maybe,' said Johnny.

'Not for any of us,' replied Natalya. 'Jake was not safe, he took risks – we all knew that. Now he is gone and that is a good thing.'

Johnny and Luke were silent.

'Sam really does rule this place, doesn't he?' said Ethan.

'Totally,' said Luke. 'He'll never see Jake as reliable now.

And on a team you have to be. It's vital. Everyone's depending on you up there. It's not a place to get complacent. Mess up in a formation or a stack? That's what kills skydivers. It's never the equipment. It's always human error.'

'Or stupidity,' said Johnny.

Silence.

But it was so loud, it was deafening.

'It is down to Sam,' said Natalya, finally breaking the silence. 'It is his call. We have to trust his decision. We all know that.'

'But that's just it, isn't it?' said Johnny. 'We *do* trust his decision. Which means we're screwed because we now don't have enough members to make up a skydiving team.' He leaned over the table and raised a glass. 'Here's to Jake – who ruined everything by being a tit.'

9

It was late afternoon. After the incident with Jake the day before, Ethan was happy it had all been fairly quiet. He was just getting onto his bike to head home when the sound of footsteps on gravel made him turn. A man wearing sunglasses and an expensive-looking dark suit had emerged from a black saloon car and was striding towards the café. He was younger than Sam, older than Luke – probably mid thirties. And his blond hair was swept back. He looked like an accountant, albeit one with a sense of style.

Sam came out of the café and shook the man's hand, then turned and spotted Ethan. Sam said something to the man, nodded, then came over.

'Ethan,' he said. 'Good day?'

Ethan nodded, and noticed that the man in the suit was still looking at him.

'Excellent,' said Sam. 'And it's about to get a whole lot better. You jump today.'

Ethan hesitated. It wasn't that he didn't feel up to it; it had just taken him by surprise. He shook his head a little to clear his mind, to think about what Sam had just said.

'Having second thoughts?'

Ethan shook his head again, realizing Sam had mis-interpreted his hesitation. 'No,' he said. No way was he backing out. He wanted to be like Johnny and the rest of the team. He wanted to be that good. And it was the first time in his life he'd felt this strongly about anything.

'Then follow me.' Sam headed off towards the hangar without another word.

As Ethan followed him, he noticed that the man in the suit was still looking at him, his sunglasses revealing nothing but reflected sky. Then Ethan was through the hangar doors and any thoughts as to who the man in the suit was were gone. This was it: he was about to skydive.

No one else was around. The last group to jump were now waiting outside for the minibus to take them to the plane.

'Sit. Watch,' said Sam, pointing at the TV in front of a row of plastic chairs. The screen flickered and Ethan sat down. He'd spent every day since taking the job watching people skydive. He'd heard them talk about it, scream about it, cry about it. He'd even caught bits of the DVD he was about to watch. From first jumpers to seasoned skydivers, they'd all passed through the café, the reception, the shop. And there was one thing he'd realized above all else: skydiving was ninety-five per cent waiting and five per cent adrenaline. If the conditions weren't right, no one jumped.

Today the conditions were right.

The TV was showing a tandem jump. Over a thumping rock soundtrack, the camera panned out from the buckle on a parachute harness to reveal an excited twenty-something girl. She gave a thumbs-up. The scene cut to the interior of a plane, the girl sitting quietly, seriously, between the legs of her instructor – who was smiling and acting very relaxed. Next scene they were sitting at the open door of the plane, feet dangling out, 12,000 feet up in the air. The girl was still sitting between the legs of her instructor and had her head back. He nodded at the camera, and then they jumped. The camera turned blue, spun, then focused on the girl. Ethan couldn't work out if she was actually smiling or if the wind was just pushing her face into an impression of The Joker. Finally the instructor looked at the camera, crossed his arms, then pulled a cable and disappeared. The film finished with the girl on the ground, leaping around and screaming.

'Simple, really,' said Sam as the film ended. 'You'll love it. Trust me.'

Ethan glanced up at him. He looked as imposing as ever, but Ethan could see that he meant every word. Not just about loving the tandem he was about to do, but about trusting him.

'How many times have you jumped?' Ethan asked.

'I've lost count,' said Sam. 'I went over the four thousand mark years ago.'

There was no bragging in what he said. It was just simple fact. Ethan was in the presence of a man utterly unlike anyone he'd ever met before. Sam seemed scary at first, but Ethan had come to realize that there was a lot more to him than the rough, tough exterior. He really cared about those who jumped at FreeFall. And he especially cared about Johnny and the rest of his team.

Sam showed Ethan the kit. 'This is a tandem rig,' he explained. 'It's larger than a solo rig because it has to hold two of us. It also needs to be able to grab enough air to support two and give the experienced skydiver enough control. After all, it takes us from a hundred and twenty mph to ten mph in just a few seconds.' He looked Ethan up and down. 'You weigh around thirteen stone, right?'

'Spot on,' said Ethan.

'Limit for a tandem is sixteen stone,' said Sam. 'Limit for a solo is fifteen. So don't go eating pies, OK?'

'OK,' agreed Ethan, wondering just how many pies he'd have to eat before he weighed fifteen stone. Then he asked, 'How big is the canopy exactly?' Despite knowing he was well within the weight limit, he suddenly felt a little concerned it wouldn't be big enough.

'Canopy, eh?' Sam smiled. 'Good to hear you're learning the lingo. Don't want people coming in thinking my staff are total muppets.'

Ethan grinned. It seemed Sam had a sense of humour after all.

'All you need to know is that it's big enough,' said Sam. 'Now empty your pockets and put this on.' He handed Ethan a blue and red jumpsuit. 'We can't have anything trailing from us when we're jumping,' he explained. 'It'd be dangerous and could split the canopy. The jumpsuit will protect your clothes and stop any flapping. Trust me, you don't want to be distracted when you're jumping.'

'Right.' Ethan promptly emptied his pockets, double-checking each one to make sure. No matter how good a skydiver Sam was, having him distracted at 12,000 feet wouldn't be good.

The jumpsuit was a good fit, and once it was on, Sam kitted Ethan up with a helmet and then the harness. It was a very snug fit to say the least, and he was glad he wouldn't be wearing it for too long.

Sam positioned Ethan up close and with his back to him and started to rehearse the jump. Ethan had seen people go through this numerous times. To be doing it himself felt amazing.

'Basic body position and commands are simple,' said Sam. 'Head back, legs up, arms crossed. Got it?'

Ethan had a go.

'And when we leave the plane, just arch yourself back-wards with your legs between mine. Right?'

Ethan nodded.

'When we're clear and stable, I'll release the drogue chute. That's the one that will eventually pull out the main canopy. It also helps to stabilize the freefall. I'll tap again and you pull your arms out like this, right?'

Ethan said, 'Yes,' as Sam got into a skydiving position in front of him, his legs slightly apart, his arms out in front and bent, as if he was holding something heavy above his head.

As they ran through it again, a message came through over the tannoy.

'That's us,' said Sam. 'Let's go.'

Ethan followed, and with each step wondered just what the hell he was doing.

The minibus that transported people to the runway was the wrong side of knackered, so Ethan was relieved to see that the plane itself wasn't in a similar state. Silently he followed Sam on board, sitting down between his legs. Everyone was wearing a helmet. It was loud inside, the engines mixing the air into a strangle of howls and revs and squeals. Ethan spotted Johnny opposite him. Johnny smiled and Ethan thought it made him look just a little unhinged. But he was glad his friend was on the plane.

Ethan felt Sam clip himself into his rig, clamping the two of them together, pulling in tight. A strap was then clipped to Sam. Ethan knew from what Johnny had told him that this was just like a seat belt, attaching him to the plane; it would be released at 1,000 feet. A few days ago Ethan had asked why it was released.

'Well, if the plane's shagged, you're better off jumping than crashing with it' had been Johnny's simple, smiling answer.

The pilot said something over the speaker system that Ethan couldn't understand, and the plane started to move.

He felt himself bumping off the floor as the plane gathered speed. Then his stomach disappeared and they lifted into the air.

Looking out through the window, Ethan watched as the ground fell away. He didn't think it was a good time to mention that he'd never flown before.

After a few minutes Sam tugged on the harness again,

tightening it even further. He flicked his wrist at Ethan, showing him the altimeter reading 10,000 feet. Ethan knew they jumped at 12,000.

It came around all too quickly. Ethan felt a tap on his shoulder and Sam gave a thumbs-up. Strapped in as he was, Ethan had little choice but to do as Sam did, so he soon found himself sitting with his feet hanging out of the open door of the plane.

He looked down between his feet at the ground below. Impossible to believe it was 12,000 feet away and that he was about to get back to it by falling.

Another tap.

Ethan turned to find Johnny grinning at him, and pointing at the camera on his helmet. He climbed out through the plane doorway and hung onto the edge. Ethan hadn't asked to be filmed, but he mouthed 'Cheers!' to him.

Sam shouted the commands: 'Head back, legs up, arms crossed.'

Ethan obeyed.

And they jumped into oblivion.

The world spun and flipped, flipped and spun. It was blue and green and green and blue. For a few seconds Ethan found it impossible to take in. And he couldn't breathe. Every time he tried to take in air, it was whipped away. But despite the panic he was fighting, he was also smiling. He could feel it; he was grinning so hard it felt like his face would crack.

The view changed, became stable. Earth below, sky above. Ethan could see it now they were belly-to-earth. Two and a half miles below him, criss-cross roads and patchwork fields stretched away to nothing. It all looked so tiny and so beautiful. Ethan was amazed. And he knew – right then in that moment – that he wanted to do this again. Once would never be enough.

Sam tapped his shoulder and Ethan pulled his arms open. He was skydiving!

'Shit! Shit! Shit! Shit! Shit!' he screamed. He knew it wasn't the most inspired thing to say, but he couldn't think of anything else; he'd just jumped out of a plane! Johnny came into view, and Ethan gave the camera a thumbs-up and said 'Shit!' again.

He felt his cheeks start to ache as the wind ripped past, dragging the breath from his lungs. Another tap on his shoulder. He crossed his arms and felt himself being almost ripped in half.

Ethan recognized the sound of the canopy opening and looked up as their descent was slowed to a gentle glide.

'Want to steer?' asked Sam.

Ethan was stunned by how clearly he could hear him, and he wasn't even shouting. Everything was suddenly so quiet now that they were no longer plunging through the air. They were drifting with the wind now, so the roar that had echoed in his ears during the freefall was totally gone.

Before he could refuse, Ethan had his hands clamped to the yellow loops attached to the steering lines of the canopy. He found that the slightest tug with either hand could alter their course.

'DZ's over there.' Sam pointed, and Ethan was able to make out the airfield. 'I'll take over when you get us close enough.'

'You sure?' Ethan asked, hardly daring to believe Sam would let him take control up here even for a moment.

'Wouldn't say it if I wasn't, Ethan.'

Ethan felt himself grinning even harder and, with a faint tug left, brought them slowly round.

A few minutes later, Sam took over, and as the ground approached, he shouted, 'Feet up, knees up!'

Ethan did exactly that and they glided in, landing with a brief slide onto their backsides.

Johnny was in front, filming the landing.

Sam unclipped Ethan and they stood up. It was all Ethan could do not to yell and scream and jump around like a loon. He felt amazing, on top of the world, completely and utterly alive.

Johnny walked over, still filming. 'As I said, life's too short not to,' he said, a huge smile on his face.

Remembering that moment high above the earth, the sensation of falling from the plane, Ethan could think of only one thing to say.

He swung round to face Sam. 'When can I do it again?'

Sam and Johnny looked at each other and grinned.

10

Ethan was sitting on the sofa with his mum and Jo, watching the DVD of his jump. It was a couple of hours since he'd done the tandem with Sam, but he was still buzzing. And Jo hadn't stopped laughing.

'Check out your face!' she said. 'You look hysterical!' On the screen Ethan's face was being buffeted by the wind, his cheeks rippling.

'I was doing a hundred and twenty miles an hour,' he told her. 'It's pretty difficult to keep a straight face!'

'I can't believe that's you,' said his mum. She was sitting on the edge of the sofa, her hands clasped together. 'Weren't you scared?'

'Not really,' said Ethan, and he wasn't lying. 'You don't

have time to be scared. Sam just gets on with it, takes you through the training, and before you know it you're at the door of the plane! Then you're out. It's such a rush!'

'No way am I ever doing that,' said Jo, watching as Sam pulled the ripcord and the main canopy exploded behind them. 'It's insane.'

'It's amazing,' said Ethan. 'Best thing I've ever done.'

The screen flicked to Ethan and Sam coming in to land.

'Sam looks very forbidding,' said his mum. 'Does he ever smile?'

Ethan laughed. 'He's terrifying, but great.'

As though in response to Ethan's mother's question, Sam looked at the camera and smiled. Ethan didn't think he'd ever forget that moment. To have people like Sam and Johnny proud of what he'd done . . . It felt great!

The DVD finished and Ethan asked, 'Want to watch it again?'

His mum and Jo nodded and he pressed PLAY.

The screen showed Ethan in the plane, strapped to Sam. But as they watched the footage again, the flat shook to the sound of the front door slamming shut. Dad was home.

Ethan saw his mum's eyes close, her head fall forward a little. He moved to stop the DVD before his dad came into the lounge, but he was too late.

'What's this then? Playing happy families, are we?'

Ethan turned. His dad was leaning against the doorframe, finishing off a can of lager. For a moment no one said a word. The only sound came from Ethan's tandem skydive on the TV.

'That your new boyfriend?' His dad was pointing at the TV with the can in his hand. 'Bit old for you, isn't he?'

Ethan said nothing. He wasn't going to let his dad ruin this. No way. So he went over to the TV, ejected the DVD and put it back in its case.

'I hope I haven't spoiled anything,' said his dad. 'Put it on, son. I want to see it.'

'It's finished,' said Ethan.

As he made to leave the room, his mum reached up and touched his hand. 'I'm really proud of you.'

Ethan smiled. 'Thanks, Mum,' he said, and headed for the door.

But his dad was blocking the doorway. 'Where are you going, son? Come on, let me watch it. Make me proud,' he said sarcastically.

'Get out of my way,' said Ethan, and heard his mum and Jo coming up behind him.

'Ethan,' said his mum. 'Don't . . .'

He stared at his dad. For a moment no one moved, then his dad stepped to one side, a fake smile slapped across his fat face. 'After you,' he said.

Ethan edged his way past, but as he did so, his dad snatched the DVD from his hand.

He snapped round. 'Give that back.'

His dad looked at the DVD, then waved it in front of Ethan's face. 'I just want to watch it, son, that's all.'

'Don't call me that. Don't call me son,' said Ethan. He lunged for the DVD, and missed.

His dad laughed, then held the DVD out. 'Go on, then,' he said. 'Take it.'

Ethan reached for the DVD and his dad threw it down the hall. It clattered into the front door.

Ethan turned in fury. 'You bastard . . .'

But his mum immediately stepped between them, pushing Ethan away. 'Don't,' she said. 'Please, Ethan, don't let him spoil it.'

'Yeah, listen to Mummy,' said his dad, and laughed.

Ethan moved towards his father, but his mum resisted and he thought better of it. Instead, he went to pick up the DVD. It seemed fine. He turned round to see his dad still sneering at him, but his mum was smiling. And so was Jo. And that was enough.

The day after the tandem jump Ethan was helping out in the shop at FreeFall. The buzz was still ripping through him.

Johnny had come in to buy a magazine; he was staring across the counter at Ethan.

'What?' said Ethan.

'Think you've got it bad, mate,' said Johnny.

'Got what?'

'The addiction. Some people jump once and that's enough for them – been there, done that, got the T-shirt. But others – *you*, for example . . .'

'What about me?'

'You want up again, don't you?'

Ethan nodded.

'Can't think of anything else, can you?'

Ethan shook his head.

'Like I said,' Johnny sighed. 'You're addicted, Eth.' And with that, he turned to leave.

Ethan called him back as some of the other regular sky-divers came to look around the shop.

'I've been thinking,' he said. 'What do I do next – you know – if I want to get into this? At least if I know what it'll cost, I'll have something to aim for.'

'The AFF,' said Johnny. 'Accelerated Freefall. It's the course we all did: Kat, Natalya, Luke. Even Jake.'

'Sounds cool,' said Ethan.

'Oh, it's cool all right,' said Johnny. 'Zero to hero in a week.'

'A week? No way.'

'That's why it's called accelerated,' said Johnny. 'If the weather's good, in one week you're jumping solo. There's lots of one-on-one tuition. It's pretty intense. Loads to learn. No time to think. Hell of a rush.'

Ethan remembered hearing a few people talking about the AFF, but he'd never taken a booking for it. 'Why don't more people do it?'

'Because it costs about fifteen hundred quid,' said Johnny. 'And that's a lot of cash.'

Ethan ran the figure around in his mind. It didn't get any smaller. 'Bollocks,' he said.

'Steep, isn't it?' said Johnny. 'Got anything tucked away?'

Ethan shook his head. 'You've seen where we live. We all chip in together. We're not exactly poor, but no way have we got that amount of cash just sitting in the bank . . .'

'What about the job?' asked Johnny. 'Could you save up?'

Ethan shook his head. 'It's a great job, but I'm hardly raking it in.' He attempted a smile. 'Hey, at least I managed to bag a free tandem. I mean, how many people can say that, eh? And a couple of weeks ago I'd never have thought I'd be able to do something like that.'

'There's nothing stopping you doing another tandem,' said Johnny. 'Or you could do a static line jump.'

'I guess,' said Ethan. He knew about static line jumps, but he wasn't really interested. Jumping from a plane and having the canopy open automatically just didn't seem to have the same buzz about it as skydiving. And you didn't get the freefall rush either. It was just a jump from the plane and then a glide down. That was it.

Ethan tried not to think about how much he wanted to do the AFF – and how much he couldn't afford it. He smiled at Johnny. 'Anyway, thanks for the DVD. Couldn't stop watching it last night. The soundtrack sucked though.'

'We use the same one for all the DVDs,' said Johnny. 'Even the training one. Can't beat a nice bit of eighties metal!'

Ethan turned and saw Sam's head round the door; he was looking at Johnny. 'Got a minute? I've a little job for you. Right up your street, I think.' Then he glanced at Ethan. 'And, Ethan – make sure you're in early tomorrow. Seven thirty, OK?'

'Yeah, no worries,' said Ethan, and Johnny followed Sam out of the shop.

Ethan thought again about the AFF and felt like he'd been kicked in the stomach. The tandem had been amazing, had totally blown his mind. He didn't want to just do that again; he wanted to skydive properly, do what Johnny did. But fifteen hundred quid? No chance, he thought. No chance at all. He spent the rest of the day trying not to think about skydiving.

For him, it was just impossible.

The next day Ethan arrived at FreeFall dead on seven thirty, skidding to a halt beside the café. To his surprise, Johnny was already there, sitting outside, shades on. He smiled, waved. Ethan returned the gesture.

'So,' he said, slipping into a chair in front of Johnny, 'what's this all about? Why are you here? Did Sam ask you to be in early too?'

Johnny just grinned and pushed his shades back. 'You still thinking about that skydive?'

Ethan nodded. 'Too right I am. Can hardly think of anything else. Bit of a pisser about the AFF, though.' He still felt gutted.

'True,' said Johnny.

'I'll get over it,' said Ethan. 'I've been thinking I might do it next summer. You know, celebrate the end of school with it or something. If I keep working here and maybe take another job as well, I should be able to save up enough.'

Johnny nodded thoughtfully then leaned forward. 'Look,' he said. 'Here's the thing . . .'

'What thing?'

'It's all been taken care of.'

Ethan didn't understand. 'What do you mean? What are you on about? What's been taken care of?'

'You. The AFF. It's sorted.'

'Shut up,' said Ethan. 'And don't be a dick.'

'I'm not being a dick,' Johnny insisted. 'It's true. That's what Sam wanted to see me about yesterday. He wants me to help him put you through the AFF.'

Ethan opened his mouth to speak, then shut it again. He couldn't believe what he was hearing. Surely Johnny was just taking the piss.

'Sam will be teaching you,' Johnny told him. 'He's the business, as you know. Doesn't miss a trick and doesn't let you jump unless he's confident you're not going to spin out and kill yourself.'

'You're not serious, are you?' said Ethan, but Johnny simply went on:

'I'll be doing the filming. I need the practice anyway. We'll be able to assess every single jump you do, show you what you're doing wrong, what you're doing right. And you'll have a nice little souvenir at the end, won't you? A little bit of Ethan Hollywood all of your own.'

At last words formed in Ethan's head. 'But . . . who?' he asked. '*Who's* sorted it? This doesn't make sense . . .' And it didn't. He'd spent the whole of yesterday dealing with the fact that he wouldn't be able to do his AFF until next summer at the earliest, and now here was Johnny telling him he'd be doing it right away. It sounded nuts.

A throaty growl interrupted his thoughts as Sam pulled up in his Defender and climbed out.

'Ethan. Johnny,' he said, striding over to them. 'Ready?'

'I sure am,' said Johnny, standing up. 'Ethan's still in shock, though, aren't you, mate?'

Ethan looked up at Sam and slowly got to his feet. 'How am I supposed to pay for this?' he asked. 'It's OK you helping me out by teaching and filming and stuff, but it's still going to cost, isn't it? And I just don't have the cash. I really don't. I mean, fifteen hundred quid . . . that's—'

'A lot of money, I know,' said Sam, cutting Ethan off. 'But hasn't Johnny told you? It's all sorted.'

Ethan nodded. 'Yeah, he said, but—'

'Then here's a little tip: shut up and accept it, right? I have ways of getting extra funding when I need it. That's all you need to know.'

'But I'll still have to pay it back,' said Ethan.

'No,' said Sam, 'you won't. That's what "sorted" means. I've also arranged cover for you this week so you don't have to worry about work. All you need to think about now is keeping your eyes and ears open, listening, learning and making sure you don't die. Got it?'

Ethan stood there for a moment, trying to take it all in. The tandem – that had been pretty crazy. But now this! How on earth had Sam sorted out the costs? And why? It didn't make sense, but Ethan didn't want to ask any more questions in case Sam got annoyed and changed his mind. It started to sink in. He was going to learn to skydive . . . bloody hell!

Adrenaline raced through him. 'You're serious, aren't you?' he said, and as he looked up at Sam, he saw a flicker of a smile cross his face.

'I'm always serious,' said Sam. 'So sort your shit out and I'll see you and Johnny in the hangar in ten.'

He went over to the café door, unlocked it and disappeared inside.

Ethan turned to Johnny. 'I'm actually going to be learning to skydive? For real?'

Johnny nodded, and came to put his arm across Ethan's shoulders. 'Not just skydive,' he said, 'but skydive *with the best.*'

'Sam?'

'No,' said Johnny. 'Me.'

11

'The AFF course,' Sam began, 'takes you from beginner to category eight qualified skydiver in eight jumps.'

Ethan was sitting in the hangar, Johnny next to him. He was fully rigged up and hanging on Sam's every word. Outside, the day was clear; sunshine was streaming in through the windows. 'Eight jumps?' he said, thinking it hardly sounded enough.

Sam nodded. 'Today we're doing ground training,' he went on. 'You'll do your first jump tomorrow.'

Ethan immediately felt disappointed. He was impatient, wanted to jump now, get back into the air, feel the sky rushing past him, experience again that strange moment when the world below just seems to sit there, perfectly still, not getting any closer, your brain unable to compute that you're at terminal velocity, falling at around 120 mph.

Johnny went and stood next to Sam. Ethan thought how different they were – Sam with his startlingly short hair, hard face and unflinching stance; Johnny looking like an advert for why extreme sports make women want to sleep with you.

'Sam's going to be leading on this,' Johnny said. 'I'm helping out. When you do your jumps, you'll leave the plane with both of us. We'll help you get a feel for the air, sort your positioning out, that kind of thing. And I'll be filming it all too. So at least you'll look good.'

'It'll give us something to analyse on the ground,' said Sam, ignoring Johnny's comment. 'Just another way of being extra thorough. The quicker you get the details right, the better you'll be when you're up there.'

'It'll also give us something to laugh at,' added Johnny.

Ethan noticed a smile start to flicker across Sam's face, but it was gone as quickly as it had appeared. He was beginning to understand the man a little more now, and since the jump he felt he could trust him absolutely.

'As Sam said,' said Johnny, 'today's ground training.' He went over to the hangar wall and pulled out what looked to Ethan like a tea trolley.

'What the hell's that?'

'The perfect way to make you look a total knob,' said Johnny. 'We'll be using it to show you the basic moves you'll need. You lie on top of it – that way you can practise the correct positions and movements in freefall.'

'Are you having a laugh?' Ethan looked doubtfully at the trolley.

Johnny shook his head and Ethan saw a rare seriousness on his face. 'If you can't do it down here, and do it well, then there's no way we're going to throw you out of a plane,' he said. 'It's human error, not equipment failure that kills. Skydiving is only as dangerous as you make it. Get the basics right, and you can do this stuff without even thinking about it. It becomes instinctive. You'll be fine.'

Ethan remembered Luke saying something similar about human error versus equipment failure. He listened even more intently to everything Sam and Johnny were saying.

Sam looked at him, his eyes hard. 'Questions?'

Ethan shook his head. 'Not yet anyway.'

'Good,' said Sam. 'You've learned your first lesson: shut the hell up. It's the only way you'll learn. I'll tell you when you can ask questions. Until then, just listen to us and do what we say. Understand?'

'Totally,' said Ethan, and meant it.

Johnny bent down and picked up a skydiving rig. 'By the end of today you'll know what this is, inside and out. You'll know how to read an altimeter. You'll know how to exit an air-craft and how to do a freefall – the correct body position, hand signals, canopy control – everything.'

Ethan nodded. Sam knew his stuff, that was obvious, but so did Johnny. He was a flash git – everyone knew it – but he was also an astounding skydiver. And Ethan could see that Sam had a lot of time for Johnny, despite the fact that they were different in almost every way. Johnny lived and breathed skydiving. What he didn't know, you didn't need to know. Ethan wondered if he'd ever be like that; hoped he would.

Johnny interrupted his thoughts. 'Tomorrow, and for the rest of the week, you'll be jumping from twelve thousand feet. Forecast is good – we shouldn't have any problems. For each of your AFF jumps, we'll be in constant radio contact, so we can guide you down, help you correct what you're doing. Jump eight, your last jump, will be your first solo. You'll be entirely on your own. Complete that, and you're qualified. However . . .' He paused and looked at Sam.

'What?' said Ethan.

'Qualifying to jump solo doesn't mean you can then just get into any plane and start throwing yourself out whenever you want,' said Sam. 'After AFF you have to do a further ten consolidation jumps before you're classed as capable, experienced and safe. With each of those jumps, one of us will jump with you.'

Ethan saw a smirk slide across Johnny's face. 'And it'll take a miracle for you ever to make it look as good as I do.'

Sam didn't respond, but Ethan laughed.

It all felt so unreal. He couldn't believe he was sitting there, listening to Johnny and Sam, learning to skydive. And somehow he'd got all this training for free. Somehow, Sam and Johnny had sorted something out. He had no idea how or why. But he knew Sam well enough to realize that any more questions about it would not go down well.

What followed was a day so intense, Ethan felt like his brain would burn up. Sam and Johnny pushed him hard. Lying on the trolley, he practised the freefall body position again and again. Sam didn't mince his words. If Ethan got something wrong, he knew all about it. Sam wouldn't accept anything less than perfection. And that perfection had to become instinctive.

What really intrigued Ethan, though, was that in the midst of the info-dump he was undergoing, Johnny and Sam seemed really interested in who he was. When they weren't telling him stuff or demonstrating something, they were asking questions – not just to make sure he was remembering what they were teaching him, but about his background, how he'd come to be there at FreeFall with them, learning to skydive.

'Everything's important,' Sam had said over lunch. 'Not just who you are, but *why* you are. I don't want to put just anyone in the sky and throw them out of a plane attached to a silk bag. That'd be irresponsible. I want to know why they're in the air in the first place, what kind of person they are, their motivation. Understand?'

By the end of the day Ethan's mind was leaking terms he'd never heard before. He found himself rattling off phrases like he knew them: AAD, body position, burble, cut away, RSL, terminal velocity, wave off, and the term used to describe people who don't jump – wuffo. He was never going to be a wuffo ever again. That felt good.

Sam had drawn the day to a close with a 'Well done, Ethan,' and a firm shake of the hand, before driving away in his Defender. Now Ethan was sitting on a bench outside the hangar, his head resting against the wall.

'So,' said Johnny. 'How are you doing?'

'I'm knackered,' said Ethan, and meant it. 'Sam's a hard-arse, isn't he? Really drives stuff into you like your life depends on it.'

'That's because it does. Sam lives and breathes skydiving. He's done it all his life.'

'You're no different,' Ethan told Johnny.

'Oh, I am,' he said, sliding down next to Ethan. 'I've been jumping for two years. I'm a qualified rigger. I can do formation stuff and solo. But Sam? He's a god.'

'Yeah. A scary one,' said Ethan. 'But that's the funny thing about him. He's this terrifying perfectionist but at the same time you can't help liking him. What's his story?'

Johnny shrugged. 'He doesn't speak much about his past, his military life. But I know he's done plenty of HALO and HAHO jumps, and that's some really serious shit. He's one of the most experienced skydivers in the business.'

'HALO?' asked Ethan.

'High Altitude, Low Opening,' Johnny explained. 'Used by special forces when they want to get in behind enemy lines nice and quickly.'

'Sounds pretty intense,' said Ethan.

'You've got that right,' Johnny agreed. 'You're jumping at over thirty thousand feet. You have to carry oxygen cylinders because you can't breathe that high up. You also have to wear special thermal kit to stop yourself freezing to death on the way down.'

'Nice.'

'Yeah. It's pretty difficult to pull a ripcord if you're an icicle doing a hundred and twenty.'

'So how low's the low opening?' asked Ethan.

'Real low,' said Johnny. 'When you eventually release your canopy, you're under two thousand five hundred feet.'

'Freefalling for over twenty-seven thousand feet? That's crazy!'

'Sure is. And pulling your canopy at under two thousand five hundred doesn't allow any room for error.'

Ethan was quiet for a moment; then he looked at Johnny. 'Imagine it – freefalling all that way. Unbelievable. You fancy it?'

'Do I really need to answer that?'

Ethan grinned. 'No,' he said. 'Not really. So what's HAHO?'

'High Altitude, *High* Opening,' said Johnny. 'You jump from the same height, wear thermals, but you need more oxygen, because you release your main canopy pretty much immediately after leaving the aircraft. You can be up there for some time.'

'That'd be amazing!' said Ethan. 'Like flying!'

'Sam described it just like that,' said Johnny. 'He reckons a HALO jump is the closest thing to nearly dying, because you're just plummeting and you can't really believe you're going to survive. But a HAHO is totally different. The advantage of HAHO is that you can leave an aircraft outside a hostile area and land silently inside enemy territory. There's no danger of the noise of the aircraft alerting the opposition. Also, they're safer. Easier to control. Higher survival rate.'

'Survival rate?'

Johnny nodded. 'HALO is pretty dangerous. Screw that up and you hit the deck. A few people have died doing it. Anyway,' he went on, 'looking forward to tomorrow?'

'Like you wouldn't believe,' said Ethan.

'It's a whole different ball game now,' Johnny told him. 'But just remember what we said and you'll be fine. And if you thought doing a tandem was incredible, wait till you find yourself under your own canopy.'

And when the time came, when Ethan actually found himself at the door of the plane at 12,000 feet, Johnny on one side, Sam on the other, everything Johnny had told him, everything he'd felt during the tandem, was blown out of the sky. This was a totally different experience. In the tandem jump, the decisions had all been made by Sam. Now, even though Sam and Johnny were with him, Ethan decided when to jump. And he wasn't strapped to anyone at all.

The call came, and Ethan jumped.

He fell . . .

. . . tumbled . . .

. . . tried to stabilize . . .

Around him the world spun and flipped. The plane appeared, disappeared.

Green Earth . . .

Blue sky . . .

Green again . . .

Arch your back, Ethan . . . he told himself.

Stable! Air rushing past, blasting away all sense of sound.

Ethan felt his arms buffeted by the wind as if he'd stuck them out of a car sun roof at eighty.

Johnny and Sam used hand signals. Ethan recognized them from the intense training of the day before. Understanding burst in his brain and he responded, adjusted his body position, checked his altimeter.

This feels natural, he thought; *like I'm meant to be up here, doing this*. But what really grabbed him was the sense of freedom. Even with Johnny and Sam falling with him, he was out there and in control of what was going on. It was up to him to get his positioning right, to pull the ripcord. And it felt brilliant. Nothing could ever touch this.

More hand signals. Time to deploy the canopy. Ethan looked down to the handle at the end of the ripcord. He knew he had to make sure he had firm contact. He gripped it hard, just as Sam and Johnny had taught him in the hangar, raising his other hand above his head for symmetry, to stop himself from spinning out.

Everything was in the next movement.

He pulled the handle hard and downwards. Any other direction and the wire could snag in the steel piping it ran through, the pin wouldn't pull, and the main canopy wouldn't deploy.

As soon as he'd pulled the handle, he pushed both arms out to the side.

Symmetrical.

Stable.

Crack!

Ethan felt his whole body being pulled upwards as, above him, his canopy burst open, caught air, inflated. Johnny and Sam were nowhere to be seen; they'd spun off to find some clean air to pull their own rigs.

'Ethan. You OK?'

For a second Ethan had no idea where the voice was coming from. He was breathless, disorientated, buzzing like hell. Then he remembered the radio. It was Johnny on the other end.

'Fine,' he said. 'I'm fine.'

'Spotted the DZ?'

Ethan quickly glanced around. There it was. How small it looked. 'Got it. Now what?'

Sam's voice came over the radio too. 'Remember what you learned yesterday. Just stay on your current heading,' he said. 'You're doing fine. Remember to use those steering toggles. Try it. Track right.'

Ethan pulled the right steering toggle. He felt himself turn to the right. He eased off, tried the left toggle, turned left. Wow! He was in control of this thing! Unreal!

'Great,' came Sam's voice again. 'Keep doing that so that you're on course for the DZ, OK? But remember, you're not aiming to land on it. You're aiming for the field just off to the right.'

Johnny's voice crackled in. 'It's a bigger target than the DZ and it keeps you out of the way of those who know what they're doing. Like me.'

Ethan laughed, looked down at the fields below, and started to gradually alter his course.

The world was getting closer and everything was quiet. The wind pushed him along, and slowly he drifted down, down, down.

'Right,' came Johnny's voice. 'I'm down. Perfect landing, obviously. How are you feeling?'

'Awesome! How am I looking?'

'You're on a good heading,' said Johnny. 'Stay on that line and I'll meet you in the field, OK?'

'No worries,' said Ethan.

'OK. Just remember to turn into the wind and flare as you come in, just to slow yourself down. Not too much, though;

I don't want you collapsing your canopy and breaking a leg on your first jump.'

Ethan looked down. He could see Johnny waving up at him, walking from the DZ to the field. And it was getting closer. He was amazed by how the Earth could seem so far away, and then, in seconds, come racing up to meet him. He let the wind take him. The field was clearly visible, and with the occasional adjustment he was dead on course. Following Johnny's instructions to the letter, he turned into the wind for his final approach.

He felt the wind slow him down. Then he pulled the toggles together, felt the canopy buck a little – and he was down.

His first landing. His first solo landing.

Bloody hell . . .

Johnny strolled over.

'Ready to go again?'

Ethan didn't even need to reply.

12

'Recap,' said Sam, eyes hard. 'You're up to level five now. What have you covered?'

Johnny had just gone to grab a drink and Ethan was alone with Sam in the hangar. It was the third day of his AFF and his feet had, quite literally, hardly touched the ground.

Ethan felt like his brain had hardwired itself to anything and everything to do with skydiving. He went through all that Sam and Johnny had taught him, demonstrated hand signals, body positions, used correct terminology. Everything he'd learned had stuck. No detail was missing. Ethan felt that skydiving was as much second nature to him now as walking and breathing.

Sam nodded when he finished. 'You learn quick,' he said.

'But don't get complacent. Remember, heights don't kill, the ground does. And that will only kill you if you forget your drills, lose concentration, or try to show off. Remember the seven Ps: Perfect Prior Planning Prevents Piss Poor Performance.'

Ethan remembered. But then Sam had a habit of repeating everything until whatever he'd taught you became instinctive. Ethan also remembered what had happened to Jake; how close he'd been to bouncing, as skydivers called it – landing at an unsurvivable speed.

Johnny came back into the hangar, and handed Sam and Ethan a bottle of water each. Then Sam let Johnny kick off with what they were doing next.

'The three-sixty-degree turns were excellent, Eth; nicely done,' Johnny said. 'Level six is more fun though – it's front-loop time!'

Ethan looked at him. 'Front loop?'

'Mid-air somersault,' explained Johnny. 'You flip yourself over while you're in freefall, then stabilize.'

'You'll be doing some tracking too,' said Sam. 'That's what we call it when we zip forward through the air, rather than just freefalling. You use it if you're trying to put distance between yourself and other skydivers. Or if you just like going fast.'

'What's after that, then?' asked Ethan. 'If this is level six, what's left?'

'Level seven is where you'll put the whole lot together,' said Sam. 'You'll do your damnedest to pull off a decent exit from the aircraft, follow our hand signals, do a front loop, stabilize, turn three hundred and sixty degrees left and right, then track away and deploy your canopy.'

'And level eight,' said Johnny with a big smile, 'is hop 'n' pop. You're on your own from exit to landing.'

'And that's it?' said Ethan. 'Qualified?'

'Ten more consolidation jumps, and you're certified,' Sam told him.

Ethan felt even more excited now that he was so close to finishing. Was his life really becoming this cool? Apparently it was, and he was loving it!

Sam raised an eyebrow at him. 'You keeping on top of it all? You seem to be.'

Ethan stared back. What could he say? That for the first time in his life he felt like he was doing something really worthwhile, something he was good at, perhaps even better than good? That he loved the sensation of freedom you got when jumping, of being right out there at the very edge of what life was about?

Say any of that and I'll sound like a total prick, he thought. So, 'It's great,' he said. 'I'm loving it. You think I'm doing OK?'

Sam nodded. 'Yes.' Then he pointed at Johnny. 'You check we're on for another jump.' He turned back to Ethan. 'You go wait outside. I'll join you in a minute. I just need to make a phone call. When I come out, I'll be asking questions, and I won't be impressed by anything other than the correct answers. Got it?'

Johnny was out the door sharpish. Ethan followed.

'Who's that?' asked Ethan as he and Johnny headed for the plane for his level seven jump that afternoon. He'd completed his level six just before lunch. The weather was still holding out. If it stayed this good, he'd be able to do his level eight tomorrow. Fantastic!

He pointed over to the car park, where a man in a suit was standing beside a nondescript black saloon car. Ethan instantly recognized him as the guy he'd seen shaking hands with Sam the day he'd done his tandem. Today he was holding a pair of binos in his left hand.

Johnny glanced over, following Ethan's gaze. 'That's Gabe, Sam's friend,' he said. 'Though he's not very sociable. Why?'

Ethan wasn't sure, but he had a feeling that the man was watching them. 'I've seen him before,' he said. 'He was here when I did my tandem. And I think he's watching us.' The words sounded so stupid once they were out that he immediately wished he'd kept his mouth shut.

'That explains it,' said Johnny, a smirk sliding effortlessly onto his face.

'It does?'

'Absolutely! My fans come in all shapes and sizes.'

Laughing, they climbed into the plane. Ethan glanced back at the man. His binoculars were raised now and trained on the aircraft. Joking aside, thought Ethan, it was odd. But he soon forgot about the stranger, not least because of who was waiting for him in the plane. Along one side sat the rest of Johnny's team, all rigged up in matching kit: Luke, Natalya and Kat.

Kat looked up at Johnny, then shot Ethan an electrifying smile. 'We've been hearing so much about Sam's new golden boy that we figured we should come and check out his progress.' She leaned back against the inside of the plane, checked her ponytail. 'Apparently you're on your level seven

– and ahead of schedule too. Perhaps all the good things we've been hearing are true?'

Ethan didn't quite know how to take Kat's words. He hadn't seen her since Sam had bollocked Jake, and she hadn't seemed too happy with him then. Now she was smiling, beaming almost, but he couldn't help noticing an edge – not so much to her voice, but to her words. *Golden boy?* What the hell was that about? He was in no way Sam's golden boy – doubted anyone was. *Kat's probably still pissed at me about Jake*, he thought.

Johnny rested a hand on Ethan's shoulder as they sat down. 'He's a natural, aren't you, mate?' he said. 'Born to it, I reckon. Like me.'

Kat laughed. 'The only thing *you're* born to is self-appreciation.'

Again that edge, Ethan noticed. What was her problem? Was this really about Jake? Ethan wondered if he was just imagining things, reading something into what Kat was saying that just wasn't there. He decided to ignore it, and focused on Natalya and Luke instead.

Luke was staring at his altimeter. He looked like he was convinced it wasn't working; or that if he stopped looking at it, it would stop working, just to piss him off.

Natalya, though, gazed right back at Ethan.

Ethan nodded and gave her a smile.

Natalya nodded back, but said nothing. She didn't need to, he thought. It was her eyes that did all the talking. They seemed to stare right through him, like she was sizing him up, looking for flaws. He looked away, but found himself glancing back at her a few times. And each time, he found her still staring at – no, *into* – him. It unnerved him. What the hell was she thinking? If I were Johnny, thought Ethan, I'd be convinced she fancied me. The thought brought a smile to his face that finally made Natalya turn and look elsewhere.

Luke was still busy going over his kit. He checked every buckle and clip once, then did so again in exactly the same order. Then again. He looked up. 'Hey, Eth,' he said. 'Want me to check your kit?'

'We've got it covered,' said Johnny. 'But I'll let you know if his lapels need doing. You did bring the steam iron, didn't you?'

Everyone laughed.

'There's nothing wrong with making sure everything's right,' said Luke. 'But I'm afraid I left the iron in the hangar.'

'That is a shame.'

'Indeed. But I'm sure we'll survive. We always do.'

'Crumpled lapels and all! We really are something, aren't we?'

Ethan liked the way the team ribbed each other. It was one of the things that made them work so well together.

Sam pulled himself into the plane and sat down next to Ethan. He looked over at Luke. 'At least one of you is bothered about the seven Ps,' he said. 'So, are you all up here for a reason or just to piss around?'

'To support Ethan,' said Kat, then slowly turned and rested her eyes on him. 'Isn't that right?'

Ethan smiled back, but he knew that his eyes weren't joining in. Yeah, there was definitely an edge to Kat. But so what? It was her problem, not his. 'Yeah, that's right,' he said. 'Kat's really trying to make me feel part of the team – aren't you, Kat?'

Kat gave him a sweeter-than-sweet smile as the pilot called through, and then the plane was taxiing for takeoff.

A few minutes later, they were airborne, and Ethan spent the rest of the flight totally focused on his next jump. He ran through the exit procedure, flicked through the hand signals, mentally rehearsed the forward roll, the 360-degree turns, deploying his canopy, and when the time came, he didn't hesitate to jump . . .

The level-seven jump went well. Sam told him so, and so did everyone else – even Kat. Only one jump remained. And for that, Ethan would be totally on his own.

The next day, when he headed out to the plane for his level-eight jump, Ethan found himself sitting in the back of the minibus with Sam and one other skydiver. Sam was there to supervise his safe exit from the plane, but he wouldn't be jumping this time. The thought didn't scare Ethan as much as he would have expected a few days ago. He knew what he was doing now, and any fear he felt just kept his mind on the job. It was a useful emotion to have and he never wanted to get to the stage where he wasn't at least a little nervous. Johnny was staying on the ground to film him landing his level eight.

Ethan looked at the other skydiver. Whereas he himself was dressed in borrowed kit from FreeFall, none of which was all that flattering, the other skydiver was in black, head to toe, with a black helmet, mirrored visor down. When Ethan looked over, he caught his own reflection in the visor.

The man nodded; Ethan nodded back. Then the minibus arrived at the plane and soon they were taxiing down the runway.

The flight was smooth: no bumps – not that Ethan cared. He was jumping at 5,000 feet, opening at 3,500. Sam quizzed Ethan with a few questions, checked his kit, made sure everything was good. Ethan knew it took about ten seconds to fall the first 1,000 feet, then another five seconds for every 1,000 from then on. That gave him about fifteen seconds of freefall time. It wasn't much, but it was more than enough. All the other stuff he'd been doing during his previous jumps, such as 360s and front rolls and tracking, was about improving his confidence in the air. But jumping at 5,000 feet didn't allow time to do any of that. This time he'd be totally focused on what the level-eight jump was all about: executing a clean exit, getting stable, deploying the canopy, then making a good landing in the field by the DZ.

That was all there was to it.

Simple.

The call came from the pilot. They were now on the jump run – five minutes to exit. Ethan felt adrenaline rip through him, and started the countdown in his head.

Five . . .

He began to run through everything he'd been taught by Sam and Johnny: how to exit, how to arch his back to flip over and stabilize in flight.

Four . . .

He rehearsed how to deploy his canopy, and what to do if he had to cut away.

Three . . .

His dad's face flickered momentarily in his mind, telling him he was a waster, a mistake. But Ethan knew better now; knew just how wrong his dad was, had always been. He pushed the image away.

Two . . .

He focused on the sense of self-belief and purpose that Johnny and Sam had given him. Skydiving was fast taking over his life. He was determined to be the best.

One . . .

He knew he could do it. He wasn't backing out now. Time to focus . . .

Zero . . .

Ethan jumped . . .

. . . and his exit was smooth. He fell from the plane, saw it above him, arched his back to flip himself over and stabilize. The view was more vivid than on any other dive he'd done, like he was even more aware of what was around him because he was up there alone.

Shit, I'm alone . . . Ethan felt his face break into a smile. He beamed. And then he laughed.

This is it! I'm really skydiving! YES!

He checked his altimeter, eye-balled the DZ, kept himself stable. The air rushing past felt like it was trying to rip his head off: 4,000 feet; 3,900 . . . 3,800 . . . 3,700 . . . 3,600 . . . 3,500 . . .

Ethan pulled the ripcord.

No sound had ever made him feel so relieved as this one – his canopy bursting into life above him, pulling him from 120 mph to 10 mph in a matter of seconds.

He checked everything, made sure the toggles were

working OK, banked left, right, pulled himself round to head towards the DZ.

Something caught his eye, far off and above him. It was the other skydiver.

Must've left soon after me, he thought as he saw the final moments of the diver's canopy opening. But that wasn't important. All that mattered was this moment.

He'd just jumped from a plane. On his own.

Ethan was on top of the world.

13

Ethan landed smoothly as Sam jogged over, Johnny in tow.

'Well?' Sam asked.

Ethan grinned, pulled his canopy in, and rolled it up to take it back to the hangar.

'Reckon he enjoyed it,' said Johnny.

'Then we consolidate,' said Sam. 'We can get a couple of jumps in today if you're interested.'

'Oh, I'm interested,' Ethan replied.

'Good,' said Sam. 'I'll go sort out a fresh rig for you.' And he turned to walk back to the hangar.

Johnny followed, calling for Ethan to hurry up. 'I'll book us into the next available space,' he said. 'Sam's coming with us as well. You must've impressed him.'

'Really?' said Ethan. 'I thought you did the consolidation stuff on your own.'

'You do,' said Johnny. 'You'll be doing it all by yourself. We're just coming along for the ride. But you need to know one thing . . .'

'What's that then?' asked Ethan.

Johnny smiled. 'If Sam's coming, then you're really in the shit!'

Ethan stopped mid-step. 'Why's that?'

'It's simple,' said Johnny. 'If you're average, Sam leaves you alone. Not interested. Better things to do. But if you show promise, then he can't help himself; he goes all out to make you better and better. And that's hard work because he's never happy with anything but perfection.' He stopped and smiled. 'After all, look at me!'

Ethan laughed. All the way back to the hangar he was quizzed on his first solo, but inside he was thinking about what Johnny had just said. He couldn't help but feel a little proud that somehow he'd impressed Sam. He knew that wasn't easy. He wasn't quite sure how he'd done it. Everything had happened so fast since he'd first met Johnny. Now here he was, a qualified skydiver.

Luke came out of the hangar to meet them.

'Well done, Eth,' he said. 'Welcome to the club.' He reached out and shook Ethan's hand. 'Sam's told me you're off up again in a bit so I've sorted you out a new rig. Johnny – you can repack your own.'

'Don't you want to do it for me?' asked Johnny. 'I never get the creases right, not like you.' He attempted a hurt look and kicked a stone disconsolately.

Luke smiled, shook his head and took Ethan's rig. 'Grab some scoff. It'll be a couple of hours before you're in the air again.'

Ethan thanked Luke as the man in black walked past. His visor was up now, but Ethan still couldn't see much of his face. Ethan nodded as he headed towards the car park.

'Ah,' said Johnny. 'Your first fan! Trust me, it's a nightmare: the adoration, the sex . . .'

'He was the only other skydiver in the plane when I went up with Sam,' Ethan explained. 'For some reason no one else was jumping. Still, it was nice to have the thing as private as possible. Helped me to focus.'

'Hungry?' asked Johnny.

'Always,' said Ethan.

Before they headed off for Ethan's first consolidation jump, Sam quickly grilled him on a few drills and hand signals, and ran him through a set sequence for the skydive. Then he checked Ethan's rig, pulling the clips to make sure they were secure. Finally he said, 'For this jump, I want to see a clean exit, stable position, and then two three-sixties, left then right, good deployment of canopy. Johnny and I will follow you in.'

'And we're jumping from thirteen thousand?' asked Ethan.

Sam nodded. 'You've shown you can skydive solo. That's what the level-eight jump is all about. Now you need enough air time before deploying your canopy to practise your skills. And that's what consolidation is for. This is where you really get the chance to prove yourself.'

Ethan was quiet – not scared, just focused, running through everything Sam had said.

Johnny looked at him. 'You'll nail each jump, mate,' he said. 'Not as quickly as me, obviously, but I'll be there to help. And I'll make sure I get your good side on camera.'

Ethan couldn't help but smile. 'I have a good side?'

'I'll let you know,' said Johnny.

'Here's the minibus,' Sam growled, shaking his head at Johnny. 'In.'

The rush of air as the plane door was pulled open slammed into Ethan and momentarily took his breath away. He suddenly felt very aware of the height he was jumping from: all there was between him and the ground below was the few centimetres of the plane's skin beneath his backside. He closed his eyes, squeezed them shut so hard that pin-pricks of light stabbed his brain, then breathed deep and slow.

13,000 feet . . . Easy . . .

The call came. Ethan was first to jump, with Sam and Johnny following. He'd be first out of the plane, first to fall from 13,000. He avoided looking round at all the other faces in the plane, the eyes of both seasoned jumpers and newbies.

And then he jumped.

Air caught him, pulled at him, the sound of it battered his ears. He saw the plane above him, and then two other dots in the sky, before arching his back, flipping over.

Earth below, sky above. Sky everywhere.

Rock 'n' roll!

Ethan got himself stable, then spied Johnny and Sam coming in, tracking across to him till they were close. He got the thumbs-up from both of them. Knowing he was getting it right made him feel a lot more confident.

Johnny grinned, then turned upside down, feet pointing straight up, keeping himself stable with his arms and hands. Ethan burst out laughing, the sound swept away by the wind.

Johnny flipped back to the stable position, then turned again so that he was just sitting in the air, as though relaxing on an invisible chair. Then he stabilized again.

Ethan looked at Sam, who gave a hand signal that told Ethan to do a 360.

Ethan did two – one left, one right. Then he returned to the stable position, found the DZ below, and got on course. All he had to do now was deploy. But he still had a few seconds of freefall left.

And each second made his smile grow and grow.

He checked his altimeter. It was time to deploy. He looked at Johnny and Sam. Both nodded and sped away from him to give him space. Then he reached round with his right hand and pulled.

That sound again – bed sheets flapping in the wind – then total silence, almost eerie. Ethan didn't know if his face was aching because of the freefall and the wind, or because he just couldn't wipe the smile off it. In the end he didn't even bother trying. He just kept his eyes on the field next to the DZ, and guided himself in, correcting his canopy now and again with a tug of a toggle, until the ground rushed up to meet him. He pulled both toggles, and landed, not entirely gracefully, on his arse.

He quickly got to his feet, started to pull in his canopy. Adrenaline was still coursing through him from the dive and it felt better than good. He could taste it; his fingers tingled. He caught sight of Johnny coming in for a perfect landing. He made everything look easy, look good. When he was clear, in came Sam, and Ethan was blown away by the speed at which he zipped in, how he then pulled up into a perfect touchdown.

Johnny waved to Ethan and walked over to meet him on the way back to the hangar. Sam sent a casual salute.

'I said you'd nail it.' Johnny clapped Ethan on the shoulder. 'You're good up there, man, you really are.'

'You serious?'

'Dead.'

Sam called over. 'Wait up, lads.'

Ethan and Johnny stalled as Sam marched over to join them, canopy over his shoulder like a huge dead jellyfish.

He looked at Ethan and smiled. 'You should be proud of yourself, Ethan,' he said and reached out to shake Ethan's hand. 'Well done.'

Ethan felt as though his arm was about to be ripped off. 'Thanks.'

'I never say that unless I mean it,' said Sam, still gripping Ethan's hand. 'You've a natural talent for this. Don't waste it.'

'I won't,' said Ethan, but the words didn't exactly express how he felt right then. Getting such praise from someone like Sam – with his experience, his perfectionism – was amazing. Ethan had never been so damned proud in his life. For the first time ever he felt like he'd actually achieved something worthwhile. And he knew then that he didn't just like sky-diving, he was addicted to it – just as Johnny had guessed.

By the time Ethan had thought of anything intelligent to say, Sam had gone. He turned to Johnny, shaking out his hand to get the blood flowing again. 'I wasn't expecting that.'

Johnny smiled, set off walking again. 'Remember what I said? You're in the shit now, mate; Sam's really got his teeth into you.'

A shout brought them both up sharp. They looked round to see someone trotting over from the side of the DZ.

'Jake,' said Johnny. 'What's he doing here?'

Ethan saw where Jake had come from. 'Kat's over there.' He pointed. 'He must've been talking to her, watching us jump.'

'Having fun, are we? You and Sam enjoying yourselves with the rookie?' Jake yelled.

'Nice to see you too, Jake,' said Johnny. 'What are you doing here? Aren't you still grounded?'

'Don't give a shit. Like I'm going to listen to Sam. His judgement's totally out. He's losing it in his old age.'

'Come on, Eth,' said Johnny, and carried on past Jake.

Jake stepped in front, blocking their way; nodded at Ethan. 'He my replacement?'

'What's going on with you, Jake?' asked Johnny. 'Why are you really here?'

'I'm asking if this rookie is my replacement; if Sam's eyeing him for jumping with the team.'

'No idea what Sam's thinking,' said Johnny. 'He's just helping Ethan skydive. That's his job, remember?'

'I remember all right,' said Jake, getting up close. 'I remember how you were always his favourite. Is that what this is? Another little Johnny clone for Sam to look after, eh?'

'Hey,' said Ethan. 'Leave it.'

Johnny laughed. 'Jake, shut up and piss off. You're talking out of your arse.'

Jake pushed him, and Ethan stepped in. 'I said leave it.'

'Look, head back to the hangar,' said Johnny, looking at Ethan. 'I'll sort this out.'

'Yeah, that's it, Rookie,' said Jake as Ethan hesitated. 'Do what Johnny tells you. Head back to teacher. Go on, like a good little boy.'

Ethan looked at Jake's sneering face, and didn't see the boot put out to trip him up. He caught it with his left foot, tried to keep his balance, fell forward and slammed into the ground.

'What the hell did you do that for?' he shouted, and pushed himself up, but he was caught in his canopy and fell back, drowning in his rig.

Jake laughed. And laughed. And laughed. Then turned and jogged back over to Kat.

Johnny reached down and helped Ethan to his feet, untangling him. 'You all right?'

Ethan nodded. 'What is his problem?'

Johnny and Ethan watched as Jake said something to Kat, then jumped into his Porsche and sped out of the car park.

'He's got an unfortunate flaw,' said Johnny, helping Ethan pick up his rig.

'What's that then?'

'He's a tosser.'

Ethan saw Johnny smile.

'Forget Jake,' said Johnny. 'He's just jealous, that's all. You ready for another jump?'

Ethan nodded. It was the one question to which he knew the answer would always be 'Yes!'

14

By the end of the day Ethan was exhausted; he was already in bed when his phone rang. He'd been relieved to find his dad absent when he got home – expecting to find him in front of the TV again, ready for another argument. But tonight he was spared.

Mum was out working. Jo had called him into her room for a chat. She was in the middle of another of her weird paintings. Ethan had stared at it in fascination. He could see that it was way cool, but he just didn't get what it was supposed to represent. That didn't matter though; he knew he didn't have to understand it to support her.

Now, lying on his bed, listening to his phone ringing, he checked his watch. Eleven thirty. No one ever phoned him this late. He didn't recognize the number.

He didn't answer and the call went to answerphone.

A moment later, the phone rang again.

Ethan picked it up, stared at it. The flat was empty now; Mum wasn't back from work and Jo had gone out with her mates. A thought struck him – what if it was Jo using someone else's phone because her own was dead? What if it was an emergency?

He answered. 'Yes?'

Silence.

'Hello?'

Ethan could hear something in the background. Wind buffeting metal. Whoever it was, they were calling from FreeFall – he'd recognize the sound of the hangar doors anywhere. They were loose and always rattled in the wind.

A whisper: 'I said I'd make you pay, Rookie.'

'Jake?'

Laughter.

The phone went dead.

Ethan didn't know how Jake had got his number, but it was the fact that he had called from FreeFall that bothered him most. What was the rich tosser up to now? Ethan had a feeling that it wasn't anything good. And since it was him Jake had called, Ethan felt that it was up to him to go and stop him.

Instinct took over. He was up, out and cycling along the road to FreeFall before he knew what he was doing. It was a dark night and the lights on his bike were fading. As they flickered in the gloom, he willed them to stay alive just long enough.

Then they died.

But Ethan pushed on, pedalled hard, the wind in his eyes. All he could think about was Jake and the trouble he could cause at FreeFall without anyone there to stop him. The bloke was a total idiot. This was probably some kind of revenge or something. Whatever it was, Ethan was determined to sort it out.

He swung the bike round a sharp corner. Bright light flooded the road, blinding him. A car horn blared and the sound of screeching tyres shattered his concentration as a car swung past, only missing him because he swerved into the verge. He felt his front tyre smack into something hard and lurched to a stop.

Jeez . . . that was close . . .

For a few seconds he sat on his bike and tried to calm down. Then he looked at his front tyre. It was totally flat thanks to a jagged rip. FreeFall was still a fair distance away, and time was of the essence. He pulled out his phone, punched in a number.

'Yeah?'

'Johnny?'

'Ethan, look, can I call you back? I'm a bit . . . busy . . .'

A girl giggled in the background. Typical Johnny.

'It's Jake,' said Ethan. 'I think he's at FreeFall. He just called and—'

Johnny came back bullet-quick. 'When?'

'Just now. Said something about making me pay, then hung up.'

'You sure he's at FreeFall? Did he tell you?'

'No,' said Ethan, 'but I could hear the hangar doors

115

rattling in the background. He's there, I know it. He could be messing with the rigs or something.'

'Have you called Sam?'

'Uh-uh. Didn't want to be on the receiving end if it turns out Jake's just pissing around.' Ethan was all too aware of how Sam would react if he thought someone had wasted his time.

'Too right,' agreed Johnny. 'I'm on my way. I'll pick you up in five.'

'Look, I'm halfway there already—'

Johnny cut in, 'You were going on your own?'

'Yeah,' said Ethan. 'But my bike's got a puncture. I'll just leave it behind a hedge or something.'

Ethan listened as Johnny explained to the giggle what was happening then came back on the phone with, 'Where are you?'

'Couple of miles out of town on the main road.'

'Sorted,' said Johnny.

Ethan hung up. Then he lifted his bike over a hedge into a nearby field, did his best to memorize exactly where he was so that he could fetch it in the morning, and waited.

Five minutes later, Johnny pulled up on his bike, engine buzzing the night. He handed Ethan a helmet. 'Jump on.'

Ethan had never been on a motorbike before. The instant he sat down, he wanted one.

'Hold on tight – put your arms round me if you want.'

Ethan hesitated.

'It's OK, Ethan, you're not my type.'

Smiling, he held onto Johnny's waist.

The bike revved and zipped away into the dark, spraying stones and dirt across the road.

It didn't take long to reach the old army base. At the security gate, Johnny explained that he'd left some of his kit behind. The guard smiled and waved them in.

As the airfield came into view up on their right, Johnny slowed the bike, pulled it to the side. Killing the engine, he turned to Ethan. 'We'll push it from here, arrive silent, OK?'

Ethan nodded, climbed off.

They edged forward, pushing the bike together along the road, then right into the car park. Johnny nodded over to an old shed and they rolled the bike into the shadows behind it, pulling off their helmets and leaving them on the pillion.

'I bet Jake's just trying to wind me up,' Ethan said softly. 'Has he always been such a dick?'

'He's always liked showing off,' muttered Johnny. 'He likes to have the upper hand. But he could have been a great skydiver if he hadn't decided to focus on being a tosser instead.' He pointed to the rear of the shed. 'We'll sneak through there, then make our way round to the front of the hangar. If Jake is here, we should be able to find him without being seen.'

As they crept off, a clatter from ahead rattled the dark.

'Stay here,' hissed Johnny, and before Ethan could say anything, he had slipped away into the darkness.

But Ethan didn't like being left behind. And he'd never been good at waiting for something to happen. So he quickly followed—

And nearly collided with Johnny coming back.

'I told you to stay.'

'I'm not a dog.'

Johnny looked at Ethan. 'I know Jake's pissed you off, but going out looking for a fight isn't like going out on the pull. When you want a fight, you're almost guaranteed to get laid – out!'

'I just don't like being messed about, that's all,' said Ethan. 'Is it Jake?'

Johnny nodded, his face grim. 'Him and two others I don't recognize. They're in the hangar.'

'What are they doing?'

'No idea,' said Johnny. 'But we're going to phone Sam.'

'How about calling the police while you're at it?'

Johnny shook his head. 'If we call the police and this is just Jake being a prick, they'll do us for time wasting.'

Ethan watched as Johnny pulled out his phone, scrolled through the numbers and hit CALL.

A 'Yes?' hissed into the air, and Johnny handed the phone to Ethan.

'Your gig, mate; you'd best tell him.'

Ethan took the phone and explained everything to Sam. Two minutes later he killed the phone and handed it back to Johnny with a nod. 'He's on his way.'

'No surprise there,' said Johnny. 'So what do you want to do now?'

'Well, we either hang about and wait for Sam,' said Ethan, 'or we get on and do something. Let's see if we can find out what Jake's actually up to.'

Just then they both saw a shadow stroll out of the hangar

and into the moonlight to smoke a cigarette. They watched, unmoving, until the figure flicked the cigarette butt away and turned back. The dying cigarette cast a faint red arc in the darkness.

Johnny nodded towards the hangar. 'Let's go.'

The hangar doors were large, sitting like sliding cat flaps in two even bigger doors for aircraft moving in and out of the hangar. Ethan and Johnny crept past the open doors and hid behind a large bin and a pile of discarded pallets. From there, they could see what was going on inside the hangar without being spotted themselves. They saw torches cutting the dark like light sabres and heard laughter echoing in the air.

Jake was with two other men. They were both large guys, taller than Ethan, and they were dressed in black, with long leather jackets that finished just above the knee. They looked to Ethan liked they'd popped along to Criminals 'R' Us to get dressed up before heading out. From this distance, the only difference between the two was that one had blond hair, the other black. They were busy pulling the parachutes out of their packs and shredding them with Stanley knives.

'They're messing with the rigs,' said Ethan.

'Yeah,' Johnny muttered. 'They're shredding everything. Harnesses, canopies – all ruined. The bastards.'

They heard Jake shout at the other two to hurry up.

Ethan could hardly bear to sit still and watch as more rigs were destroyed. At last he spoke. 'We need to keep them here until Sam arrives,' he said. 'I reckon he'll want to have a word or two with Jake.'

Johnny nodded. 'And your plan for that?'

'We lock them in,' said Ethan.

'Nice,' agreed Johnny, nodding appreciatively.

'And simple,' added Ethan.

15

'It's easy . . .' Ethan had almost convinced himself. 'You take this side of the hangar; I'll sneak round the back and come up the other side. That'll give me a chance to check the back doors are locked so they can't escape.'

'Used to trapping criminals in the act, are you?' said Johnny.

'When you see me at the other hangar door,' continued Ethan, 'wait for my signal.'

'Ooh, a signal!' said Johnny. 'How James Bond!'

Ethan smiled. 'I'll raise my hand. You wave back to indicate you've seen me. Then we push the doors together – fast! – and shut them in. OK?'

'Just like that?' said Johnny.

'Just like that,' repeated Ethan. 'Ready?'

Johnny nodded.

With a deep breath, Ethan scooted along the side of the hangar. There were two doors at the back and one more on the other side. All were still securely padlocked. Soon he was round at the front of the hangar again. He heard Jake laugh. It was a sound that made him want to punch him hard.

He looked across the doorway. Johnny was just visible on the other side. Ethan raised his hand and Johnny waved back.

Shoulder hunched against the door, Ethan pushed it hard. His heart pounded as he drove it along, willing it shut with everything he had. It screeched loudly in the night as he heaved it across.

Inside, a shout went up: 'The doors are shutting!'

Ethan heard footfalls approaching, but that simply made him go at it even harder. He wasn't going to let Jake win. With a loud yell, he gave the door a final push and saw Johnny do the same.

Then, just inches from closing, something stopped the doors in their tracks.

'Shit!' panted Johnny. 'They're on the other side!'

'Then shut up and keep pushing!' cried Ethan. 'Push!'

Ethan could feel someone shoving the door the other way. His feet were slipping, his muscles were hurting now, and he'd already split his knuckles on the door. But he heaved again. He was so close . . .

Suddenly he felt his door give way, heard Johnny yell, and saw him flung backwards hard onto the ground.

Jake's companions rushed through the gap and hurled themselves at Johnny.

Ethan abandoned the door and ran to help his friend, but Johnny was already on his feet and ready for them.

The one with the blond hair reached him first, but Johnny dodged to the left, crashing his elbow into the side of the man's head as he moved. Mr Blond stumbled and fell head-first into a wall. Johnny immediately whipped round as the other, dark-haired man came at him. This time, he stepped right and used his left leg to sweep Mr Black's legs from under him. The guy landed hard and face-first on the ground. Ethan winced.

Johnny turned to Ethan. 'Get out of here! Now!'

Ethan shook his head and ran towards Johnny, keeping a careful watch on the two men, who were now pulling themselves to their feet. He was ready to pile in, despite the size of Mr Blond and Mr Black. Johnny was a mate, and to Ethan, that mattered more than anything.

'I mean it,' said Johnny. 'Sam'll be here in a minute. I can handle this!'

'Two against one?' said Ethan, guessing Jake was leaving the rough stuff to these two gorillas. 'No chance!'

The men were on their feet now and making for Johnny.

He was turning, ready for another attack. But they were approaching him more cautiously this time, and Ethan didn't blame them. Having seen the way Johnny had taken them both down, he made a mental note not to get on the wrong side of him. It was obvious that he knew how to fight, and was used to handling himself when things got out of hand. This wasn't the light-hearted Johnny that Ethan was used to. He was seeing a whole new, darker side he had never guessed existed.

'I said get out of here!' Johnny shouted, but before Ethan had a chance to respond, the two men launched themselves at him. This time they were prepared. Johnny's blows didn't seem to make a dent. Mr Black reached in, grabbed him and threw him to the ground. Then they both laid into him, feet first.

As Ethan ran into the fight, he heard the kicks making contact, saw Johnny hunch into a ball on the ground.

The men were too busy kicking three levels of shit out of Johnny to see Ethan bursting out of the dark. He went for Mr Blond first, hoping the weight and momentum of his body would throw the guy to the floor. It didn't. In fact, it felt like running into a brick wall. The man half turned towards Ethan, paused mid-kick, spat, then smacked him across the face with the back of his hand, dropping him to the floor with a broken lip, his cheek stinging like hell. Then Mr Blond turned back to Johnny as if Ethan was of no account. But Ethan's attack had bought his friend some time. Now he was up on his feet again, tackling Mr Black. Ethan knew Johnny had a good chance one on one, so he immediately launched himself at Mr Blond once more, dragging himself up onto his back.

The guy spun round, trying to shake Ethan loose, but Ethan had locked his arms around his neck. Mr Blond swung left and right, but Ethan hung on, frantically trying to work out what his next move should be. He caught sight of Johnny ducking a punch from Mr Black and swinging back with a kick to his stomach. This wasn't the movies, this was real,

Ethan realized, and if he let this gorilla get the advantage, he was screwed. The man was heavier and stronger and would probably rip his head off quite happily before attacking Johnny again. So he couldn't let Mr Blond get the upper hand. He wasn't one for fighting dirty, but under the circumstances, he reckoned 'dirty' was his only option. There were no rules here, no referee to call foul. All that mattered was survival.

He figured his best option was to hang on and try to do some damage at the same time. And that meant going for the face. Ethan could feel adrenaline burning through him as he clawed upwards with his hands, found an eye-socket, and pushed a thumb in hard.

The man staggered backwards with an agonized yell. Ethan pushed harder and then stretched across to reach the other eye.

Mr Blond twisted and turned, reaching round for Ethan, but Ethan knew what would happen to him if he let go, so he just dug in harder and scrambled higher.

As Mr Blond continued to try and prise Ethan off his back, Ethan felt the damp warmth of blood on his hands. He held on for as long as he could, but with his hands now wet with blood, he finally slipped and fell to the ground.

Mr Blond bellowed with anger, but Ethan was up super-fast and onto his back again, this time reaching for his ears and twisting as hard as he could. The man stumbled left and right, screaming, swearing and clutching the sides of his head as blood poured down from his damaged ears. Ethan scrabbled for the face again – but with the weight on his back, Mr Blond finally stumbled, lost his footing and fell.

Ethan's world went dark as the man landed on him, slamming the air out of his lungs like he was a burst bag of crisps.

Then there were lights. Stars bursting everywhere. Blinding him.

Ethan was trapped under Mr Blond and gasping for air. The weight of the man was ridiculous – like he was made of lead. Ethan tried to wriggle out from under him, but he couldn't budge, so he grabbed his ears again and hoped that would be enough to get him to move. Mr Blond bellowed and Ethan pulled harder. The man clawed at Ethan's hands and swore.

Ethan tried to crane his head round to see Johnny. Unfortunately Mr Black seemed to have his friend pinned in the dirt, arms pulled out to the sides and trapped under his attacker's knees. As Ethan watched, the man raised his head and brought it down with a crack on the side of Johnny's fore-head. Johnny struggled no more and Ethan knew he was out cold.

Where the hell is Sam? he wondered. *Just where the hell is he?* It felt as though he and Johnny had been fighting for hours, though he knew it could only have been minutes. Desperation gripped him and he kicked out, bucking his body like he was being electrocuted. Mr Blond rolled to the right and Ethan could finally breathe again. He dragged himself to his feet and tried to catch his breath as the man started to pull himself to his knees. Blood was running from his ears and eyes and dripping over his shirt. He looked up at Ethan, snarled. Mr Black was turning as well now, and Ethan could see that Johnny was still out for the count.

Ethan knew this was it. If he let Mr Blond hit him, he was a dead man. And, probably, so was Johnny. So he kicked Mr Blond in the groin with his left foot. Then again. The man doubled over.

Ethan didn't think twice: he sent another boot in, and launched the guy backwards, his head slamming into the ground. Ethan stumbled forwards, ready to go in again if need be, but it was clear Mr Blond wouldn't be getting up for a while. He was out cold.

Ethan spat blood and looked over at Johnny. He was relieved to see him moving, albeit slowly. Then he looked up at Johnny's attacker. The man was as big as Mr Blond, if not bigger. And he was smiling. He looked at Ethan and beckoned him forward with a wave of the hand.

Ethan was knackered. He didn't know if he'd survive another fight. But what choice did he have? He raised his fists and advanced. Then something hammered into his leg. It came out of nowhere, catching him hard across the side of his left knee. Pain shot through him and he dropped like liquid, screaming. He rolled around on the floor, breaths short, taking the pain, holding his knee. The leg was dead, numb; he couldn't stand up. Then a voice broke the moment.

'Looking for me, Rookie?'

Ethan glanced up to see Jake staring down at him. Hanging from his left hand was a thin plank of wood. He was doing his best to be gangster cool, with a cigarette dangling limply from the corner of his mouth. A long black coat added to the effect, though it didn't suit him.

'Why are you doing this?' spat Ethan, trying to sit up.

'What's the point of ruining Sam's kit? And those gorillas of yours nearly killed Johnny! Are you mad?'

Jake strolled over, rested a foot on Ethan's shoulder and pushed.

Ethan fell back, still dazed from the pain in his knee. Jake leaned forward, and Ethan felt his lungs being compressed; wanted to throw up. He looked at the other two men. Mr Blond was beginning to move; Mr Black was standing over Johnny, who was also stirring now. Every time Johnny tried to get up, the goon simply pushed him back to the ground.

'I thought you might turn up if I called,' said Jake, drawing hard on his cigarette before blowing the smoke down into Ethan's face. 'Thought it would add to the fun if you saw what I'd done. Didn't expect Johnny to come too. Bit of a bonus, that. And now I get to give you a kicking as well as ruin Sam's life. Fucking excellent.'

Ethan struggled against Jake's foot, fighting for breath. 'It's not my fault Sam threw you off the team,' he panted. 'It's not anyone's fault but yours.'

Jake raised the plank, menace in his eyes. 'Want some more of this, do you?' But before he could bring it down, Ethan saw his chance and went for it. Grabbing Jake's foot, he twisted hard, turning with it as he went. Jake went down, the plank and the cigarette spinning off into the dark.

Ethan saw Mr Blond watching – though luckily still too dazed to do much. Mr Black wheeled round to see what was going on – and that was enough to allow Johnny to clamber to his feet. Now the man was torn between helping Jake and stopping Johnny.

As Jake struggled up onto his knees, Ethan leaped to his

feet and smashed in with a kick, hard and fast, aiming for Jake's stomach. Jake squealed and toppled backwards, coughing in pain. Ethan didn't give him a chance to recover. As he tried to get up, Ethan kicked him back down. Jake wasn't really fighting any more, but Ethan was beyond caring. He was locked in the moment now. It was all that mattered: he couldn't hear or see properly, his body was in pain, there was blood in his mouth – and all he wanted to do was keep raining in the kicks and punches, take all his anger out on Jake till there was nothing left. Nothing at all.

But somewhere at the back of his mind a warning sounded: he knew he had to back off – stop before he lost control completely. He staggered backwards, aware now of Jake's groans. The other two men were now trying to deal with Johnny, who was just about managing to stay out of their reach.

Then Ethan spotted the plank Jake had used against him. Calmly he walked over, picked it up, came back.

Jake looked up at him. 'No . . . don't—'

Ethan broke the plank across his knee with a crack that signalled the end. Enough.

Only apparently Mr Blond wasn't following the same script, because as Ethan looked down at Jake, he felt huge arms wrap around him from behind. The stink of tobacco breath caught in his nostrils and stubble rasped against the back of his neck as he was lifted bodily off the ground.

Suddenly the arms released him, but Ethan wasn't given a chance to escape. Two fists pounded into the sides of his neck, dropping him to the ground, where he landed next to Jake.

Ethan turned to see the man spit and smile, crack his knuckles, flex his neck. Then he reached down and picked up Ethan as though he weighed no more than a child. Ethan struggled, but this time it was useless. Mr Blond had him tight, arms pinned.

Jake pushed himself to his feet and wiped blood from his mouth. He held one half of the plank in his hand.

'Screw Sam and screw you!' he hissed, and he launched the end of the plank at Ethan's stomach.

The blow made Ethan retch. He folded up, pain racing through his body, coughed, tasted bile in his throat, felt sick, scared.

Mr Blond refused to let him fall, just held him tight for more of the same.

Jake came in with another blow from the plank. It hurt just as bad. Ethan heard Jake laugh. Then he puked. It stung his throat, and he could see blood in it.

'Nice.' Jake laughed as Mr Blond dropped Ethan face down in his own vomit.

Ethan stayed where he was. He knew he was deep in shit and that there was fuck all he could do about it. Moments later, Johnny was thrown to the ground next to him. Johnny looked at him, attempted a smile, but said nothing. Then Ethan saw Jake and his goons looming above them and knew what was coming next.

The screeching of tyres split the night and finally ended the fight. Ethan turned his head to see what was going on and saw headlights burst round the corner of the hangar like fireworks. Gravel and dirt scattered as Sam pulled his Defender up sharp, kicked the door open and hurled himself towards the boys like a raging bull.

'Another time, Rookie!' said Jake, and he and the two goons bolted.

Sam skidded to the ground. 'Ethan? Johnny? You OK?'

Ethan sat up, coughed, shook his head to clear it, then nodded.

'We'll live,' said Johnny.

'Well, you look like you've been shat out of a bear's arse,' said Sam. He turned back to Ethan. 'What's Jake done?'

Ethan pointed at the open doors to the hangar. 'They've killed the kit, Sam,' he said. 'Ruined it.'

Sam stood, ran over to the doors, turned back, face hard. 'Can you walk?'

In answer, Ethan and Johnny pulled themselves to their feet.

'What state are they in?' asked Sam. 'I saw Jake was bleeding. What about the other two?'

'Not great,' said Johnny, stretching his back. 'Same as us.'

'Right,' commanded Sam. 'Defender. Now.'

He turned, and Ethan and Johnny clambered into the back seats. The engine thrummed into life with a heavy growl.

'They headed off down there.' Johnny pointed, leaning over the front seats. 'Down the grass airstrip. They must've cut across the fields to get here or something.'

'What about the fence that surrounds the place?' asked Ethan.

'It's just a fence,' said Johnny. 'It's not patrolled or anything. Not any more.'

Sam kicked the Defender forward, headlights sweeping the night.

'There they are!' yelled Ethan, spotting three figures running ahead.

Sam dropped a gear, accelerated.

Suddenly Ethan spotted something else just in front of Jake and the two men. It was a helicopter. 'Shit!'

Sam looked at Ethan. 'What's up?'

Ethan said nothing; just pointed.

Sam saw the helicopter. 'You're kidding me,' he said.

The blades were just starting to spin.

'Told you he was a rich kid,' said Johnny, looking at Ethan. 'The tosser *flew* in.'

Sam gunned the Defender.

Ethan gripped the metal rail behind the front seats to stop himself lurching back into Johnny. He could see Jake just ahead, closing in on the helicopter, its blades now a blur.

Sam swung the Defender round, trying to block Jake's route.

Jake dodged, and before Sam could make another pass, he'd reached the helicopter.

Sam rammed the gearstick forward and made to go after Jake. 'Too late, Sam,' said Johnny. 'Look.'

Leaning from the open door of the helicopter, Jake waved a one-fingered salute.

And from the Defender, the three of them returned the gesture.

Back in the office, Sam quizzed Johnny and Ethan on what had happened. They explained everything – from Jake's phone call, through discovering what was going on, to the moment when their plan went to shit and they got their arses kicked.

'Lucky I turned up when I did,' said Sam.

They nodded.

'And I'm to understand that neither of you started the pushing and shoving, right?'

Ethan and Johnny nodded again.

'Why didn't you just bolt? Fighting isn't clever or glamorous. Most of the time it's best to just hit hard and run away. How did it get out of hand so quickly?'

'They grabbed me first,' said Johnny, 'before I could do anything about it. Ethan just jumped in to help. I don't think they were expecting it. Then it all kicked off.'

Sam turned to Ethan. 'So Jake phoned you and you decided to come over here, but you *weren't* looking for a fight?'

'No,' said Ethan firmly, slowly realizing that he was in an awful lot of pain. 'I just wanted to stop him doing whatever he was doing. I figured that whatever it was couldn't be good. Didn't figure he'd have two other blokes with him.'

'That was your first mistake,' said Sam. 'Always plan for what might happen if everything goes to shit. That way, when it does, you might be able to get out of it.'

Ethan felt this was suspiciously like getting a bollocking – which didn't seem very fair, considering he and Johnny had done their best to save the rigs.

'Can you remember where your bike is, Ethan?'

Sam's question pulled Ethan from his thoughts and he simply nodded.

'Good. I'll give you a lift. You both did well tonight. Thank you.'

Ethan looked at Johnny. Had they really just heard that?

Sam got up from behind his desk. 'Move it, you two. I've a busy day tomorrow. Even more so now that I've got to sort out the damage done by Jake and his pals.'

As they headed for the door, Ethan asked, 'What are you going to do? Call the police?'

'That's for me to think about, not you,' said Sam. 'And for now we keep this in the team. I'll find my own way of dealing with Jake. In my own time. Now shift it.'

16

Johnny came over to Ethan, sat down, grabbed the Coke can from his hand and took a sip.

'Help yourself,' said Ethan.

'Thanks, I will,' said Johnny, taking another swig before handing it back.

They were both sitting outside the hangar, rigged up and ready for another jump, their second of the day. FreeFall was busy, business was good. It was a couple of weeks since the run-in with Jake, and despite the damage to the rigs, Sam had managed to call in a few favours and everything was running smoothly. Nothing about Jake's unwelcome visit had been mentioned since. They had cobbled together a believable cover story to explain their bruises – a run-in between a tree and Johnny's motorbike.

Ethan's final two consolidation jumps had gone by so quickly and smoothly he'd hardly noticed them. He was now diving solo and getting in at least one jump a day, depending on the weather and how busy things were at FreeFall. He'd even had the chance to fly a Raider, which had been scary as hell but a total blast. Luke had laid it on thick with the instructions for flying such a responsive canopy. Ethan had listened carefully, and it had paid off because the thing had handled amazingly – like it was hardwired to the wind; you directed it, it didn't hesitate. And it was tiny – no bigger than a fashionable daysack when it was packed up, little larger than a power kite when deployed. And, as Johnny had said back when Ethan had met him on his first day at FreeFall, small, fast and scary.

A shadow fell across Ethan and Johnny and they looked up to find Sam standing over them, binoculars in his hand.

'Another good jump, Ethan,' he said. 'Well done.'

'Thanks,' said Ethan to Sam's back as he headed off to his office.

'A man of few words,' said Johnny, and Ethan nodded. 'Incidentally, are you trying to make a habit of impressing him?'

Ethan turned at Johnny's question. 'What do you mean?'

'Well, just look at you. It's like you belong here or something. From tandem rookie to skydiver in just a few weeks. It's pretty impressive.'

'No it's not,' said Ethan, shrugging. 'It's like most things: do what you're told to do and do it properly and you'll probably be OK at it.'

'Don't sell yourself short,' said Johnny. 'Sam really is impressed. So am I. You remind me of someone brilliant.'

'Who?'

'Me.'

Ethan laughed. 'How do you cope with being you?'

'It's hard,' said Johnny. 'You wouldn't be able to hack it. The girls, the glamour; it's tough.'

'You bear it well, all things considered.'

Another shadow cast itself over the conversation. This time Ethan and Johnny looked up to see Kat. She too was rigged up.

'Hey,' she said, and sat down opposite them.

'Kat,' said Johnny. 'How's Jake?'

Kat looked at him. 'Is there ever a moment in your life when you think before you speak?'

'Never,' said Johnny. 'So what was the attraction anyway?'

'He drove it,' said Kat, and stalked off.

Ethan went after her, catching up with her in a few strides, racking his brain for a topic of conversation.

'So you bought one yet, then?' he came up with, falling into step beside her. 'You know, one of those fancy skydiving helmets you were talking about?'

'Yeah. Ordered it yesterday. Arrives at the weekend.'

'What's it like?'

Kat stopped and looked round at Ethan. 'It's like a helmet, Ethan. You put it on your head.'

The conversation had dropped dead, so he asked, 'You OK?'

'What, apart from being boyfriend-less?'

Johnny came up and butted in. 'You're better off without a tosser like that, especially after what he did.'

137

Kat turned on him. 'He made a mistake,' she said. 'That's all. What, like you're the perfect skydiver? You've never messed up? Not even once?'

'I'm not talking about the skydive,' said Johnny.

Ethan looked at him. 'Sam said he'd deal with it.'

'She has to know,' said Johnny, and he turned back to Kat. 'We found him ruining the rigs. Him and a couple of other blokes built like trolls.'

'Shut up,' said Kat.

'It's true,' Ethan told her. 'They ruined stacks of stuff. Sam was able to sort it out, but the damage was pretty bad. It got a bit rough. Jake must've had a fair few bruises on him.'

Kat shook her head. 'Jake wouldn't do that,' she said. 'And the bruises . . . he said they were from a bar fight he got into. Anyway, he's all mouth. Doesn't have the balls.'

'You believe what you want,' said Johnny. 'And then ask Sam.'

For a moment no one said anything. The silence stretched on as Kat scowled at them both.

Again Ethan desperately thought of something to say to break the awkwardness. 'So how did you get into skydiving exactly?' he asked Kat.

'Same as you,' she said, shrugging. 'Tandem, then AFF. It's not that difficult really, you know. Anyone can do it.'

'Oh, I wouldn't be so sure,' said Johnny. 'Ethan's a natural. Not as good as me, obviously, but still pretty brilliant. Aren't you, Eth?' He slapped Ethan hard on the back and Ethan shrugged, looked at Kat, attempted an apologetic smile.

The look Kat returned was cold, her eyes narrow. 'It takes more than a few jumps and an ego to make a skydiver,

Ethan,' she said flatly. Then she headed for the minibus as it pulled up to ferry the next group of jumpers to the plane. It was pretty clear to Ethan that she wanted him to shut up.

'Come on, Eth,' said Johnny. 'We're jumping too.' Then he shouted ahead to Kat, 'If you want, I'll go first – show you how it should be done.'

'You're so full of shit,' said Kat without looking back.

Ethan and Johnny watched her walk away.

'Prickly today, isn't she?' said Johnny. 'Ready?'

'Sure am,' said Ethan, and the two of them followed Kat into the minibus.

Ethan found himself alone with her in the back of the plane. They were over the DZ and everyone else had jumped. Johnny had done so in a particularly elaborate fashion, faking being shot and then stumbling backwards out of the open door with a deathly scream that neither Ethan nor Kat could hear because of the wind. Ethan was still laughing about it when Kat stood to go.

Ethan waved, smiled.

Kat looked back, but didn't return the wave or the smile. She was obviously still angry about Jake. But there was nothing Ethan could do about it. At least she now knew the truth about what Jake had done to the rigs – not that she believed it. So he just smiled again, and watched as she stood at the door, ready to jump.

Suddenly the plane lurched. Ethan felt it buck beneath him and drop. He landed back in his seat with a heavy thump. And at the same time, he saw Kat stumble, try to catch herself . . .

Fall.

She cracked her head against the edge of the plane door as she did so. Ethan didn't hear it, but seeing it happen was enough to make his stomach flip. Then her body just sort of slumped and slid round the edge of the door and out into open air. But as she fell, her rig caught on the door – it was the nightmare scenario. Ethan watched helplessly as Kat's main canopy pulled open, then tangled, and became nothing more than a useless bag of silk, the lines twisted.

He was instantly reminded of what had happened to Jake. He remembered what Luke had said about the AAD: it would deploy at 750 feet and catch Kat before she hit dirt. But if her canopy was still flapping around, it could just as easily get tangled with it and fail.

Ethan ran over to the door. He could just make out Kat plummeting downwards, spinning out of control towards the Earth. Her canopy was towing behind her like a huge scarf – it would have to be cut away. Ethan knew only one person had any hope of reaching the handle on the harness to release the canopy and then deploy the reserve.

So he leaped out after her.

He arched, flipped, stabilized. He could see Kat far off and below to his left. She was still spinning, totally out of control. All he could think about, his entire focus, was Kat and how he was going to stop her smashing into the ground. He pushed his arms back and shot forward, accelerating fast, tracking across the sky like an Exocet missile.

It seemed to Ethan that the next few seconds stretched out for ever. Kat was so far away, and had such a head start on him. He checked his altimeter: 9,000 feet pinged past. Then 8,000.

Suddenly he was level with Kat. She appeared so abruptly in front of him that he had to really struggle to keep himself stable. Now, though, they were falling at the same rate, 120 mph – terminal velocity. She was spinning wildly and Ethan had to get close enough to deploy her canopy – which meant really, really close. So with little movements of his body here and there, he gradually, ever so gradually, edged forward.

Ethan checked his altimeter. Checked it again. They'd pinged past 7,000 feet now. They were running out of time. He had to hurry, get in before they both hit the dirt.

He could almost hear the seconds ticking by.

His best bet, he figured, was to aim for the handle that would cut away the main canopy. That way, even if he wasn't able to pull the reserve, Kat's AAD would sort it out, and he'd have enough time to push away and deploy his own canopy.

6,000 feet . . .

So, with a final move, Ethan brought himself in towards Kat, reaching out to grab her with both hands.

But he came in too fast, too hard, and didn't have a chance to stop himself and slow down. The thump as he connected with her sent a shockwave through him, and he felt something in his left shoulder pop. Then his arm went numb. Dead to the world.

5,000 feet . . .

Now they were both in trouble: Kat was out of control and unconscious, and Ethan had one arm totally out of action. Amazingly, he'd managed to keep hold of Kat with his right hand, and it was on the handle that would cut away Kat's canopy. Keeping himself calm, Ethan managed to get them both stable; then, with a huge yank, he tugged the handle.

4,000 feet . . .

Kat's main canopy disappeared above. She and Ethan continued to plummet downwards at 120 mph.

Ethan saw the handle to pull Kat's reserve. With a deep breath, he lunged for it, felt his fingers close round it, and yanked.

Kat, still unconscious, disappeared, swept up above him by the explosion of her reserve. But all Ethan could think about, as he tracked away to find some safe air, was that he was seriously in the shit; with his arm out of action, he was unable to reach his ripcord to release his own canopy. He twisted round, but his arm hurt like hell, wouldn't move. He tried again, but the movement sent him into a spin and he floundered in the air, unstable. Ignoring the pain, the panic, he righted himself, got back on track for the DZ, then had another go, tried to reach across, couldn't . . .

Ethan checked his altimeter. He'd just pinged past 3,000 feet.

SHIT!

17

He didn't have time to think about how bad everything was. What he had to do was get the hell out of the deep shit he found himself in. The thought that in saving Kat's life he could soon be ending his own really pissed him off.

Get a grip, he told himself. *Focus.*

Unable to reach the ripcord for his main canopy, he was now reliant on his reserve. There were two ways to activate that: use his good arm, the one still keeping him stable, to pull the toggle and release the reserve; or do nothing and trust the AAD to do its stuff. If he reached over to pull the toggle, he'd spin and lose control. The spin could cause the lines to twist and that would be it – bounce time. But if he did nothing and the AAD failed, he was dead anyway.

The altimeter pinged again – he'd just passed 2,000.

He didn't like leaving things up to fate and his equipment. He gritted his teeth and went for the toggle. But, as expected, the movement of his good arm spun him violently to the right, straining his neck. He tried again and again, but each time he came within inches of the toggle, then spun again.

Ethan heard his altimeter ping. He'd zipped past 1,000 feet. Everything was now down to the AAD.

Ethan closed his eyes . . .

. . . and felt himself yanked from 120 to 10 mph in seconds. His knackered arm flapped around, then smacked him hard in the face. The sensation stung. He didn't mind though. It meant he was alive.

As Ethan glided gently to the ground, in the silence underneath his reserve canopy, he screamed. It was all he could do. He'd saved someone's life, nearly killed himself in the process, but survived none the less. It was definitely something to scream about.

When he landed, he was still screaming. The reserve, not being very manoeuvrable, had placed him a few hundred metres away from the DZ, so he just lay there for a few moments, trying to take it all in. He'd never been so close to death. It wasn't something he ever wanted to experience again. But now that he had, now that he'd been seconds away from oblivion, he felt that something monumental had changed for him. OK, so the skydiving had given him a chance to see what he was capable of, to realize that there was more to life than worrying about exams and his dad. But what he'd just done – saving Kat, saving himself – had made him feel more alive than ever before. In fact, it was as though he'd been asleep his whole life and had only now fully woken up. He took a deep breath, held it, breathed out. He felt absolutely and completely aware of every part of his body, like every single bit of who he was buzzed with life. Everything around him looked clearer, the colours brighter, the air fresher. He knew then that skydiving wasn't just a part of his life, it *was* his life.

Ethan heard a motorbike pulling up close, then someone jogging over.

'I hope you're not dead, because if you are I'll have to ride back and get the minibus to shift your sorry carcass.'

Ethan looked up to see Johnny grinning down at him. 'Nope,' he said. 'Not dead. Not even slightly.'

'Anything broken?'

Ethan waved his one good arm. 'This one works fine, the other one doesn't. I felt it pop when I bumped into Kat.'

Johnny sat down, helped him to sit up. 'You saved Kat's life, Eth.'

'And the AAD saved mine,' said Ethan. 'Kat OK?'

Johnny nodded. 'Yeah, but she's gone to the hospital for a check-up. Sam spotted her first. He was watching the plane when she jumped. He knew something was wrong right away.'

'So he saw me jump out after her?'

'It was unbelievable, Eth, just insane . . .' Johnny paused. 'You know you could've been killed?'

'Wasn't really thinking about that,' said Ethan. 'I saw Kat fall from the plane unconscious; didn't really have much choice but to go out after her.'

They heard the rumble of a large engine and turned to see

Sam's Defender come to a standstill a few metres away. Sam got out, leaving the engine running, jogged over, nodded. 'Ethan.'

'Sam . . .' Ethan nodded back.

'Can you walk?'

Ethan nodded again.

'His arm's shot though,' said Johnny. 'Guess he'll be following Kat to the hospital.'

'Help me get him into the Defender,' said Sam, looking at Johnny.

Johnny nodded, unclipped Ethan from his rig, then helped Sam pick him up and walk him round to the passenger side.

'I'll leave the bike at the café and then get in the back,' said Johnny.

Ethan watched as he jumped on his bike, kicked it into life, spun it through 180 degrees, flinging dirt skyward, then sped off back to FreeFall, kicking out a quick wheelie on the way.

Ethan laughed, even though it hurt.

'He's a one-off,' Sam muttered, gesturing at Johnny. 'Don't think I've ever seen him without a smile on his face.' Then he clambered into the driver's seat and looked Ethan dead in the eye. 'What you did, Ethan, was absolutely bloody idiotic.'

Ethan opened his mouth, closed it, didn't know what to say.

'You are extremely lucky that you both survived. I'm not even going to bother listing the number of things that could've gone wrong. I'm amazed nothing did. You should, by all accounts, be dead. Both of you.'

'But—' said Ethan.

'No buts,' interrupted Sam, his voice hard. 'You need to understand that it's as much luck as skill that you got away with it. By jumping out after Kat you put both your lives at risk – I could have been dealing with two dead skydivers.'

Ethan looked at him. He couldn't believe what he was hearing. Was Sam really saying he'd have done better to let Kat fall – possibly to her death?

'You shouldn't have tried to go after her, Ethan. It was very brave and it took a lot of skill, but also, you got lucky. Frankly, I've never seen anything like it before and I hope I never do again. Understand?'

Ethan nodded.

'Good,' said Sam, and put the Defender into first gear. But before he pulled away he turned back to Ethan.

'What?' snapped Ethan. He was still reeling from the bollocking he'd just been given.

'Well done,' Sam said, reaching out to rest a heavy hand on Ethan's good shoulder. 'Bloody well done.'

Having picked up Johnny, Sam drove Ethan to the hospital. On the way he asked Ethan, 'Got a mobile on you?'

Ethan nodded.

'Good,' said Sam. 'Then I suggest you call your parents. They'll want to know what happened.'

'No chance,' said Ethan. 'Mum's working and would only freak if she knew. She's got enough to worry about as it is. If she starts thinking skydiving's dangerous . . .' His voice faded and he stared out through the windscreen. If his mum found out about this, she'd panic, maybe want him to stop skydiving. He couldn't let that happen.

'What about your dad?' asked Sam.

'What about him?' Ethan countered.

Sam looked across at him. 'Like that, is it?'

Ethan nodded.

'Your call,' said Sam. 'If you're sure.'

'I'm sure.'

It wasn't long before Sam pulled into the A&E bay. It seemed that the story of what had happened in the air had already swept through the medical staff like wildfire.

Ethan was soon sitting with Johnny and Sam as a doctor examined him. The doctor listened quietly while Ethan told him what had happened. Ethan noticed his eyes widen at specific points in the story. But then he did something to Ethan's shoulder that not only hurt like hell but sounded pretty horrible too. Something slipped into place and Ethan found he could move his arm again, though it felt sore.

The doctor stood back, adjusted his stethoscope, then turned to look at Ethan. 'I'm assuming, young man, that I don't need to tell you just how lucky you are to be not simply alive, but pretty much unscathed.'

Ethan shook his head. Sam had made that fact all too clear.

'Normally,' explained the doctor, 'I would expect two people who'd essentially collided in mid-air to be in various bits and pieces in the morgue. However' – he shook his head wonderingly – 'it seems that you have come as close to dying as is possible – and lived to tell the tale.'

Ethan attempted a smile, and the doctor smiled back.

'Your young lady friend, as is to be expected, is somewhat grateful for what you did,' he said.

'Where is Kat?' Ethan asked. 'I'd like to see her.'

'She's in better shape than you,' said the doctor. 'Mild concussion. Doesn't remember much apart from standing up in the plane and then waking up on the ground. I'll have a nurse take you to see her.'

Ethan looked up at this. 'Really?'

The doctor nodded. 'You dislocated your shoulder, that's all. Mild bruising. However' – and he looked hard at Ethan at this point – 'you will need to rest.'

Sam looked up at the doctor, who returned the stare.

'He'll be on a course of painkillers and anti-inflammatory tablets,' he explained. 'I recommend a minimum of four weeks' rest, to give the shoulder a chance to mend. I trust you will be able to make sure this adventurous spirit can be otherwise engaged until then?'

Sam gave him a simple 'Yes.'

'Good,' said the doctor, and quickly but carefully put Ethan's arm in a simple sling. 'Any questions?'

Ethan looked at his arm. Four weeks' rest! *Damn.*

'Would I be able to see Kat now?' he asked.

Kat was lying on a bed, fully clothed. Natalya was with her. When Ethan walked in with Johnny and Sam, it felt like they'd stumbled into a seriously private, hear-any-of-this-and-you're-dead conversation.

Kat looked up, pushed her hair out of her face. She attempted a smile but she looked awkward, embarrassed.

Natalya gave Kat a hug, then came over to Ethan. 'You are either a brave fool or foolishly brave,' she told him.

'I think probably a bit of both, don't you, Ethan?' said Sam.

Ethan did a good impression of a goldfish, his mouth opening and closing as he tried to think of something to say and failed.

'Kat OK?' asked Johnny.

'More than,' said Natalya. 'She survived the whole thing and does not remember any of it.' She turned back to Ethan. 'You saved her life, Ethan. That she will not forget.'

'And neither will we,' put in Sam.

'He's such a hero, aren't you, Eth?' said Johnny. 'But then he had me to learn from, so how could he be anything else?'

Natalya looked at Johnny and shook her head with the ghost of a smile. 'I will leave you with her,' she said. She glanced at Ethan, nodded, then disappeared through the swing doors.

'She's so intense,' said Ethan.

'Exciting, isn't it?' Johnny grinned. 'Makes me feel all tingly.'

They went over to Kat's bed. Sam was looking down at her, face stern. Ethan tried to smile but it felt forced, like it was a smile he was wearing, not one he actually meant.

'M'lady,' said Johnny, 'we bring you your knight in shining armour.' He glanced at Ethan. 'Well, we bring Ethan. Hope that's good enough. Apparently he saved your life.'

Ethan smiled, said, 'Hi,' but could think of nothing else. Kat looked pretty good, considering what she'd just gone through. Waking up to find you'd been seconds from being killed must be a fair shock, he thought.

'You had me scared up there, young lady,' Sam told her.

'It was an accident,' she said. 'I just slipped and hit the door, I think. Ethan knows more about what happened than I do.'

'That was it really,' he confirmed. 'You banged your head.' He grinned. 'Pity that shiny new helmet of yours didn't arrive today.'

'Ironic, isn't it?' said Kat. 'The week I go and order one is the week I have an accident.'

'It's not irony, it's fate,' said Johnny, sitting down on the end of her bed.

'In what way's that, then?' asked Kat.

'Don't know,' said Johnny. 'But it sounds good, doesn't it? All mysterious and stuff. Like me.'

Sam said, 'Well, now that I see you're OK, I'm going to make a phone call. I'll be back in five.'

Johnny stood up. 'I'll come with you.' He turned to Ethan and Kat. 'Body . . . needs . . . chocolate . . . must . . . eat . . .'

Then Kat and Ethan were alone. Ethan looked at Kat, smiled, looked back at the floor, then out the window, and finally took an exceptional interest in the pattern of the curtains. He could have said a lot about what had happened – what it had been like to see Kat fall from the plane, how every single second seemed to be burned into his brain with such clarity it was like watching a movie in high definition – but he just couldn't find the words. At last he looked at Kat again.

'Thank you,' she said, breaking the silence. 'What you did, it was amazing.'

'As Johnny would say – "I know," ' replied Ethan.

'I mean it. I'm alive because of you. I shouldn't even be sitting here. I didn't wake up until after I'd landed, and even then I had no idea what had happened. And now it seems you're more injured than I am.'

'I'm all right,' said Ethan. 'Just got to rest the arm for a few weeks, that's all.'

'What about skydiving?'

Ethan shrugged. 'Don't know,' he said. 'Just have to wait it out, I guess.'

'That sucks,' said Kat. 'I'll be in the air before you. That doesn't seem right, seeing as it's my fault you're injured.'

'Think you'll be nervous?'

'I'd be more nervous if I could never jump again,' said Kat.

Ethan smiled. He wasn't handling this well, and he knew it. He wasn't cut out to be the hero. He'd just reacted, that was all; it was instinct.

'I'm really sorry, Ethan,' said Kat. 'I was a cow to you before the jump and then I put your life at risk. Unbelievable.'

'It's OK. To be honest, I'm as stunned as you are by all this,' said Ethan. And he was. It wasn't like he'd planned any of it. Kat had fallen, he'd gone after her. At the time he hadn't really thought about what he was doing. All he'd known was that he had to save Kat. And he'd done that. 'I just jumped out after you,' he told her. 'You'd have done the same. Anyone would.'

Kat laughed. 'You really think so?'

'Sure,' said Ethan. 'I was just there at the time, that's all. Anyway, how long do you have to stay here for?'

Kat shuffled slightly on the bed. 'To be honest, I don't actually need to be here at all. There's not a scratch on me. They're just keeping me in overnight for observation. I think it's just because they like coming in to ask me about what happened. No one can really believe it.'

'It's quite a story, isn't it?' said Ethan, grinning. 'You flying through the air unconscious, me flying in to save you. We'll be on the front page of the newspapers before we know it.'

'If you were Johnny, I'm pretty sure photographers and reporters would already be here,' said Kat. 'You know he's not going to shut up about this for about a million years, don't you?'

'It'll be fun to hear how the story gets exaggerated in the telling,' said Ethan. 'By the end of the week you'll have been jumping without a parachute.'

They both laughed. Ethan couldn't help feeling a little proud of what he'd done. Even Johnny hadn't done anything like that – which was saying something. And as icebreakers went, having your life saved certainly seemed to work: Kat was being more friendly now than she'd ever been. The only bummer in the whole thing was that he wouldn't be skydiving for a month. Skydiving had completely taken over his life. He lived it and breathed it. He spent every waking moment thinking about it, and at night he dreamed of falling through the sky with a big fat smile on his face. So what would he do with himself for the next four weeks?

'You OK?'

Ethan looked at Kat. 'Just thinking about the skydiving,' he said. 'Can't believe I won't be able to do it for four weeks. Seems like for ever.'

'It's not that long,' said Kat. 'Anyway, that's not as long as Jake's got to wait, is it?'

Ethan looked at her. 'He's only been banned from jumping at FreeFall. Sam can't stop him jumping elsewhere, can he?'

'No,' said Kat, 'but what he did can. Word gets round, Eth.

And messing with rigs is the sin of all sins in skydiving.'

'So he's really screwed?'

Kat nodded. 'Totally.' She laughed. 'Anyway, you've got more important things to worry about. Like your addiction.'

Ethan looked at her.

'Johnny's right about that. I can see it in your eyes,' she continued. 'Skydiving does this to people – takes them over completely. You're addicted, Ethan. Join the club.'

Ethan grinned. 'Nuts really, isn't it? I've only been doing it for a few weeks, and look at me!'

'Don't knock it,' said Kat. 'When you find something that you not only love doing, but do well, it's a great feeling. You're lucky.'

'We both are,' said Ethan.

18

'You've a face on you like a slapped arse,' said Sam when he next saw Ethan at FreeFall. 'How's the shoulder?'

Ethan was back at work. His shoulder felt fine. All he could think about was the fact that he couldn't jump. For four weeks. It bugged the hell out of him.

'Fine,' he replied. 'Aches a little, that's all.' He moved his shoulder as if to prove a point, winced.

'Yes, I can see how everything's just fine,' said Sam. 'So listen.'

Ethan was struck by the purpose in his voice. It sounded like he had a plan.

'You're a damned good skydiver, Ethan. Don't let your impatience ruin it. Give the shoulder enough time to heal and you'll be back in the air. But if you don't rest it, you'll knacker it up completely. Don't let that happen.'

Ethan nodded.

'I mean it,' said Sam. 'Wind your neck in and deal with it. See this as an opportunity. Get to know the regulars better, read up on skydiving, get a better understanding of every-thing. Just because you're not jumping doesn't mean you have to stop learning. Right?'

'Yeah,' said Ethan.

'And a warning . . . Don't think for a single second that I won't know if you book in for a jump. You may be qualified, and you may not need my permission any more, but nothing gets past me at FreeFall, OK? And if I find out you've jumped before your four weeks are up, I'll ground you for the rest of your life.'

Ethan could see from the look on Sam's face that he meant it. But then Sam always had that look on his face: hard, unmoving, unwavering.

'Now that's sorted,' said Sam, 'I've arranged for you to meet up with Luke after work. He'll be waiting for you in the hangar. Head over there as soon as you shut up the shop.'

'What am I meeting him for?' asked Ethan.

'Luke's offered to help keep your mind off the fact that you won't be jumping for a while.' Sam looked at his watch. 'He's going to train the hell out of you instead. Now get your arse over to the shop and open up. You're losing me business.'

As usual, Ethan wasn't given a chance to reply – Sam was already heading off to his office.

The shop was busy, and with every customer that came in to

buy kit, Ethan felt more and more envious. Since completing his AFF, he'd hardly gone a day without a jump. It didn't seem fair – like he was being punished for saving Kat's life. He was glad when the time came to shut; he headed off to the hangar, wondering what Luke had planned 'to keep his mind occupied', as Sam had put it.

Luke was waiting for him when he arrived. 'Hi, Ethan,' he said. 'Good day?'

'It was a day,' replied Ethan. 'What are we doing?' He couldn't be bothered with the small talk. He was grumpy, and he doubted there was much anyone could do about it.

'Formation drills,' said Luke. 'And you need to get this shit absolutely right on the ground before you can even consider doing it in freefall.' He walked over to the hangar wall and pulled out one of the trolleys Ethan had used during his AFF. 'Once I've shown you the basics, we'll lie on these,' Luke explained. 'As you already know from your AFF, you lie flat on them, as if in freefall, and try to move smoothly between each formation.'

'I'm going to learn formation stuff?' said Ethan. 'Why? I didn't think I was ready.'

'Sam's idea,' said Luke, 'and he thinks you are. He also wants to make sure you don't stagnate while you're resting that shoulder. We'll be running through all the usual sky-diving drills as well as the formation stuff. Got it?'

Ethan nodded. If Sam thought he was ready, then he wasn't going to say no. As he headed towards the trolleys, he thought about the team, and about Jake. Did this mean Sam was considering him as Jake's replacement? If there was anything he wanted more, then he couldn't think what it was. He pushed one of the trolleys back and forth. 'Are you sure this isn't a joke?'

'No joke, Ethan. Remember – this is all down to Sam. And I don't know whether you've noticed, but he doesn't really have a sense of humour.'

What followed then, and for the four ensuing weeks as Ethan's shoulder was allowed to recover, was training that covered just about everything Luke knew about formations and skydiving in general. Ethan knew everyone joked about Luke's obsession with the tiniest of details, but as the weeks passed, he soon saw just how useful and important that obsession was. Luke didn't just know what he was talking about, he sounded like he'd invented it. And before long, Ethan had the formation drills down to a fine art. But that wasn't all: Luke constantly quizzed Ethan on the finer points of safety, awareness in the air, and landing. He also taught Ethan how to pack his own rig.

'You'll not be able to jump with this until you pass your rigger's qualification,' said Luke as Ethan repacked his rig under Luke's watchful gaze. 'But at least this way you'll know what you're doing when you come to do the official training. And knowing it won't do any harm, will it? Means you've a better understanding of how your rig works.'

Ethan agreed. Everything Luke showed him he absorbed, memorized and practised. And if he wasn't at work, he was reading up on skydiving, chatting to more experienced skydivers, hanging out with Johnny; anything, just so long as it was about being in the air.

Ethan was obsessed. He knew it.

* * *

It was a bright Saturday morning when Ethan finally rode his bike into FreeFall with a grin on his face like a melon slice. The four weeks was over. He was jumping today.

He was just climbing into the minibus with Sam when Johnny arrived.

'Couldn't miss your first jump,' he said as he sat down next to Ethan.

Two other faces appeared.

'Luke . . . Natalya . . .' said Ethan, surprised to see them.

Luke nodded back; Natalya, as usual, just stared at him with those intense, penetrating eyes. But there was something new in her gaze, Ethan thought. It was as if she was looking at him with a little respect. And maybe she was. Maybe his insane rescue of Kat had given him a little kudos. If so, he wasn't about to complain.

'And Kat,' said Luke as Kat jumped in behind.

Kat looked at Ethan. 'Figured it'd be nice to jump out of a plane with you and actually remember the experience,' she said. 'And I've got this.' Ethan smiled as she held up a new skydiving helmet. It was bright red, with a full-face visor.

'Nice,' he said, nodding at it.

'Cost over three hundred quid,' said Kat. 'Can't really believe I've spent that much.'

'When you're a slave to freedom, money doesn't matter,' said Johnny.

'Slave to freedom?' queried Ethan.

'I can't believe I said it either,' said Johnny. 'Sounds good though, don't you think? I'm so . . . mystical.'

Luke turned to Sam. 'I reckon we should do some of the

formation stuff with Ethan. He knows it now. All he's got to do is put it into practice in the air.'

Sam looked at Ethan. 'Couldn't agree more,' he said. 'You OK with that, Ethan? Reckon your shoulder is up to it?'

Ethan nodded. 'Totally. Never felt better.'

'I'll make sure I'm careful,' said Luke. 'The movements are pretty slight anyway. It's not like I'll be trying to pull your arm out of its socket.'

'I'm OK with anything so long as I get to jump,' said Ethan.

'Ah, just listen to him,' said Johnny. 'He's all excited!' Then he hugged Ethan dramatically. 'I'm so . . . proud of you . . . son . . .'

Ethan pushed him away, smiling and shaking his head. Then the minibus set off and he felt his stomach lurch. This was it . . .

The call came through – they were over the DZ. In the minibus, Sam had given them the order of things: Luke was to do some simple two-person formation stuff with Ethan; Johnny, Kat and Natalya were free to do whatever they fancied; Sam was going to follow Ethan and Luke, just to keep an eye on things and assess Ethan's performance.

Johnny, Kat and Natalya were at the door of the plane. They nodded at Ethan, then jumped.

Ethan took his place at the door with Luke. He wasn't even given time to think about what he was doing. It was all instinctive. He followed Luke's hand signals, got into position.

Jumped.

Ethan didn't need to scream – the adrenaline searing

through his veins was doing it for him. As he accelerated to terminal velocity, he looked up to see the plane above become nothing more than a black dot.

Seven and a half seconds later, he was doing 120 mph.

He arched his back, flipped over, got stable. Luke was just away to his right. On seeing Ethan get into the stable freefall position, he tracked over.

Luke gave a hand signal and they both flicked themselves into the first position – facing each other, holding hands. With a nod, they switched to the next position – Ethan holding Luke's left ankle with his left arm, Luke doing the same to Ethan. Then back to the first position.

Luke grinned. Ethan smiled back as he spotted Sam, who was tracking in to join them. And so they finished their freefall as a three-point star.

Ethan looked at Sam, then back at Luke. Jumping alone was a rush, but jumping with others, people who trusted him in the air . . . this was something else.

Sam nodded at Luke and Ethan. They checked altimeters, then broke the star formation, bursting away from each other like fire crackers.

Ethan made sure he had clean air above and around him, checked his altimeter, pulled the ripcord.

The unmistakable crack of his canopy catching air filled his ears as he was pulled into a steady glide. Then everything was peaceful, and he could enjoy the gentle return to Earth.

Back at the hangar, everyone was talking. Ethan loved every-thing about being back in the air – even being on the ground afterwards. After a jump, it was impossible to come down from the high for hours. It was a rush like nothing else. And, he realized, this was the first time that he'd felt a part of the team, rather than just a tag-along.

Sam called for everyone's attention. 'Right,' he said. 'Next weekend you're all going to the skydiving competition in France. I've got some business of my own in France so I'll head out earlier, but I'll meet you there.'

'What skydiving competition?' asked Ethan.

'The one in France,' said Johnny. 'The one Sam's talking about. Jeez, how you gonna learn anything if you don't listen?'

'So how come you all know about it and I don't?'

'Because I didn't tell you about it,' said Sam.

'But I'm invited?' asked Ethan, unable to hide his smile.

Sam gave a nod. 'Not just invited; I've booked your ticket.' Ethan wasn't given a chance to respond as Sam was already speaking to the whole team again. 'Let me make one thing clear,' he said. 'You're not there to compete as a four-way team, with Ethan instead of Jake, and Johnny filming. Despite what you all might think, Ethan isn't ready to take Jake's place just yet . . . He will be soon enough, but we're not going to rush it. Got it?'

Everyone nodded and Ethan grinned. A skydiving competition in France! Fantastic! Ethan realized he'd progressed quickly, but knowing that Sam was considering him as Jake's replacement felt amazing. He opened his mouth to say something, but the look Sam gave him made him shut it immediately.

'You'll all be doing this for the experience. Go out there, get a feel for how a competition runs, and check out what you're up against for when you do eventually enter as a team. Right?'

Nods all round.

'Good,' said Sam. 'Now, to make it interesting . . .' He paused, and everyone leaned closer. 'I've already entered you in a couple of categories – call it your instructor's prerogative.' He looked at the gang, one by one, then explained, 'Johnny, you're in for freestyle solo, Luke you're on accuracy, Kat and Natalya, you're on two-way.'

Ethan looked at the team. They were all smiles.

Sam stepped back and winked. 'And if you find a way to win something in the process, that's a bonus. Right, travel arrangements . . .'

Ethan, like the rest of the team, was hooked on Sam's words. He knew he'd have to get his mum to agree to let him go, but couldn't think of a reason why she'd say no. This was such a great opportunity – he knew she'd understand that. And Dad wouldn't have any say in the matter.

'As I've said, I'll meet you out there,' said Sam. 'Everything is arranged and paid for. Your tickets are in my office, as are details of the accommodation. If you don't mind, I'll leave Luke to deal with all that, as usual.'

'Don't you trust me?' asked Johnny.

'In a skydive, yes,' replied Sam. 'In my office, no.'

'It's a fair point,' said Johnny.

'And well made,' added Kat.

Ethan couldn't help himself. 'But how's all this being paid for?' he asked.

Sam's look was steely. 'I have my contacts. They like sponsoring the right team. Perform well, they'll stay on board.'

'They the same contacts who covered my AFF?' Ethan wanted to know.

'They are. And before you ask, they like staying anonymous.'

'But you booked my tickets without asking,' said Ethan. 'How'd you know I'd be free?'

'I didn't,' said Sam. 'I just made a big assumption.' He turned to leave, but stopped and looked back at the team. 'One more thing,' he said. 'Any takers for a night jump?'

19

'Night jump?' asked Ethan. 'I'm guessing that's exactly what it sounds like, right?'

'Absolutely,' said Sam. 'These guys haven't done one for a while and it'll do them good to have a little refresher. You've not got enough experience yet so I'll take you tandem.'

'When are we doing it?' asked Ethan.

'At night,' said Johnny. 'That's why we call it a night jump.'

'And to think I once found you funny,' said Ethan, sighing theatrically.

'I'll arrange it for tomorrow evening,' said Sam. 'I've already checked with the pilot and he's free. Luke?'

Luke looked at him enquiringly.

'Can you sort out the LEDs and glow sticks?'

Luke nodded, and Ethan asked what an LED was.

'If you're flying a plane at night, spotting a skydiver is pretty impossible,' said Sam. 'LEDs – light-emitting diodes – are bright enough to make sure we stand out well enough to be avoided.' He turned back to Luke. 'Give Ethan an idea of what a night jump involves. The rest of you read up on it. I doubt any of you can remember much about the potential effects of hypoxia on your night vision, or anything about the dark zone.'

Natalya spoke up. 'Hypoxia is a restricting of oxygen to the brain that happens in most people above seven thousand feet. It can potentially make your vision cross-wire and slow your thinking, but this is usually not a problem unless you are doing a high-altitude jump. At night, however, it can make it difficult to focus or judge distance. This can be very dangerous, particularly when coming in to land.'

Sam nodded his approval, then said, 'See you tomorrow,' and left.

Ethan looked at Natalya. She was gazing at him intently, but as he returned her stare, she got up and followed Sam. He realized then that of all the team members, she was the one he knew the least about. She seemed incredibly loyal to the team, but apart from that . . .

'Natalya was introduced to the rest of the group through Sam,' Johnny said, almost as if he'd read Ethan's thoughts. 'No one knows anything about her. She's really private.'

'Gets on OK with Kat, though,' Ethan remarked.

'So did Jake,' said Johnny darkly. Then he grinned. 'Anyway, I'm taking bets on who she *really* is.'

Ethan raised an eyebrow.

'It's completely above board,' said Johnny, 'just so long as she doesn't find out.'

Ethan laughed. 'So who do you think she is?' he asked.

'Luke reckons she's the daughter of some eastern Euro politician bloke who's now in hiding,' said Johnny. 'He likes all that conspiracy theory bollocks. Kat's not joining in the fun. Says it would ruin their special relationship. Typical girl.'

'What about you?' asked Ethan.

'Oh, I'm odds-on favourite,' said Johnny. 'I think she's a vampire.'

'France?' said Jo.

Ethan nodded. 'It's a skydiving competition. Sam's booked me a ticket and everything!' He had rushed back home with the news, excited and breathless. Now, sitting in the lounge with Jo and his mum, he was doing his best to make it all sound very normal.

'But it's such short notice,' said his mum. 'Why didn't Sam mention it sooner? And who's paying for it all? Is there something Sam's not telling you? Because I think you should find out if there is, just in case . . .'

Ethan knew it was a little odd that it should all be booked and paid for by a completely unknown – well, unknown to him – benefactor, sponsor, whatever. But to be honest, he didn't care. He was just grateful to be going. He shrugged. 'I think Sam just wanted to make sure I'd be good enough to go before he mentioned it and got my hopes up,' he said.

His mum looked a little worried at this. 'You're taking part?' she asked anxiously.

'No way!' said Ethan. 'I'm not ready for that! I'm just going out to watch, see how competitions run, that kind of thing. It'll be amazing.'

'No kidding,' said Jo. 'I'm well jealous.'

Ethan grinned. 'You're not telling me you're interested in skydiving, are you?'

Jo shook her head. 'Nah,' she said. 'But sexy male sky-divers – particularly French ones? Those I'm interested in!'

They all laughed, and it sounded good. Laughter was something Ethan didn't hear too much of at home.

'Well, I'm sure it will be a wonderful experience, love,' said his mum. 'But do you think I should just speak to Sam about it? Find out a bit more.'

'There's not much more to find out,' said Ethan quickly, knowing that if his mum phoned Sam, he'd never live it down – certainly not if Johnny found out. 'It'll be fine, Mum. It's all sorted.'

'Well, if you're sure,' said his mum, smiling. Then the front door of the flat slammed and Ethan saw the smile falter.

Heavy footsteps sounded in the hall and they all looked up to see Dad standing in the doorway.

'Ah, a lovely family gathering,' he said, lurching against the door. 'How sweet.'

Ethan got to his feet.

'Going somewhere?' asked his dad.

'France,' Ethan heard his mum say as she got up too. 'He's going to France! Isn't that exciting?'

Ethan looked at his mum. He knew it was a desperate attempt on her part to get Dad interested in something other than drink – to maybe share a bit of what being a family was about. He loved her for it. He also knew it wouldn't work.

'You? In France?' said his dad, and laughed. 'And how are you affording that then, eh? Because I'm not bloody paying for it, that's for sure.'

'It's paid for,' said Ethan, determined to remain calm, if only for the sake of his mum and Jo. 'There's a skydiving competition. Sam's organized the tickets.'

'Sam?' said his dad, pushing himself away from the door and stumbling forward a little. 'You teacher's pet now, is that it?'

'The whole team's going,' Ethan said steadily. 'All expenses paid.' He watched as his dad just stood there, speechless. It was like he could actually see him trying to think of something to say.

'You couldn't pay me to go to that place,' his dad muttered eventually. 'All that foreign food and crap. Bloody awful. Never been abroad – never want to.' He shuffled forward and dropped onto the sofa.

Ethan felt unbelievably calm. For once, even his dad couldn't rile him. He smiled. 'Yeah, right,' he said. 'Or is it that I'm doing something you've never had the balls to do and you hate it.'

'Who'd want to jump out of a plane?' said his dad, laughing and switching on the TV. But Ethan could hear how forced his laughter was.

'You should try it,' he said. 'I'll get Sam to do a tandem with you.' Then he smiled again. 'Oh, actually that wouldn't work. You have to be fit and healthy to do a jump – so that's you screwed, isn't it?'

His dad looked up at him. 'You've turned into a right cocky little shit, you know that?' he snarled. 'And I can still knock it out of you.'

169

Ethan heard his mum murmur, 'Leave it now, Ethan, go on,' but he had something else to say.

'You're a loser, Dad,' he said evenly. 'And you hate the fact that you haven't been able to drag me down with you.'

'I'm warning you . . .'

Ethan looked at his dad and smiled. 'Warning me? How?' he demanded. 'You're pissed, Dad. You can't even pull yourself out of that sofa.'

His dad rolled himself onto the sofa arm to push himself to his feet. 'I'm going to give you such a kicking, you little . . .'

And as Ethan watched his dad struggle to stand up, he knew he would never have a hold over him again. 'Really?' he said, then he reached out, and with a gentle push sent his dad falling back onto the sofa.

The last thing Ethan heard as he left the flat was his dad swearing and Jo's stifled laughter.

It was 2200 hours the following evening and they were all gathered in the hangar for the night jump.

'Listen up. Here are your altimeters,' said Sam, handing them out. 'You'll be using your usual audible ones as well, but these are back-lit, for obvious reasons . . . Torches,' he went on, handing out small, rubberized ones. Ethan watched as the team clipped them to their jumpsuits.

'The torches are so you can check your canopy in the dark,' Johnny told him.

'Everyone's got their LEDs strapped to their legs,' said Luke, looking at Sam. 'And I've checked each one to make sure they're regulation brightness.'

'Regulation brightness?' said Ethan. 'Seriously?'

Luke nodded. 'They have to be visible for three miles in every direction – we're not the only ones in the sky.'

'Remember, everyone,' said Sam, 'we don't want those things activated until we're in the air.' He then pulled something from his pocket. 'The final bit of kit . . . Glow sticks.'

Even Ethan knew what these were – simple plastic tubes with two chemicals inside separated by a thin sliver of glass. All you had to do was bend the tube to break the glass, the chemicals would mix and the thing would glow blue or green or red or whatever for about eight hours. He smiled, remembering how his mum had given him one at Halloween and how he'd used it to read comics under his duvet.

'Finally,' said Sam, 'the dark zone. Luke?'

Ethan saw Luke open his mouth – but Johnny got in first.

'Allow me,' he said, and turned to the team as though addressing a class. 'Above a hundred feet you've a good view of the DZ because of all the ambient and moon light. The lower you get, the darker the ground looks, and once you get really close, this light is lost because of the low angle of reflection. Below a hundred, it feels like you're landing in a black hole and you can experience ground rush – which is where it feels as if the DZ is flying up at you out of the darkness. Be prepared, guys, and don't let it faze you!'

'If it's so dark, how do we see the DZ?' asked Ethan.

'It's lit,' said Sam. 'Any other questions?'

No one spoke.

'Good. It'll be lights out in a couple of minutes. Everyone activate your glow stick and cover it with this.'

Sam handed out a roll of thick duct tape, then looked at Ethan. 'We go for lights out so that our eyes are acclimatized to the darkness when we jump,' he explained. 'The lights will be off in the plane as well.'

'And the duct tape?' asked Ethan.

'The glow sticks are activated now so that we can check they're not duds. Once we're sure they're all OK, the duct tape goes on to stop the light shining in people's eyes – we pull the tape off just before we jump.'

It was yet more information for Ethan to take in, but that didn't bother him. Anything to do with skydiving and he lapped it up.

'Right . . . lights,' said Sam, and the room was plunged into darkness. They all sat there in silence for a few minutes; eventually Ethan's eyes adjusted to the gloom and he could make out the rest of the team.

'Remember,' Sam told them, 'maintain your night vision by not looking at any lights, even far-off ones. The only light in the plane will be red as that won't affect your eyes. You need to be sharp for this, OK?'

The team murmured a yes.

Sam checked his watch. 'Good,' he said. 'Let's go.'

As everyone stood up, Kat looked at Ethan. 'Excited?' she asked.

Ethan nodded. 'How many night jumps have you done?'

'Not enough,' said Kat. 'It's amazing. Everything looks and sounds and feels completely different when you jump at night. It's like you're just floating. Makes you wish it could last for ever.'

'I can make any night last for ever,' said Johnny, winking at her.

'Yeah, and for all the wrong reasons,' she said.

Everyone laughed.

'Don't knock it till you try it,' said Johnny.

Ethan grinned. 'So what's it like, jumping in the dark?'

Johnny stopped and came close, as if he was about to pass on the biggest secret of his life. 'Better than sex,' he whispered. 'Almost.'

'Now load up, everyone,' said Sam. They had driven to the plane in his Defender, lights out all the way. 'I want us up there and jumping asap.'

The team lined up and clambered on board the plane. Ethan glanced at the pilot. He wasn't the usual one. In the strange red light, he looked like the man who Johnny had once told Ethan was Gabe, Sam's friend. Ethan figured maybe Gabe was a night pilot.

Sam pulled the door shut, locked it, nodded at the pilot and sat down. Ethan looked across at Johnny, who winked before pulling on his skydiving helmet. Kat, Luke and Natalya did the same – they all had full-face helmets, Kat's still shiny new. And as the plane taxied round for takeoff, Ethan decided he had to get a full-face one too, if only because it would make him look so bloody cool.

Ethan, like the rest of the team, heard the pilot say that they were coming up to the DZ. Adrenaline fizzed through him. He wondered if it would ever feel any different; if one day he'd skydive and not get the buzz. He hoped not.

Everyone stood and lined up. Luke first, then Natalya, Kat, Johnny – with a camera helmet – and finally Ethan. Sam came over and clipped their harnesses together, pulling Ethan in tight.

Luke looked over to the pilot for the thumbs-up, then pushed open the door.

Ethan felt the air burst into the plane. All he could see beyond the door was a thick, tarry blackness. It seemed utterly impossible, unreal almost, as though they weren't flying at all, just sitting on the ground with the engines running.

He wasn't given much more time to think about it. With a nod, the rest of the team tumbled through the door in quick succession, and Ethan soon found himself staring into utter blackness.

Then he felt Sam pull his head back. He crossed his arms. And jumped.

As they left the plane, Ethan didn't know if he was terrified or excited or both. This was skydiving unlike any-thing he'd experienced before. Everything felt different. Jumping in daylight, you knew where you were going, could see the world below you. But this time, it was a jump into the unknown.

A stab of light caught Ethan's eye as Sam activated the LED.

For the first few moments he felt like he was in a washing machine. He had no idea which was up and which was down as they tumbled through the air, accelerating to terminal velocity.

Then Sam flipped them over, belly down.

Ethan was blown away by what he saw. Above, in the clear night sky, stars glittered through the dark. Below, the world was a black canvas dotted with lights like distant galaxies.

He checked his altimeter, then quickly found the rest of

the team, their LEDs pulsing in the blackness. The pilot had dropped them perfectly over the DZ – Ethan was able to make it out below. It was lit up as Sam had said it would be, and was getting closer.

Another check of the altimeter. Wind rushing past. This was it, thought Ethan, smiling. Everything he wanted was in this moment. He longed to feel like this for ever: so completely alive, buzzing with it, the metallic taste in his mouth of the adrenaline coursing through him.

He felt a tap on his shoulder; Sam was reaching for the ripcord.

Then the canopy exploded, and after the intense rush of the freefall, Ethan and Sam were pulled up into a perfectly controlled glide to the DZ.

It was eerie floating down in the blackness. Below them, lights of towns glowed, and car headlights seemed to cut the darkness into zigzags. During a normal day jump, Ethan knew where he was in the sky, how far away the ground was, but in the dark it was just like Kat had said – it felt as if he was floating there, not falling at all.

As Ethan stared into the night, trying to take it all in, he noticed it getting darker, just as Johnny had warned, and realized they were now in the dark zone. That meant the DZ was getting close.

'Knees up!' shouted Sam.

Ethan reacted, pulled his knees up hard. Seconds later the ground rushed up at them, Sam flared the canopy, and they landed gently.

'Enjoy that?' Sam asked as he unclipped Ethan.

'What do you think?' he replied. 'What a rush!'

Sam sorted out the rig and pulled in the canopy, rolling it up.

As Ethan followed Sam back to the hangar, the rest of the team landed on the DZ. A beaming Johnny soon caught up with him. 'Quite a mind-screw, isn't it?' he said. 'Just wait till you do it solo; it's a religious experience.'

Ethan laughed and raised his left hand. 'I'm shaking. I think my brain's still up there somewhere. I can't stop buzzing!'

'You're really beginning to sound like one of us, Eth,' Johnny told him. 'Be afraid. Be very afraid.'

'Nothing I can do about it,' said Ethan. 'I absolutely bloody love it!'

'Then there's just one thing left for you to try,' said Johnny.

Ethan looked at him. 'What?'

'Your first BASE jump,' said Johnny. 'You can come along tomorrow night and watch if you like.' Then he winked. 'But don't tell Sam.'

20

Ethan was waiting outside his block of flats; he recognized the van as soon as it turned into the road. It was the one he'd seen Johnny jump into when he'd first met him. Hell, that seemed so long ago now.

The side door flew open.

'Kat?'

'Well spotted,' said Kat. 'Jump in. It's not exactly luxurious, but there are a few rucksacks to sit on.'

Ethan got in. Kat slid the door shut behind him and the van sped off, sending him onto his arse. He shuffled himself round into a sitting position.

Johnny was peering over from the front seat. 'You remember The Dude?'

The driver waved back with his left hand, the little finger and thumb outstretched, the middle three fingers clenched.

'He's a legend in his own lifetime,' said Johnny. 'It's his fault I got into BASE jumping in the first place.'

'So you skydive then?' asked Ethan.

'Totally,' said The Dude. 'I've been out of the country for a while – otherwise you'd have seen me at FreeFall.'

'He's so mysterious . . .' Johnny's eyes were wide. 'By *out of the country* he actually means lying on a beach in Goa.'

The Dude laughed.

Ethan looked at Kat. 'He really calls himself that?'

Kat rolled her eyes. 'His favourite movie's *The Big Lebowski.* Ever seen it? He watches it every week.'

The Dude nodded, waved his hand again, accelerated as some traffic lights ahead turned from green to red.

'Feeling OK?' Johnny asked Kat.

'I'm a little nervous,' she replied.

'Good,' said Johnny. 'I don't want to do this with anyone who doesn't get nervous.'

The Dude reached for the stereo. 'Time for some tunes,' he said, drawling out the word 'tunes' as if it was spelled with at least a hundred *U*s and ended with 'zaaaahhhh'.

Music slammed into the van, turned up to the maximum. No one spoke, simply because you couldn't hear anything above the music.

A few miles down the road, and halfway through something that sounded like a drum kit being destroyed, The Dude turned the music down. 'We're being followed.'

'Shut up,' said Kat. 'No one knows we're doing this.'

Johnny turned to The Dude. 'Serious?'

The Dude nodded. 'Car's been tailing us for the past few miles. I've slowed down a few times to give the driver a chance to overtake, but he's just stayed behind.'

'Maybe he's just a nervous driver,' said Ethan. 'You know – doesn't like overtaking at night or something. My mum's like that.'

'Nah, this is different,' said The Dude. 'I'm sure of it.'

Kat looked up at Johnny.

'See what happens if we pull over,' he said. 'Wait till you're on a straight bit of road, then indicate and pull off the road, like we're checking a map or someone's getting out to take a piss or something.'

A few moments later, The Dude pulled the van off the road, flicking his hazard lights on as they came to a standstill. A black hatchback zipped past at way above the speed limit, the exhaust growling angrily, so low that it caught the road, sending sparks scattering across the tarmac.

'Idiot,' said Kat, looking at the disappearing tail lights.

Johnny turned to The Dude. 'Did you get a look at the registration number?'

He shook his head. 'Must've been mistaken,' he said, 'but all the signs were there. Kept his speed on mine, and never overtook, even when I slowed.'

'But who'd follow us?' asked Ethan.

Johnny sighed dramatically. 'It was probably some of my more hardcore fans,' he said. 'They get so fractious if they've not touched me for a while.'

'Did you really just use the word fractious?' asked Kat.

'And I hardly know what it means,' said Johnny. 'Sounded good though, didn't it?' He turned to The Dude. 'OK to head on?'

The Dude answered by easing the van back out onto the road. About fifteen minutes later he pulled into a lay-by.

'This is it,' said Johnny, looking over at Ethan and Kat.

The Dude jumped out of the van and pulled open the side door.

Ethan jumped out and watched as Kat and Johnny grabbed a rig each and clipped themselves in.

'Follow me,' said Johnny.

The Dude locked the van and they trailed off into the dark.

'We're here,' Johnny said after a hard ten-minute climb.

Ethan stopped. 'Where's *here* exactly?'

Johnny pointed at the view. It was fantastic. Rolling hills stretched away beneath them, dotted with specks of light. And stretching up into the sky above, just a couple of hundred metres from where they were standing, stood an enormous antenna.

'You're kidding,' said Ethan. 'You're crazy.'

'Right,' said Johnny. 'Kat? You ready?'

Ethan looked at Kat, saw her nod nervously. It was the first time he'd ever seen her look even slightly unsure of herself.

'First we check each other's rigs,' said Johnny.

'I know that,' Kat told him.

'I know you know,' he said. 'But we'll be doing everything by the letter tonight. There's no second chance with this. OK?'

Kat nodded and started to check Johnny's rig.

Ethan noticed that the rigs were much smaller than those he'd used. They were more like the size of a Raider.

'What's the difference between these rigs and the ones I'm used to?' he asked, always keen to learn something new about the sport that had taken over his life.

'These are BASE-specific rigs,' said Johnny. 'You can use converted rigs, but these are better.'

'They look no bigger than a Raider,' said Ethan.

'They're not,' said Johnny, 'but the difference is that these are low-aspect-ratio canopies – technical term which means they're bloody reliable in the opening and stable in flight. Last thing you need on a BASE jump is some highly manoeuvrable canopy above you – it'll swing you into a cliff before you know it.'

'Right,' said Ethan, and realized he had never seen Johnny so serious before. It was reassuring, but it didn't quite make him wish he was Kat.

'Sorted,' said Johnny. 'Now here's what we're gonna do.'

Ethan drew closer; he wasn't going to miss a chance to learn something from his friend.

'Kat and I are going to peg it over to the antenna. Then we'll climb as quickly as we can to the highest point and jump. Dude, you're on filming duty. Ethan – you keep a watch out. If we get spotted, we're in the shit.'

Ethan nodded.

Johnny pulled something out of his pocket and handed it to him. 'Two-way radio,' he explained. 'If there's a problem, you tell us and we bolt. Right?'

Ethan nodded again. It was a skill he'd mastered since turning up at FreeFall.

'It's just a simple press-'n'-talk job,' Johnny told him, pointing at the large black button on the side of the radio. 'It's quicker than a mobile. Saves time if you don't have to tap in a phone number.' He turned to Kat. 'A ladder leads up the antenna, but it starts about seven metres off the ground. We'll use this to get up to that point . . .'

He opened a rucksack and revealed a thick knotted rope with a three-pronged grappling hook attached to the end of it. Ethan wondered where he'd found the hook – it looked pretty deadly.

'The ladder is enclosed all the way up to a small platform. You go first, Kat, and I'll follow. OK?'

Kat nodded, and Ethan saw her shift from foot to foot.

'When you jump, you know what to do. We've practised this plenty of times.'

'Is it different from jumping out of a plane?' asked Ethan.

'You jump from a plane at speed,' said Johnny, 'so your canopy grabs air immediately. BASE jumping's different. You're starting from a stationary position and your canopy won't grab enough air until you've picked up speed.'

He turned to Kat. 'We'll be fine with this. We're jumping from one of the highest points in the country. Just make sure that when you jump, you get yourself far enough away from the antenna for your canopy to deploy safely. And throw your drogue chute out straight away; it needs to pull your canopy out asap.'

'Isn't the drogue chute packed with the canopy?' said Ethan. 'I thought it came out when you pulled the ripcord.'

'Not when you're BASE jumping,' said Johnny. 'Do that and the delay would have you bouncing before the main canopy had even been fully deployed. For this, you have it in your hand and chuck it out as soon as you jump. That way it pulls the canopy out straight away.'

'Makes sense,' said Ethan. 'As much as jumping off a huge aerial can ever make sense,' he added.

He glanced over at Kat. 'Are you sure about this?' he asked her. 'I mean, it's not like I'm there to jump out after you and pull your reserve.'

Kat smiled. 'Totally,' she said. 'And I can't expect you to be there every time I jump, can I? You're not Superman!'

'Oh, I don't know,' said Ethan, hiding a smile.

'Anyway,' said Kat, 'Johnny knows what he's doing and so do I. Nothing will go wrong.'

'I know,' said Ethan. 'Johnny's the best there is.'

'I'm pretty damned good myself, Ethan.'

'Sorry, I wasn't . . . I mean . . . Look . . .'

Kat laughed at his discomfort. 'It's fine. Don't worry. I'll be golden. Johnny's done so many BASE jumps he's lost count, and we've practised loads. OK?'

Ethan nodded.

'Thanks for the concern though,' she said, and winked.

Ethan turned and saw that The Dude had switched on the video camera. 'Eth,' he said, 'you're on film, man! Is this a rush or what?'

Ethan grinned. OK, so he was just watching, but the atmosphere was electric, like the air was crackling with the energy of what was about to happen.

'Dude? Eth? See you in a few minutes,' said Johnny. 'Kat – let's do this thing!'

Ethan watched Johnny and Kat march off into the dark towards the antenna; he was still thinking about what Johnny

183

had said. He'd never given the whole issue of grabbing air much thought before. He'd always figured BASE jumping was much like skydiving – just from much closer to earth. But now he realized it really didn't allow any room for error. If Kat didn't pick up enough speed in those first few seconds, if she didn't grab enough air, then that was it.

Game over.

21

'Everything OK?'

Ethan put the radio to his mouth, pressed the button. 'Yeah, Johnny,' he said. 'All quiet down here. You?'

'We're at the antenna,' said Johnny, his voice crackly on the radio. 'Kat's looking nervous though. Don't know if she's up for this. Might spew.'

Ethan heard the distinct sound of someone being punched.

'Scratch that,' said Johnny. 'She's fine.'

Ethan laughed. 'You're both nuts – you know that, don't you?'

'You love it,' said Johnny. 'Cutting radio contact now. I'm

going to throw the rope up. If all goes well, we'll be grabbing air in less than ten minutes.'

'Good luck,' said Ethan, but Johnny was gone. He turned to The Dude. 'Got any binos?'

The Dude reached into his pocket. 'Here,' he said. 'You'll just be able to make them out against the night sky as it's so clear.'

Ethan put the binos to his eyes. For a moment he saw nothing, just a blur of shadows as he tried to find the antenna. Then he found it, tracked up the ladder and soon spotted Johnny and Kat. 'These are amazing,' he said, stunned by how much he could see in the dark.

'They've got some kind of special night-vision system or coating or something,' said The Dude. 'Johnny gave them to me.'

'Where'd he get them?'

'Sam, I think. Pretty cool, huh?'

Ethan nodded. They were very cool indeed. He kept the binos trained on Johnny and Kat. They had now reached the tiny platform Johnny had mentioned. Ethan had no idea how high they were, but he did know it was high enough to kill them if something went wrong.

'You see them?' asked The Dude.

'At the platform,' said Ethan. 'Camera not making them out?'

'Too dark,' said The Dude. 'Should be able to get something when they jump, though. They'll be visible against the sky then. At the moment they're just blurs against the antenna.'

Ethan kept watching. He could see Kat now; she was at

the edge of the platform. Johnny looked like he was giving her a final prep talk. Ethan wondered what he was saying, how Kat was feeling. He loved the adrenaline of skydiving, but he knew that it was pretty safe – that he had a reserve canopy if necessary. Hell, it had already saved him once! But BASE jumping didn't have that. And yet, in spite of all the danger – or maybe *because* of it – he couldn't help wanting to try it for himself.

He watched as Kat turned away from Johnny – and jumped.

'Kat's gone!' he said. 'She's—' He broke off as he heard the distinctive crack of a canopy grabbing air. 'Bloody hell! She's done it!'

'Awesome!' yelled The Dude.

Ethan heard a whoop that took him straight back to the first time he'd seen Johnny BASE jumping. He pulled his binos from Kat, spotted Johnny, went back to Kat. She was coming in to land now. Ethan watched her touch down, heard her scream, saw her punch the air – and felt a little jealous . . .

The Dude was still filming Johnny, who'd just touched down near Kat.

'They're on their way,' Ethan told him. 'Look pretty happy with themselves, don't they?'

'Totally,' said The Dude. 'Unreal.'

Ethan lowered his binos as Johnny and Kat jogged over, carrying their canopies. He could see a wildness in their eyes – Kat was babbling in excitement.

'What did it look like?' she was asking Johnny. 'I thought I'd messed up, but then the canopy opened, and next thing I was just gliding down. It was un-bloody-believable! Eth, you've got to do it! You just have to!'

'You know, I think she enjoyed it,' said Ethan, smiling.

'It's the effect I have on women,' said Johnny. 'It's a burden, but I deal with it.'

Kat leaned over and kissed him on the cheek.

'No time for that,' said The Dude. 'Need to go.' And he turned back towards the van, started jogging.

Ethan looked at Johnny and Kat. 'You two need a hand with anything?'

'We're fine,' said Kat. 'More than fine. I just want to get back and see what it all looked like on film! Come on!'

Ethan watched her head off after The Dude.

'What have I done?' asked Johnny, shaking his head.

'Created a monster, I think,' said Ethan with a laugh.

They jogged back to the van. Ethan and Kat piled into the back while Johnny and The Dude climbed into the front.

'Always thought you'd fit in,' Johnny told Ethan. 'The team feels right with you in it.'

'I'm not sure I'm part of the team yet,' said Ethan. 'Not till I can jump in formation with you.'

'Oh, you're part of the team all right,' said Johnny. 'Otherwise you wouldn't be here. It was Kat who suggested it.'

'Really?'

Kat nodded. 'You're in, Ethan. No doubt about it.'

Ethan beamed. He couldn't help it. The grin spread across his face and refused to leave.

'You OK with that?' asked Johnny. 'I only ask because you don't look too sure.'

Everybody laughed.

Suddenly there was a flash of headlights and Ethan saw a Porsche come speeding round the bend. Then he heard the police sirens.

They all did.

22

'Said we were being followed,' hissed The Dude. He stamped on the accelerator, wheel-spinning out of the lay-by, throwing Ethan onto his back.

'It's Jake,' said Kat. 'I'd know his car anywhere. The bastard shopped us.'

'But that car earlier wasn't a Porsche!' Ethan yelled over the roar of the van's engine.

'It was probably being driven by his minions,' said Johnny. 'I bet Jake's been keeping an eye on us for weeks, just so he could do this.'

The Dude swung the van hard to the right and catapulted Ethan into Kat.

'Sorry,' Ethan said, pushing himself away. 'I thought you said this wasn't illegal!'

'It isn't,' Johnny shouted back. 'But climbing that antenna was.'

'Thanks for letting me know,' said Ethan, rolling his eyes. It was one thing getting involved in something that was risky. But getting chased by the police wasn't exactly something he'd include as part of a fun night out. 'What now?'

'Toolbox in the back there somewhere,' said Johnny. 'Need it.'

'What the hell for?' said Ethan, turning to look at the piles of kit The Dude had scattered in the back of the van.

'Just find it,' shouted Johnny.

Ethan could hear the sirens getting closer. With a shrug he started to search through what seemed to be bits and bobs of The Dude's life. There was a sleeping bag, a couple of tents, rucksacks of all shapes and sizes, ropes and climbing kit, a camping stove.

He looked over at Kat; she'd pinned herself into a corner of the van, bracing herself against the sides with her feet and hands. 'Toolbox?' he said, raising a hand in the air in frustration.

Kat looked around, shook her head. 'Must be your side, Eth.'

Ethan turned round for another look.

'Ethan?' said Johnny. 'We're going to need it very soon . . .'

'You sure it's here?' he asked. Through the windscreen he could see city lights ahead; at least they were nearing home.

'It's there all right,' said The Dude.

'Yeah, and so's everything else,' hissed Ethan, and had another rummage, digging through The Dude's stuff like a mole through earth. Then his hands found a box. He pulled it out. 'This it?'

Johnny turned, nodded. 'Open it.'

Inside there wasn't a single tool. Instead, Ethan was looking at a pile of number plates. He looked up and saw the grin on his friend's face.

'Done this before,' said Johnny with a wink. 'They're all sorted into pairs, so just grab one, OK?'

The van suddenly braked hard, but Ethan braced himself against the side, pulled out a pair of number plates and snapped the toolbox shut. 'Here,' he said, passing the plates to Kat, who handed them to Johnny. 'What next?'

Johnny laughed. 'Look and learn, Eth.'

Ethan hung on as The Dude accelerated again, spun down some side streets and pulled over.

'Out!' shouted Johnny.

Ethan and Kat tumbled out into the street.

'Make like you're walking back from town,' said Johnny. 'You're a couple and you've had a great night. Make it look good.'

Ethan saw The Dude quickly swap the number plates on the van as Kat slipped her arm round his waist and pulled him away. They walked round a corner into the main street.

Ethan heard the sirens, and instinct told him to run – especially when the police cars turned onto their street, lights flashing. But Kat pushed him up against a wall and snuggled in, her body warm and soft against him.

'What are you doing?' he asked.

'Saving our arses,' Kat hissed.

The police cars sped past, disappeared.

Ethan didn't move; didn't really want to.

Kat spoke first. 'OK, we're in the clear.' She pushed herself away.

'Well, that was all very cloak-and-dagger,' said Ethan. 'Done this before?'

Kat just smiled. 'See you at FreeFall tomorrow?'

'Just a minute,' said Ethan. 'How are you getting home?' He didn't like the idea of leaving Kat to her own devices. It was late and dark.

Kat pulled out her phone. 'Taxi,' she said. 'Need a lift?'

In the shop the next morning, Ethan was finding it difficult to concentrate. He'd already narrowly avoided making a couple of errors with takings at the till. The events of the night before were still buzzing in his head. The BASE jump had been exciting enough, but being chased by the police had added an edge to the proceedings. As had the brief moment when Kat had pressed herself against him – even if it had only been an act to avoid the police.

'Good morning, Ethan.'

Ethan looked up. Natalya, face serious as ever, was waiting at the counter. He nodded, said, 'Hi.'

'I have heard that you had an interesting evening last night.'

Ethan wasn't sure, but he thought he saw a faint smile on her face. He shrugged.

'Such secrecy,' said Natalya. 'A pity Jake called a few people to tell them about Kat's BASE jump.'

Ethan sighed. He was beginning to wonder if the whole world knew about that.

'You should be more careful,' Natalya told him. 'Sam does not like his team taking too many risks.'

'Sam knows?'

Natalya shrugged. 'Perhaps. Probably. Sam knows most things.'

'What have you heard?' Ethan asked her. He didn't think he'd done anything wrong. So why was he nervous?

'Nothing much,' said Natalya. 'I have not seen Sam today so I cannot say for sure what he does or does not know.'

'Why would Sam care anyway? It was Kat's decision. She didn't need his permission.'

'Maybe not. But the team is more important to Sam than you could possibly know.'

'You make it sound like he's their dad!'

'In many ways he is,' Natalya said simply.

And that answer really worried Ethan. It suddenly felt like there was something mysterious about 'the team'. Something going on that he didn't know about. And he didn't like that at all.

'Anyway, I just came in to see if you were around all day. We are having a little meeting later about the competition,' Natalya told him.

Ethan wanted to ask her more questions, but he couldn't think of any that made sense. So he just said, 'What time?'

'One, I think. In the hangar. Luke would like to do a quick check to make sure we are all prepared.'

Ethan wasn't surprised. Luke had been given responsibility for looking after the accommodation and flight details. And Luke, as Ethan now knew well, was obsessed with detail. They all made fun of it, but they respected it. After all, no one would want Johnny in charge of getting everyone to the airport on time.

'I will see you then,' said Natalya as she left the shop.

For the first time that morning, the shop was empty. Ethan found the silence deafening. It had been bad enough being chased by the police for trespassing, but now he had Sam to worry about. He didn't want to be on the receiving end of his fury. After all, Sam had kicked Jake out for taking a risk that jeopardized the team. What was to stop him doing the same to someone else?

'Ethan!'

A cheer from Johnny greeted Ethan when he arrived at the hangar. Johnny and Kat were the only ones there.

'Hey, Johnny,' said Ethan, but he was unable to disguise the worry in his voice.

Kat came over. 'What's up?' she asked.

'Everyone knows,' said Ethan. 'About last night. Jake shopped us, and I think Sam has probably found out about it. But does that matter? I mean, would Sam be bothered?'

Ethan saw a nervous glance flick between Kat and Johnny.

'Yeah, he might be,' said Johnny, none too reassuringly. 'Ah, well, I guess we should've expected it. Who gave you the heads up?'

'Natalya,' Ethan told him. 'She came into the shop this morning to let me know about the meeting.'

'Nothing we can do about it now,' said Kat. 'You jumping today?'

Ethan ignored the question. 'So what if Sam does know?'

Kat was just opening her mouth to say something when

the hangar door opened and Ethan turned to see Luke and Natalya. He wanted an answer to his question but wasn't given a chance to press any harder as Luke came over.

'This is going to be quick,' said Luke. 'I'm not going to give out tickets just in case someone loses theirs.'

Ethan couldn't help but laugh as Luke looked hard at Johnny.

'We meet here at five on Friday. Flight's at eight. I've managed to persuade someone to drive us down to the airport in the minibus. Don't forget to bring your passports. That's all you really need to know. Questions?'

'Yes,' said Johnny. 'Have you managed to upgrade us to first class?'

Before Luke could reply, the hangar doors opened once more, and Sam marched in. 'Right,' he snapped, staring at Kat and Johnny. 'I'm not here to listen to your excuses. I'm not interested.'

'Well, that's that, then,' said Johnny. 'Thanks for the chat, Sam.'

'Neither am I interested, Johnny, in your pathetic attempt at humour.'

Ethan looked at Sam, and was struck more than usual by his size and presence. The scars on his face seemed more pronounced than usual, like they were projecting his ill-contained annoyance. Ethan avoided speculating how someone like Sam had come to get such scars – they looked horribly deliberate. But right now, it was clear that Sam was furious. It suddenly seemed a lot darker inside the hangar, like he was sucking the light out of the moment.

'But—' said Johnny.

'Stand down,' said Sam. 'And for once in your life, listen.'

They were all listening, thought Ethan. What choice did they have?

'I don't expect you to stop BASE jumping,' said Sam, his voice a deep rumble, every word clear. 'But I do expect you to at least have some sense as to *when* you do it.'

'Look, if you're worried about the police—' said Johnny, but Sam cut in, and Ethan was beginning to wish he was somewhere else.

'I'm not worried about the police,' said Sam. 'You dodged them well enough. I'm worried about you.'

'We did everything by the book, Sam,' said Kat. 'We've been training for this for months.'

'And I've been training you for months to be the best there is. Did you think it was a good idea to do this only days before we fly to France?'

Ethan glanced at Johnny and Kat. They were both looking very uncomfortable.

Sam spoke again. 'You're a team,' he told them, 'and as a team you have to know where and when *not* to take risks. Haven't you learned anything?'

'I know,' said Johnny, 'but Kat was ready. If Jake hadn't shopped us—'

'Irrelevant,' said Sam. 'You've known about the competition for long enough to plan things around it. Only Ethan can be excused that.'

Ethan saw Sam shoot a glance at him, but his eyes displayed no emotion. Then he turned back to Kat and Johnny.

'You're both good,' he continued. 'I know that because I trained you. I'm not saying you could've been killed, but an accident would have made the trip a waste of time. And if there's one thing I don't like it's my time being wasted.'

Kat and Johnny remained silent.

Ethan was beginning to feel pretty confused and un-comfortable himself. Sam was talking to them like he was back in the army. This whole skydiving thing was obviously a whole lot more serious than he'd realized.

'So tell me' – Sam's voice was quiet – which, thought Ethan, made it all the more terrifying – 'am I wasting my time?'

Johnny and Kat both muttered, 'No.'

'Good,' said Sam. 'And what about you, Ethan? Have you got what it takes?'

Ethan nearly took a step back at finding himself under the full focus of Sam's penetrating gaze. But he didn't hesitate in his reply. 'Yes,' he said firmly.

'That's the end of it then,' said Sam. 'We won't mention this again. I don't want our sponsors to think they've wasted their time and money, and I don't want you to make me look like a pillock. Now sort your heads out and get in the air.'

23

Climbing out of the minibus, Ethan looked across at the airport. It was early-evening busy, and buzzing with buses and cars dropping off and picking up. The air smelled hot with exhaust fumes, junk food, sweat.

It was a week since the meeting in the hangar with Sam, and they'd all been doing as much as they could to get into the air and practise. No one had mentioned the BASE jump again – not even Johnny. Sam was now away on his business trip, so it was down to the team to get themselves ready and arrive at the competition in time.

Ethan was excited. And nervous – but not just about the competition. He'd never been on a passenger flight before. The only plane he'd ever been in was the one he'd been jumping out of all summer. He guessed now wasn't the time to start telling people that – after all, he didn't want to look like an idiot.

Luke had got out of the van first and was already standing outside the main entrance to the terminal, waiting until everyone had gathered up their kit.

'Flight's been changed,' he said when they reached him. 'We leave in twenty minutes.'

Ethan didn't understand. 'I thought we had to check in,' he said.

'Already done,' Luke said simply. 'At least we'll get there quicker. Ready?'

Everyone nodded.

Ethan started to ask more questions, but Johnny looked at him and said, 'Come on – last one on the plane fancies Luke.'

Luke didn't laugh; he just set off. 'We're boarding at gate sixteen A. It's this way. We'd best get a move on.'

The change of flight seemed strange to Ethan, but no one else seemed bothered – not even Luke, which was reassuring. In fact, the change of plan seemed to have made everyone even more excited. Ethan shrugged and followed along behind. It wasn't as though he was a seasoned traveller, used to the ups and downs of international flying. Perhaps this kind of thing was normal.

It was only when they were all on board and the door to the plane was pulled shut that Ethan realized it wasn't normal at all – because the only people on the plane were the team. Every other seat was empty.

The plane taxied along to the runway and took off. Ethan was used to the sensation of being in a plane as it went airborne, but this was different. For one thing he was sitting in a proper seat and facing forwards. For another, this plane totally dwarfed the one he was used to jumping from.

After the plane had broken through cloud, the seat-belt light flicked off and Ethan gazed out through the window. Clouds, like snow-covered peaks, stretched to the horizon. For a moment he wondered what it would be like to jump from such a height, to do one of those HAHO jumps Johnny had described. The thought made him sit back in his seat and grin.

He was about to reach for the in-flight magazine when a man with blond hair came from the front of the plane. Ethan recognized him immediately as the man he'd seen at FreeFall from time to time – Sam's friend.

Just as Ethan remembered, he was in his early thirties, smart, clean-shaven, his blond hair swept back, not a strand out of place. His suit looked just a shade over very expensive. And he looked at Ethan as if he was studying him for an exam. It made Ethan uneasy.

Johnny nodded at the guy. 'Hey, Gabe,' he said. 'Figured this was your handiwork. What's up?'

'Change of plan,' said the man, leaning against the back of Johnny's seat.

'Guessed that with the change of planes,' said Luke, getting up from his seat to come and join them. 'What's going on?'

'You're talking about this like you half expected it to happen,' said Ethan curiously. He turned to Gabe. 'Who are you? I know you're something to do with FreeFall because I've seen you there. But what's the connection?'

Kat and Natalya came over, looked at Ethan. 'This is Gabe,' said Kat. 'He looks cute, but I wouldn't exactly take him home to meet the parents.'

'Thank you, Kat,' said Gabe. He looked back at the team. 'A job's come up,' he said. 'Top priority. We're sending you in. Everything's arranged.'

'What are you talking about?' asked Ethan. 'What job? What's been arranged?'

'My apologies,' said Gabe, turning to Ethan. 'We had planned to give you longer to settle in. We would not, by choice, have involved you in this so early, but the decision has been made for us. Sam's agreed it because your progress has been – well, shall we say, unique?'

Ethan looked round at the rest of the team, his gaze finally settling on Johnny. 'So,' he said. 'What *exactly* am I involved in?'

For a few minutes – while Gabe spoke privately with the rest of the team – Ethan was left on his own to wonder what the hell was going on. Looking back, he could see how certain things had been strange from the start. The free tandem jump had seemed a fantastic and unexpected perk of the job, but now he saw there was more to it than that. Had Sam actually used it to see just how he'd respond in the air? Had Sam been watching him, assessing him from the moment he'd walked in to take the job? Had he already been thinking about a replacement for Jake?

But a replacement for *what* exactly? All Ethan knew was that Johnny and the rest were a skydiving team, but now he was sure they were more than that. For a start, it seemed pretty certain that it was Gabe who had funded his AFF – no wonder Ethan had seen the man watching him at FreeFall.

And now here they all were, on a private flight, with Gabe talking about a 'top priority' job and 'sending' them in. It all sounded top secret, military. Was Sam still in the military in some way – some *top-secret, military intelligence* kind of way? Or was that too far-fetched?

The huddle broke up and Gabe came over. 'Johnny will explain everything,' he said to Ethan. 'You can then decide if you're in.' And he made his way back to the front of the plane and disappeared; the door slid shut behind him with a faint hiss.

Johnny slipped into the seat next to Ethan. 'I've a confession,' he said.

'No shit,' said Ethan.

'We're not your average skydiving team.'

Ethan wasn't in the mood for games. He wanted to know what was going on and he wanted to know now. He'd guessed much of it, but he needed to hear it for real. 'Forget the cryptic bullshit, Johnny,' he said. 'I've already worked that out. Sam's not been training me up just so that I can have fun at a hundred and twenty mph – so why don't you tell me what's happening, what Gabe's on about, what Sam's got to do with all this, and just what job it is we're being sent on?'

'First off,' said Johnny, 'I can tell you that we work for Sam and he needs our help.'

'I thought he was going to meet us at the competition,' said Ethan.

'The competition's a cover,' Johnny explained. 'It gave

Sam a reason to be in France and us a reason to be around – just in case.'

'Just in case of what?' asked Ethan.

Johnny leaned forward. 'Sam hasn't just been training us to skydive,' he said. 'And he hasn't just been giving you a nice bit of charity either.'

'He wants me to be part of the team,' said Ethan, voicing his own conclusion. 'I'm not stupid. I always thought it was odd that someone paid for me to do the AFF. It was Gabe, wasn't it? Sam told him about me, and Gabe somehow came up with the cash to put me through.'

Johnny's usual jokey persona disappeared completely. 'We're a freefall team,' he said, 'but that's also a cover story. The whole thing was Sam's idea. He used FreeFall as a way to find the people he wanted – and he found us. We work for MI5. Gabe's our contact. He provides the cash and the sexy equipment.'

'And it was Sam who put me up for this?'

Johnny nodded. 'You impressed him, and that's saying something. We've seen you skydive, and he's right, you're a natural. Your first solo dive was excellent, and you've improved with every jump since. Plus – and this is a biggie – you fit with the team.'

'Keep talking,' said Ethan.

'Look, let's just say we've had our eye on you from the start. From the moment you did your tandem jump, Sam had us watching you. All of us.'

'You've been spying on me?'

'Not spying,' said Johnny, 'but we have been keeping an eye on you to see if you'd fit in.'

'That makes me feel so much better.'

'And so it should,' snapped Johnny, the ice in his voice surprising Ethan. 'Jake didn't make the grade, and neither did the bloke before him. But then he just fucked off into nowhere and we never heard from him again.'

'He disappeared?' said Ethan.

'Yeah – though it didn't change the fact that he wasn't good enough. But that's another story.'

'You're not even past the first chapter of this one,' said Ethan. 'Tell me more about Gabe and MI5.'

'Can't,' said Johnny.

'You'd better.'

'Seriously, I can't. That's down to Sam and Gabe. I'm not at liberty to divulge that information.'

'*You* don't even understand some of the words you just used.'

'What gave it away?' Johnny laughed. 'Look, I've told you all I can. We're skydivers and we've been trained by Sam, the best in the business, to be a covert operations team for MI5. We get to do stuff people only ever see in the movies. The only other thing you need to know is that Sam's in trouble. We're now on a heading to get him *out* of trouble. This will involve wearing lots of black, doing a HAHO jump, setting off explosives and generally causing a diversion. Interested?'

Ethan opened his mouth, shut it again. Then said, 'HAHO?'

'High Altitude, High Opening,' Johnny reminded him. 'Sometime pretty soon we're going to be leaving this plane at thirty-two thousand feet. This is just the sort of mission Sam's been training us for. He thinks – and so do we – that you should be our last team member. I can tell you nothing more than what I've already said until you decide whether you're in.' He paused, then sighed. 'I know it's not much to go on, mate, but you'll just have to trust me. I'm not making this up. And the stuff I'm not telling you – what you could be doing with your life if you joined us – well, it's pretty mind-blowing . . .'

'So I've a choice in this?' asked Ethan. He really didn't like the fact that so much had been going on behind his back. But at the same time he was psyched. Skydiving had changed his life, made him realize he could do something radically different to everyone else. And what Johnny was describing was even wilder. Joining some kind of secret military operation certainly sounded better than just sitting in an office or being a drunk like his loser dad, but he needed to know it was his own decision.

'You've always got a choice,' said Johnny. '*You* decided to take up skydiving. *You* decided to take on Jake when he killed the rigs. *You* decided to save Kat. You've been making the decisions all along. If anything, you've selected yourself.'

'I guess so. In a way . . .' said Ethan thoughtfully. 'But it's what I've selected myself *for* that's the problem. I'm not sure I understand exactly what it is.'

'I've told you everything I can,' said Johnny, 'but if you want a word of advice from a friend, forget thinking, forget trying to weigh up the pros and cons. Just go with what your gut tells you!'

Ethan sat back in his seat and, despite a strong urge to just say *Count me in*, decided to play devil's advocate. 'What if I say no? What then?'

'We drug you and you wake up back home, stinking of booze.'

Ethan frowned. He couldn't tell if Johnny was bullshitting or not.

'Eth, mate,' said Johnny seriously, 'none of this is a joke. I – we – are asking you to join us because we want you to be a part of the team. But if you want out, you've got that option.'

Ethan already knew he wanted to be involved. He wanted it more than anything he'd ever wanted in his whole life. But he needed to be sure he'd thought it over fully. What he decided now would change everything. This was no longer just a hobby; something fun to do that sounded cool and sexy when you told girls about it. This was a career, a whole new life – important, exciting and very, very dangerous.

'Ethan—' Johnny began.

And then the words were out before he had a chance to stop them. 'Fuck it,' Ethan said. 'I'm in.'

24

Johnny stood up. 'Ladies and gentlemen, we have a new team member!'

Luke was the first to respond. 'Nice one, Eth,' he said. 'Glad to have someone on board who actually takes things seriously.' He looked at Johnny, and they both smiled.

'Cheers,' said Ethan; then he winked. 'But I'm only in it for the girls.'

Luke and Johnny laughed.

'You made the right decision all the same,' said Natalya. 'I am pleased you have joined us.'

For the first time Ethan saw a genuine smile on her face. It suited her, he thought.

'Don't think Jake could call you a rookie now,' said Kat.

'Pity we can't tell him – it'd be worth it just to see the look on his face.'

'You're over him, then?' said Ethan.

'Was never on or even under him,' she joked.

'Enough of the emotional stuff,' said Johnny. 'Let's get down to business. Luke?'

Ethan listened up. So did everyone else.

'The situation is this,' Luke began: 'an encrypted hard disk has been stolen. It contains sensitive information that, were the encryption to be broken, could prove damaging to certain parties.'

'If it's encrypted, what's the problem?' asked Ethan, hoping he didn't sound like a total knob. 'Isn't that supposed to mean no one can read it unless they're the right person with the right code or something?'

'Yup,' said Johnny. 'But Gabe reckons this was an inside job. Which means there probably *is* someone with all that. Sam was sent in to recover the disk *before* the encryption could be broken and the info sold to the highest bidder.'

'So where's Sam now?' asked Kat. 'Why call us in?'

Luke went on, 'The person suspected of stealing the disk was tracked to a small island off the coast of France. Sam was HAHO'd in a few hours ago to get the disk back. But he's now communicated that the situation has changed and is critical. He needs urgent support to complete the mission.'

'Which is where we come in,' said Natalya. 'Right?'

Johnny nodded and looked at Ethan. 'Like I said, the sky-diving competition was the perfect cover for Sam to leave the country and for us to follow on in case it turned into a full-on shit-storm – which it has.'

209

'So eloquently put,' said Kat, shaking her head.

'So we were sent to the competition just in case Sam needed us?' Ethan asked.

Luke nodded. 'No one would suspect a thing,' he said. 'Gabe got the communication from Sam as we left FreeFall. The jet was being held in reserve, just in case this kicked off.'

The more Ethan heard, the more unreal it all seemed. He'd just found out he was a member of a special ops team working for MI5. It was like something from the movies; something that only ever happened to good-looking actors on the big screen – oh, and as it turned out, him! He felt himself grinning like an idiot and tried to focus. 'You've still not explained how we're involved,' he said. 'Or what's in the files on the disk.'

'The contents of the files are on a strictly need-to-know basis,' said Johnny. 'And Gabe doesn't want us to know. Which means none of us needs to ask. All we have to do is help Sam. He's arrived at the target destination but is unable to locate and extract the disk without being compromised.'

'Why?' asked Natalya. 'What has happened? Did Gabe not know the situation before he sent Sam in?'

'The situation's changed,' said Johnny. 'There are more x-rays on the ground than originally thought and it's now too risky for Sam to act without a diversion.' He looked at Ethan and grinned. 'Which is where we come in.'

'X-rays?' asked Ethan.

'Enemies,' explained Kat, then turned to Johnny. 'And by "compromised" you mean killed, don't you?'

Johnny nodded and looked at Ethan. 'You keeping up with this? It's a lot to take in.'

'Yeah,' said Ethan, smiling. 'It's not every day you become part of a covert ops team, is it?'

'Shit happens,' Johnny said with a shrug.

The plane dropped suddenly and Ethan heard the engines squeal a little, felt his stomach flip. It had been doing that a lot in the past few minutes.

'This situation Sam's in . . .' he said. 'Does it mean we have to take guns with us?'

'For a start, we use the term *weapon* rather than *gun*,' said Luke. 'And, no, we won't go in armed. We never do. The job of the team is always to try and slip in under the radar, not to go in and take people out. We need to be invisible. Weapons have a habit of making people very obvious indeed. But we will be taking in explosives to create a diversion.'

'He means we'll blow shit up,' said Johnny.

'Sounds dangerous,' said Ethan.

'Comes with the territory,' Johnny replied, 'and it's all part of the fun. Anyway, who wants to live a life that's risk-free? Better to live as a lion for a day than a lamb for a year, right?'

'That's cheesy,' said Ethan.

'I know,' said Johnny. 'Can't believe I said it.'

'True though,' Kat put in quietly.

'If the op goes well, we'll still be going to the competition,' Luke added. 'It's all part of the cover story.'

Ethan looked at the team – *his* team – four people he now counted as the best friends he'd ever had. He was about to jump from a jet with them – on a mission for MI5 to rescue the toughest bloke he'd ever met in his life. Just a few weeks ago he wouldn't have believed it was possible, wouldn't have believed he could have the skills for such a mission. But it was and he did. He was confident of that. Sam – the team – wouldn't have chosen him otherwise. All he had to do was stay sharp, stay focused, and remember everything he'd been taught.

'OK,' he said, 'ignoring the lion/lamb thing, I do have one more question.'

'What's that?' said Johnny.

Ethan smiled. 'What's the pay like?'

25

'We go in thirty,' said Johnny. 'Let's move.'

The team moved to the rear of the plane.

'You're with me,' Kat told Ethan. 'We're going in tandem.'

'Tandem?' said Ethan. 'But isn't this a high-altitude jump? I didn't know you could do that.'

'Well, you can,' said Kat, 'and we can't have you doing one without any prep. Natalya's got no experience of doing tandems and she's taking the explosives in anyway. And you're too heavy to go with Johnny or Luke. So it's me.'

'Explosives?'

Kat nodded. 'Natalya's the expert in that area. Seems to know more than Sam, and that's saying something.'

'I can't work her out,' said Ethan.

'You're not the only one.' Kat led him through a door and down some metal stairs. 'I'm probably her closest friend and all I know is that I know nothing about her. This way.'

They went through another door, and immediately Ethan noticed the temperature drop.

'At this altitude we'll be jumping with oxygen,' Kat explained. 'And it's very cold so we'll be wearing thermals. I'm sure you'll look very sexy in them.'

Ethan found himself in a section of the plane that had been entirely stripped of anything comfortable. The walls were just metal plates and struts riveted together. And the sound of the plane's engines had seriously risen in volume. To speak and be heard, everyone had to shout.

Johnny nodded at them. 'I'll give Gabe eight out of ten for kit prep,' he said.

'Only eight?' queried Ethan, trying to stop his teeth from chattering.

'He left my lucky teddy bear behind,' said Johnny.

Luke pulled out a map, laid it on the metal checker-plate floor. 'This is the DZ,' he said, pointing just below a patch of dark green on the map as everyone else gathered round. 'We'll be nicely hidden by the trees and we're only half a click from here, which is where Sam and the disk are. Our job is to draw attention away from that point and allow Sam sufficient time to get in and recover it.'

'Click?' asked Ethan.

'Kilometre,' translated Kat.

'What is "here" exactly?' asked Johnny. 'Doesn't look like much on the map.'

'That's because it isn't,' said Luke. 'In fact it's what's left of a fifteenth-century castle. It's built right above these sea cliffs here. This is what our satellite picked up,' he added, producing some black and white bird's-eye-view photos of the castle. Ethan couldn't quite believe he'd just heard Luke refer to a satellite as though they owned it.

'Main access to the castle is from the beach, here,' Luke went on, pointing at the map again. 'This line here is a path that runs from the beach up to the clifftop.'

'Looks lovely,' said Johnny. 'When can I move in?'

Luke ignored him. 'We HAHO into the DZ, then we're on with the diversion. RV is the beach. Sam is to meet us there. I'll contact him when everything kicks off.'

At this, Natalya piped up. 'I have spoken to Gabe and checked the kit,' she said, her face as serious as ever, though she sounded excited. 'We have more than enough detonators and P4. To secure the beach, we are taking anti-personnel mines – Claymores.'

'And how do we get off the beach when we're done?' asked Kat.

'One of the packs we're taking contains two inflatable canoes,' said Luke. 'A sub's on course to pick us up at dawn.'

'A sub?' said Ethan. 'You're joking, right?'

Luke shook his head.

'What if the beach is compromised?' Natalya asked.

Luke rested a finger back on the castle, then dragged it up a little to rest on a small black shape nearby. 'In that case we leave from here,' he said. 'It's the old watchtower.'

'Thanks for the added colour there,' said Johnny. 'You see, Eth? It's not just fun, it's a learning experience too!'

Ethan leaned closer to look at the map, then back at the

pictures of the castle. The watchtower was perched right at the top of the cliffs behind the castle ruins.

'How do we get down those?' he asked. 'It'll take ages to climb.'

'It would . . .' said Kat, looking across at him. 'Actually if we go that way, you'll be doing your first BASE jump sooner than you think! But we'll only do that if everything goes tits up – our aim is to make sure it doesn't, OK?'

Ethan couldn't think of anything to say to that so he kept his mouth shut.

'That's it,' said Luke, bringing everyone back to the task in hand. 'Final point to remember is that this is a covert op. We need as little contact with the x-rays on the island as possible. We get in, provide Sam's diversion, and get out. Understood?'

Talk over, everyone leaped into action. They started to sort through bags of kit Ethan had never seen before, handing out various bits and pieces to each other, checking everything once, twice and then a third time. And they were getting changed out of their everyday clothes, into stuff that looked considerably more hardcore.

Ethan turned to Kat, who was now dressed in black combat trousers, a black jacket and black boots. The outfit made her look scary as hell.

'Why's it so cold?' he asked, finding it impossible to stop shivering.

'No heating,' said Kat. 'No point making the luggage nice and cosy. Don't worry, though – this'll sort that out.' She handed him a pile of clothing. 'You'll need to strip and put the black kit on first,' she explained. 'You'll be in that for the mission after we land. It's a pretty fab material actually: breathable, as close to silent as you can get, and completely waterproof.'

'Doesn't look waterproof,' said Ethan, holding up the jacket and trousers.

'What were you expecting?' asked Kat. 'Oilskins?'

Ethan examined the other piece of clothing, which looked like a jumpsuit, but was padded and much heavier. 'What's this?'

'Once you're dressed in the other kit, pull that on over the top,' Kat told him. 'It's a silk-lined, thermal-insulated suit. It'll stop you turning into a six-foot ice-pop when we jump.'

'It's that cold out there?' Ethan felt pretty chilly as it was, and they were still in the plane.

'It sure is. We're jumping from a jet travelling at hundreds of miles an hour, thousands of feet up. The wind-chill factor's going to be pretty extreme.'

'Point taken.'

'Then get a move on,' said Kat. 'And if you're embarrassed about getting your kit off in front of me, I promise I won't grope you or tell anyone if I see anything weird.'

'There's nothing we—' Ethan began, then saw the smile on her face. 'Ha ha,' he said, and started to get changed.

When he was finally dressed, Johnny came over with some more kit.

'Boots and socks,' he said, handing them over. 'They're your size, trust me.'

Ethan took them. They too were black. And the boots had a high ankle and the mother of all treads.

217

Johnny smiled at him. 'They're not general issue. Government couldn't really afford to have squaddies running around in these things. They're an adaptation of an Italian mountain boot. Couple of hundred quid a pop.'

Ethan slipped on the socks – two pairs: one a silk lining sock, the other a thick wool sock with padded sole – then eased on the boots, laced them up. They felt absolutely amazing – snug, comfortable, warm.

'They won't require any breaking in, either,' said Johnny. 'Leather's been specially treated. Kat?'

She turned round.

'Just so you know,' said Johnny, 'Ethan has a tendency to scream like a big girl when he's doing a tandem. And his language is simply appalling.'

Kat laughed. 'I'll look after him.'

Johnny went back towards Luke, who Ethan could see was now talking to Natalya and looking through some large black holdalls.

'Right, Ethan,' said Kat. 'The rig.'

'It's a tandem rig,' said Ethan. 'Bigger canopy because of the additional weight.'

'Exactly. We need to get it adjusted just right so we don't cut off our circulation when we're gliding. It'd be pretty embarrassing to land with you dead.'

For the next few minutes Kat pushed and pulled at Ethan, clipping him in and making sure everything felt right, comfortable.

'How's that?'

'Fine,' said Ethan.

'Now the oxygen.'

Ethan looked at the large, black, canvas-covered box in Kat's hand. She handed him a face mask.

'We'll both get our oxygen from this,' she said. 'All you need to remember is that there's more than enough in here for us both. Don't panic and start breathing like you're about to die; you'll use it up quicker, or hyperventilate and pass out.'

'Not good,' said Ethan.

'Right,' agreed Kat. 'Flying in with you unconscious wouldn't be as easy to control. I might even have to cut you loose, drop you before we get there.'

Ethan looked at Kat. Was she serious? 'I'll make sure I stay awake and alert,' he promised.

'All you need to remember,' said Kat, 'is that when we jump, you have your head back and your arms crossed, just like you did with Sam. That'll allow me to flip us over, get our descent under control and deploy, without having you destabilize us.'

Ethan felt a hand on his shoulder. It was Luke.

'Sorted?'

Ethan nodded. 'I'm fine,' he said. 'Totally.'

'Good,' said Luke. 'Remember we've all been watching you, not just Sam and Gabe. If we didn't think you were up to it, you wouldn't be here.'

'No,' said Johnny, coming over with Natalya. 'You'd be sedated at the front of the plane, utterly unaware of just how cool we really are.'

'Are you serious?' asked Ethan.

'Deadly,' said Johnny.

For a few moments Ethan was silent, thinking about that.

Then he looked up and said, 'Right, so tell me about the jump. I've done plenty at twelve thousand. How different is it at thirty-two thousand?'

Everyone smiled at him. It felt really good.

'The big difference,' began Kat, 'is the amount of time you'll spend in the air.'

'You've been skydiving up until now,' Luke continued. 'Forty-five-second freefall, followed by about five to ten minutes in glide. This isn't a skydive. We leave the plane and deploy canopies immediately.'

'So how long are we in the air?' asked Ethan.

'We'll be gliding across approximately thirty miles,' said Luke, 'so we'll be in the air for about two hours.'

Ethan did a double-take. 'Two *hours*? No way!'

'Way,' said Johnny. 'You'll love it. Everyone knows what they're doing, including you. It's just another jump, but from a little bit higher, is all.'

'Gets pretty surreal though; particularly when you're drifting through cloud,' said Kat.

'Here . . .' said Luke, handing Ethan a watch. It looked bomb-proof, Ethan thought as he put it on his wrist. 'And this is a tactical throat mic.'

Ethan looked at the next piece of kit in his hands. It looked like a length of black elastic attached to a wire, a battery pack, an earpiece and two small cylinders that pointed inwards.

'It's designed for operators in the military,' said Luke, 'and you wear it round your neck like this.'

Ethan watched as Luke put one on himself, securing it round his neck. He felt like he was watching a demonstration of some new gadget on a weird military TV shopping channel.

'These two things here' – Luke pointed at the cylinders – 'are the dual transponders or throat mics. If you want to talk, just press both of them against your throat and you're on.'

Ethan copied Luke, and put on the throat mic.

'It'll block out most ambient noise,' continued Luke as Ethan slipped the earpiece in, 'and will even pick up a whisper.'

'Yes,' Johnny said, his expression serious and business-like. 'The throat mic is the product of choice both on and off the battlefield. Thank you, Luke.'

Ethan laughed.

'Anyway' – Luke ignored Johnny as best he could – 'you've probably seen plenty of these things being used in bad action movies by macho actors.'

'You know – the ones that look like me,' said Johnny, checking Ethan had put the thing on properly.

'We'll be on a chat-net,' said Luke. 'It means everyone can speak at the same time.'

'So don't go telling Kat you think Luke's a dick,' said Johnny, 'because he'll hear you.'

'We'll be tumbling out of the plane in close formation, one after the other,' Luke continued. 'Aim is to get out, find space and pull the canopy quickly. Once we all know where we are, we'll head off.'

'So how do we know where we're going?' asked Ethan. 'And how do we keep close when we're jumping in the dark?'

Johnny began to answer, but the call came through from the pilot.

'No time for any more explanations,' said Luke. 'We're good to go.'

26

Luke called everyone over, and Ethan followed Kat, who leaned closer and said, 'We may take the piss, but Luke's generally our reason for staying alive. If he doesn't check it, don't use it. OK?'

Ethan stood with everyone else as Luke did his rounds. And after what Kat had just said, he looked at Luke in a new light. He knew from experience that he was into the detail, but to know he was so vital to everything the team did made him listen all the harder. After all, Ethan was pretty keen on staying alive. He was amazed at just how thorough Luke was. Nothing got missed. He pulled Johnny up for a pocket left undone. The pocket was empty, Johnny had protested, but that didn't matter, not to Luke. He even checked Kat and Natalya's hair.

'When are you two going to cut this off?' he asked. 'It's always a tangle risk, you know that.'

'So's Johnny's,' said Kat.

'Seriously though – long hair and this kind of activity don't mix too well.'

'We tie it up well,' Natalya pointed out. 'And you are forgetting that our cover relies on the fact that we do not look like the kind of people who would do what we are about to do.'

'Hmm . . .' Luke sounded unconvinced. He glanced at Ethan. 'OK?'

'Fine,' said Ethan as Luke checked him over carefully.

'Remember about the oxygen. Don't gulp it. Breathe normally. It may feel weird, sound weird, and it doesn't taste great either, but it's fine.'

'Got it,' said Ethan.

'Good,' said Luke, and clapped him on the shoulders with both hands. 'You're part of the team now, Ethan.'

Ethan nodded and smiled. He knew he couldn't back out now – he didn't want to.

Gabe appeared through a door at the rear of the hold. 'We depressurize in a few minutes,' he said, 'so I'm going to be brief . . .'

Ethan listened closely. He didn't want to miss anything. Whatever it was they were about to do, whatever it was he'd agreed to be involved in, he wanted to be clear on every last detail. He knew it was dangerous – that much was obvious. All the more reason to make sure he didn't let everyone else down – or make a tit of himself.

'Right, you all know what you're taking with you, but I'm

going to run through it again – partly for Ethan's sake, and also to make sure you don't get your faces shot off because I didn't tell you everything.' Gabe crouched down beside the two large black holdalls they were jumping with. Luke would carry one, Johnny the other. Each holdall contained two black bergens. Gabe explained that, on landing, Luke, Johnny, Natalya and Ethan would take a bergen each. Kat got off lightly – for this mission only four bergens were needed, so she wouldn't be carrying.

Gabe turned to Johnny and Luke. 'Your bergens contain the BASE rigs. Everything checked?'

Johnny and Luke nodded.

'Good,' said Gabe. 'Lose those, and your emergency exit is screwed . . . Natalya,' he continued, 'your bergen contains everything you'll need for the diversion – P4 explosive, detonators and Claymores. Has it all been checked?'

Natalya nodded. 'The equipment is all OK,' she said, 'but I am not happy about our lack of protection. What are we to do if they shoot?'

'Make sure they don't see you,' said Gabe. Then he turned to Ethan. 'Your bergen will contain the two inflatable canoes.'

'OK,' Ethan replied. 'But what about Sam? Don't we need to know where he is?'

'All you need to do is focus on the mission,' said Gabe. 'Sam's more than capable of looking after himself. He's made a career out of it. Just provide the diversion he needs and get the hell out. Right?'

The pilot buzzed through with the final call.

'OK, we're about to depressurize,' said Gabe. 'Everyone to oxygen. Now.'

'Ethan, put this on,' said Kat, handing him a face mask.

'But it's not connected,' Ethan pointed out.

'And it won't be until we know the oxygen in the bottle is flowing. And we need to check the seal on your mask, OK? Can't have the thing leaking when we're outside the plane.'

She reached over, blocked the hole where the tube attached with her hand. 'Can you breathe?'

Ethan shook his head. He didn't like the sensation.

'Good,' said Kat. She did the same with her own mask before grabbing the bottle, turning it on and staring at the dial. Then she took the tube attached to the bottle and put it up to her eye.

Ethan was about to ask what she was doing, but Kat got in first. 'This way we can feel if the oxygen is flowing,' she told him. 'Just because the dial gives a reading doesn't mean it isn't defective.'

'Oh, right . . .' Ethan was stunned by the attention to detail. It almost made him feel safe. Almost.

'If we put these on and the oxygen flow is screwed, then when the cabin depressurizes we'll be in a state of hypoxia within a minute, dead in two.'

Ethan didn't say a thing. Dead in two minutes?

'And don't worry about the farting,' added Kat.

He looked at her, not sure if he'd heard her right. Farting? What the hell did that have to do with anything?

'Once this thing's unpressurized, all gases expand,' Kat explained with a grin; 'even oxygen under a tooth filling – causes it to explode. You're lucky; we checked you out – no fillings. Must be all that flossing.'

Kat attached the tubes to the face masks and nodded.

Ethan nodded back. He could taste the oxygen coming through.

Kat turned to the rest of the team, gave the thumbs-up. Ethan did the same, even though it made him feel like a complete idiot.

He saw Gabe grab a cabin mask, put it on.

Then the hold was depressurized.

The temperature dropped even further, and Ethan looked at Kat, who nodded to confirm the plane had indeed depressurized. All he could now hear was the sound of his breathing as he sucked in oxygen, and the noise of the plane. When pressurized, the cabin was sealed in a sound-tight vacuum. Now that it was depressurized, the vacuum had gone and the noise of the plane was loud to the point where Ethan wondered if it would actually hold together.

He could tell that the plane was getting in line for the jump. The inside of his mask felt wet. Then his goggles started to steam up.

Kat came over and got his attention, signalled for him to do as she did. Then she lifted the bottom of her own goggles for a few seconds to allow them to clear. He copied as she strapped him into the tandem harness. That done, the team lined up in their jumping order. Ethan looked at them as they organized themselves. All kitted up, they were a frightening sight. He was used to seeing them in normal clothes or their fancy skydiving suits. But now they were head to toe in black, rigs strapped on, any kit they were jumping with strapped around their legs. Soon they were holding onto each other for stability, their heavy kit pulling them from side to side.

This is it, thought Ethan. *When Kat jumps, I go with her. I'm just cargo.*

His attention was suddenly caught by a sucking, howling sound, and he looked over to see Gabe pulling open a door in the side of the plane. Outside, there was nothing but blackness. It took him back to the night skydive, the sensation of jumping into nothing.

A tap on his shoulder, and Ethan felt himself being pushed forward as Kat and the rest of the team lined up. He and Kat were at the front. They would be first out of the plane.

For a moment Ethan felt shock and fear take hold as he peered out through the door. Wind was blasting into his face and he knew that outside was a fall of 32,000 feet.

All he had to remember was to breathe easy, cross his arms, put his head back. Simple.

Then Kat pushed forward.

And they toppled out of the plane.

Ethan had no idea where he was. He was blinded by the blackness and deafened by the sound of the wind outside the plane. Everything was darkness and noise, and he could do nothing about it. Whatever happened, it was all down to Kat. He'd saved her life once. Now *his* life was in *her* hands.

Ethan spotted the flash of the plane's lights directly above him, but then they were gone, and he realized that Kat had arched her back, flipped them over belly-down. He knew she would now be checking around to make sure that they had clean air above; that she wasn't going to deploy the canopy and end up piling into another member of the team.

A moment later, he heard the reassuring crack of the canopy blasting out above them, grabbing air, and he was pulled into quick deceleration. It always felt like he was travelling upwards in the sky, but he knew that wasn't happening; they were just slowing down. And 120 to 10 mph in under ten seconds was some serious braking.

As they slowed to a glide, Ethan could feel Kat moving. He visualized what she was doing: using a torch to check the canopy, making sure the lines weren't snagged, caught or twisted, looking at the altimeter.

Her voice sounded in his ear. 'Ethan, you OK?'

He reached up and pinched the comms device round his neck. 'Yeah,' he said. 'Fine. That was quite something, being first out.'

'We had to be,' said Kat. 'We're heaviest, so we'll be at the bottom of the stack.'

'You mean we're doing a stack formation?' asked Ethan. He'd seen skydivers doing this at FreeFall. They'd position themselves to basically stand on top of each other's canopies. It looked bloody difficult at the best of times. Doing it in the dark at 30,000 feet must be almost impossible.

'Yeah,' said Kat. 'Didn't have time to explain on the plane. It's how we make sure we don't lose each other. We glide in, in stack formation. We're all on GPS, so we can use that to guide us to the island and the DZ. You'll hear the rest of the team coming in now. Johnny's first.'

Ethan just caught the faint flapping sound of a canopy, then heard Johnny's voice over the chat-net.

'Kat, I'm coming in.'

'OK,' she said. 'Eth, you might feel a faint tug from above;

it's just Johnny locking his legs into our lines. No need to panic.'

Ethan felt the tug as soon as she finished speaking.

'I'm on,' came Johnny's voice again. 'Natalya? Luke?'

'Coming in.' That was Luke.

Finally Natalya drifted in and they were all locked in formation.

'Ethan, you need to check the dial on your oxygen bottle,' said Kat. 'Make sure it isn't in the red.'

Ethan didn't ask what they'd do if it was, just did exactly as she said. It wasn't in the red. Then he tried to imagine what they all looked like: four canopies drifting down through the clouds, high above France, and on target for a tiny island somewhere in the vast darkness.

He couldn't help but smile, then laughter bubbled up inside him.

'What's so funny?' asked Kat.

'Not funny, just fantastic,' said Ethan. 'I can't get the grin off my face. This is awesome!'

Kat laughed too. 'Glad you're enjoying it. Now, I'm afraid this journey might get a little uncomfortable; two hours hanging from a rig isn't something you want to do every day.'

Ethan could already feel his legs aching.

'Pull your leg straps down,' said Kat. 'Get them halfway down your thighs.'

Ethan did as she said and immediately felt better.

'She's getting frisky,' came Johnny's voice over the chat-net.

'Just don't want his balls pinched to hell on the descent,' said Kat.

'Thanks for the concern,' said Ethan, and everyone else laughed. But he didn't care. He'd never felt so alive in his life, and hearing everyone laugh over the chat-net just made him feel even more like a part of the team.

As they continued on their journey down through the night sky, he thought back over the past few weeks. His life hadn't just changed, it had altered course completely. Like most people he knew of his own age, he'd headed into summer feeling bored, directionless, wondering what the hell he was going to do once all the exam stuff was out of the way. And now, just a few weeks later, he was a member of a covert ops team, on a mission to rescue Sam. It felt impossible and brilliant. Ethan imagined what his dad would say if he knew, thought about the look on his face, and found himself laughing again.

Kat's voice pulled Ethan from his thoughts: 'Eth?'

'Yeah?'

'We're OK to come off the oxygen now, OK? We've just dipped below twelve thousand.'

'That went quickly,' said Ethan. 'It feels like we've only been gliding for a few minutes.'

'More like an hour,' Kat told him. 'You're enjoying it then?'

Ethan pulled off his oxygen mask. His face was wet, and the air hitting it froze the moisture instantly. 'Too right,' he said, despite the sudden cold. 'It's brilliant! I mean, what's not to love about this?'

'Couldn't agree more,' said Kat, and Ethan felt a sudden kick of g-force as the stack started to pull a turn to the left.

Kat spoke again. 'I could stay up here for ever. Nothing

matters when you're riding the wind; everything's so peaceful, everything makes sense.'

'Most people wouldn't agree though,' said Ethan. 'Doing this would seem completely nuts to them.'

'The main problem with skydiving is that you have to be sexy to do it,' Johnny chimed in. 'That's why I'm so good. And why so few people skydive.'

'You must tell me how you manage to be so modest,' said Ethan.

'It can't be taught,' said Johnny. 'You either have it or you don't. It's a natural talent.'

'Skydiving's an exclusive club,' said Luke, coming in on the chat-net. 'And no one can argue that being part of something exclusive isn't appealing.'

'And that is why it is so great,' agreed Natalya.

'Exactly,' said Kat. 'It's one of those things you just know hardly anyone else is ever going to do. Like this – I mean, who gets to do a stack formation at nearly thirty thousand feet?'

'So, Kat, how did you get into all this?' asked Ethan. 'Why skydiving? What do your parents think about it?'

'They encouraged me,' said Kat. 'They were tired of me getting into trouble, doing stupid things. This way they knew I was getting a thrill and that it was legal. And besides, it got me out of their hair. All they had to lose was a few quid.'

'She sounds so daring, so dangerous,' said Johnny. 'So like me.'

'No one's like you, Johnny. You're definitely a one-off.'

'Sounds like your parents are pretty cool,' said Ethan: his own parents could never afford to pay for him to skydive – his dad would just think it was beer money wasted.

'Honestly, I hardly see them,' said Kat. 'I spent most of my time with the housekeeper.'

Ethan laughed. 'Housekeeper? We don't even have a house!'

At this, the chat-net crackled with laughter from everyone in the stack.

'We're at five thousand now,' said Kat. 'Ethan, that's the island over there to the left.'

Ethan looked down to where she was pointing. He could just make out some faint lights far below them in the gloom. He knew they were now gliding over the sea. If he was honest, he didn't want it to end, but then his thoughts turned to their mission and he felt a jolt of adrenaline hit his system. He could taste the metallic flavour of it on the edge of his tongue – part fear, part exhilaration.

He loved it.

Kat's voice brought him back to the present. 'We land in five. Remember: legs up and land on your arse!'

27

Out of the darkness, Ethan saw the ground rushing up to meet them. The stack had broken up a few minutes before to allow everyone to glide in safely. Now they were seconds away from landing.

As they came in, the grass looked like a smoky blur.

'Legs up, Eth!' said Kat.

The ground came up fast, but Ethan felt Kat pull the canopy into a perfect touchdown. He landed on his backside, but it felt more like he'd simply sat down on the grass than completed a two-hour drop from a jet thousands of feet above. Around him he saw Johnny, Luke and Natalya touching down, each of them swooping in neatly like an owl on a kill.

Within seconds, Kat had him unclipped and, like the rest of the team, was quickly bundling up the canopy.

'Ethan, catch!' said Luke, throwing something to him. 'And again.'

Ethan caught both items. The first was a small black pouch with a zip around three sides. The second was a tin, much like a shoe polish tin.

'That's a silk stuff sack,' said Kat. 'Unzip it and stuff in the canopy, rigs and thermal suits – which we can take off now, by the way.'

Ethan did as he was told. The bag unfolded easily to something ten times its original size and, after stuffing the canopy and everything else into it, he used the compression straps to squeeze it into a small, tight ball. 'And this?' he asked, holding up the tin.

'Black face cream,' said Kat. 'No point being in all this black kit if our hands and faces glow in the dark. Don't cover yourself in it. Just use enough to break up your skin-tone, OK?'

Ethan opened the tin, stuck his finger in and then started to smear the stuff on his face as best he could. 'OK?' he asked, looking at Kat.

'Yeah,' she said. 'Just remember to do your ears and neck too, and also above the wrist.'

Ethan looked at the rest of the team busying themselves with their kit: Natalya, Luke and Johnny stowing their own canopies into the stuff sacks, then pulling the four bergens from the holdalls. It was organized, slick, done with purpose. Ethan had never felt so switched on in his life. With the rush from the flight to the island still buzzing through him, he felt more than ready to get on with the mission.

'Now we hide that lot in the trees,' said Luke, indicating the stuff sack Ethan was holding. 'By the time anyone finds the gear, we'll be long gone.' He handed Ethan a large bergen. 'Yours,' he said. 'It looks heavier than it is.'

Natalya and Johnny came over, holding a stuff sack and a bergen each. Luke pulled out a map and spread it on the ground. Then he took something out of his pocket, flicked it open, and a deep green glow spilled over the map.

'What's that?' asked Ethan. 'Doesn't look like your average torch.'

'It's not,' said Luke. 'It's a Betalight. Military issue. It's a harmless radioactive chemical that glows for about thirty years. Doesn't have an on/off switch, just this rubber cap to cover it up.'

'Right,' said Ethan, 'of course,' and decided he should stop asking questions.

'It's perfect for this type of work,' Luke continued. 'Gives us just enough light to read a map without the risk of getting spotted.' He placed a finger on the map. 'We're here,' he said. 'The drop was perfect. Which means we all owe Gabe a drink.'

Everyone looked down at the map. Ethan glanced around at his teammates and felt relieved to be on their side, rather than on the receiving end of whatever it was they were about to unleash. They no longer looked like adrenaline freaks, desperate for another rush. They seemed focused, organized, and more than a little dangerous. He already knew they were great skydivers – he'd seen that for himself – but this mission wasn't just about jumping out of a plane. It was about explosives, and rescuing Sam, and possible contact with people who would shoot first and probably not even ask any questions later. Given Sam's background, and Gabe's involvement, the team would obviously have been given training and skills that Ethan had yet to see. He wondered when he'd be getting some of that training himself.

'We're to tab – that's *run*,' Luke explained, glancing at Ethan, 'from here, through the woods and then up to the castle.'

'How far is it?' asked Natalya.

'Only about half a click,' Luke replied. 'If we get a move on, we should be there in ten.'

One thing was bothering Ethan: what if they ran into anyone? They had no weapons, no way of protecting themselves. It was the only thing that made him really nervous. He felt reasonably confident that he and his teammates could handle themselves in a fight, but what if they got shot at? 'What if we're spotted?' he asked.

'It's like Gabe said,' Johnny explained. 'We're to be as close to invisible as we can be. We go in, do our thing, get out. It's a grown-up version of hide-and-seek.'

'But there's still a chance, isn't there?' said Ethan. 'And they're armed. It doesn't seem exactly fair. I'm not massively keen on getting my face shot off.'

'The priority is the diversion,' Luke said. 'We're not here for a scrap. If you're pinged – sorry, Eth, spotted – just get out as fast as possible.'

'But if you do run into someone,' added Johnny, 'you just hit them bloody hard and run away. Got it?'

'Yeah,' said Ethan.

Luke folded up the map and got to his feet. 'Johnny, you take point.'

Johnny grabbed his bergen and jogged off into the dark. Ethan swung his own bergen onto his back and joined the rest of the team as they followed in quick pursuit.

Having made their way through the trees, hiding their rigs on the way, Ethan and the team now stood staring across the open ground to the castle on the clifftop. To Ethan, the ruins looked like a set of huge broken teeth scattered across the horizon. Kat pulled out some binos and handed them to him. They were the same as the ones The Dude had given him at the antenna.

'Check out the castle, Eth. Tell us what's up there.'

Ethan trained the binos on the ruins. 'There's one tower still standing,' he said after a moment, keen to make his description as clear as possible. 'The wall is nothing more than a pile of stones, but there's a large section completely missing, creating a huge hole. Through the hole, inside the ruins, I can see a large tent and some lights.'

'I'm guessing the tent is where the meeting is taking place and probably where the disk is being looked at,' said Kat.

'Security?' asked Luke.

'Nothing obvious,' Ethan replied.

'This is probably a makeshift rendezvous,' said Luke. 'They won't have done much prep of the site because they won't be expecting anyone to know they're here.'

'Gate-crashing,' said Johnny. 'One of my favourite pastimes.'

Ethan was about to lower the binos when he saw

movement. 'Hold on,' he said. 'I can see two guards. They're standing at the large hole in the wall.'

'Let me have a look,' said Kat, and he handed over the binos.

'The x-rays look more like doormen than anything to worry about,' she said. 'They're carrying, though. Both have M4 carbines.'

'Hardly surprising,' said Johnny. 'Even though they aren't expecting visitors, that doesn't mean they're going to come out here with nothing but a toothbrush.'

'The M4 is a variant of the better-known M16,' Luke told Ethan. 'It's been used in Afghanistan and Iraq.' He looked at the rest of the team. 'If those two are anything to go by, we can expect anyone else we spot to be carrying as well. The one advantage we have is that, as Johnny said, they're probably not expecting visitors. This place is miles from the mainland. If anyone was coming, they'd count on hearing them.'

'Unless they happened to drop from the sky,' said Johnny happily.

'All the same, we'll need to get rid of those two guards before we do anything else,' said Luke. 'If they spot us, the mission is screwed, and so are we. Kat, Natalya – you OK for that?'

Ethan saw the girls nod. Kat was still staring through the binos.

'See anything else?' asked Johnny.

'No,' said Kat. 'Nothing. Hang on . . .'

Everyone heard the hesitation in her voice.

'What is it, Kat?' asked Luke. 'What you got?'

'Birds,' she replied. 'Helicopters. Over to the right, just in front of some more woodland.'

Luke took the binos from Kat, had a look, then passed them on.

Ethan could just make out some oddly shaped silhouettes far off to the right and away from the castle. If Kat hadn't said anything, he'd never have known they were helicopters; in the dark, they simply looked like strange bits of the shadowy landscape.

'Three of them,' said Kat, taking the binos back. 'Gabe told us Sam said there were more people here than they'd originally thought. That's why he called for backup. That's why we're here. Seems they turned up in style.'

'What's the problem?' asked Ethan. 'Why would a few more people make any difference to Sam?'

'Stealing a disk from under the noses of three or four people is one thing,' said Luke. 'Doing it in a crowd is some-thing else entirely. Chances of getting pinged are pretty high.'

'But there was no mention of the birds,' said Natalya. 'Gabe would have told us.'

'I know,' said Luke, 'and that's what's worrying me.'

'You think this is more serious than we thought?' asked Ethan.

'Exactly,' said Luke. 'I'm guessing there's more people at this party than either Gabe or Sam realized. And that's going to make our job even harder. We're going to have to be damned careful just to avoid being slotted.'

Slotted, Ethan knew, meant *shot*. For a few seconds everyone was quiet.

Johnny broke the silence. 'There's no point dwelling on it,' he said. 'We need to get on with the job in hand, finish it and extract ourselves – and Sam. Right?'

Everyone nodded.

'Good,' he went on. 'So let's focus on what's really important, shall we?'

'What's that then?' asked Ethan.

Johnny smiled. 'How soon we get to blow shit up . . .'

28

Ethan couldn't help but notice that Luke was the natural leader. OK, so he had perhaps three or four years on most of the others, but there was also something else about him – a quiet confidence they all trusted utterly.

'Right,' he told them, 'this is what we're going to do. First we deal with those two x-rays up there. Then Ethan and Johnny head for the beach, secure it, sort out the canoes and contact the sub. Avoid the clear ground in front of the ruins. Go through the woods to the right of the helicopters, OK? And take some of the Claymores.'

Luke turned to Natalya and Kat. 'You two will lay the diversionary explosives, draw attention away from what Sam's got to do.'

'Just a minute,' said Johnny. 'Don't I get to blow stuff up too?'

'No,' said Luke, and ignored Johnny's obvious disappointment. 'The beach will need to be secure. That's down to you and Ethan. You'll have the Claymores anyway; just remember to point the damned things towards the enemy, OK? They'll make a nasty mess of you if you get it wrong.'

'But the explosives,' said Johnny, doing his best to sound sad. 'I'll miss the pretty lights . . .'

'Oh, you'll still see them, I'm sure,' said Kat. 'Isn't that right, Natalya?'

Natalya nodded, and Ethan saw a grin on her face.

'Anyway,' said Luke, 'Natalya's the queen of explosives. I trust her not to blow us all up in the process, whereas you might just get a little carried away.'

Johnny looked sorrowfully at Ethan. 'I hate to admit it, but it's a fair point,' he said.

'What about you?' asked Ethan, looking at Luke. He wanted to know what everyone was doing, get all the details straight in his mind and understand his place in all of it.

'Once Kat and Natalya have set everything off, I'll turn my attention to the tent. I've enough flash bangs and smoke grenades to have them wandering around in a daze for hours.'

Ethan didn't want to ask if that was a joke.

'That way,' Luke continued, 'Sam – wherever he is right now – will have plenty of cover and confusion to find the disk and get out.'

'Then we're out of here, right?' said Johnny.

'Absolutely,' agreed Luke. 'We'll paddle out from the

beach and the sub will be waiting. Nice and simple. Questions?'

There was silence.

Then Johnny said, 'Isn't this the bit in the movie where somebody says something like "Let's rock and roll"?'

And Ethan saw a glimmer of excitement on the face of the unshakable Luke. 'Yes,' he said, and turned to Natalya and Kat. 'We need those x-rays out of the way. And it needs to be done silently. Let's rock and roll.'

Natalya and Kat disappeared into the darkness between them and the castle, two black shapes slipping away through the long grass.

Luke turned to Ethan and handed him the binos. 'Watch,' he said.

Ethan focused the binoculars and brought the shadowy image of the castle ruins up nice and clear.

Nothing.

Then something: a faint blur of dark against more dark. He had them – the girls edging forward. He lifted the binos a little; spotted the two doormen outside the tent. He could see them quite clearly in the faint glow of light coming from inside. They were smoking, talking. One laughed, the other joined in.

Then they were gone.

Ethan scanned left, right, looked back. No. They had definitely gone. He lowered the binos and looked back at Johnny and Luke. 'What the hell did they just do?'

'Ask the girls yourself,' said Luke. 'Here they come now.'

Kat appeared at Ethan's side. 'Right,' she said. 'What's next?'

Ethan looked at her and Natalya. Neither of them were out of breath. 'What did you do – with the guards? Where are they?'

Natalya looked at him, cocked her head to one side. 'They are asleep, Ethan,' she said. 'Like big babies. And how the fat one snores!'

Kat laughed, and Johnny and Luke joined in.

'But they were armed,' said Ethan. 'You could've been shot.'

'And I could've died if you hadn't jumped out of the plane after me at FreeFall,' said Kat. 'Life's just full of surprises, isn't it?'

'I guess so.'

'The tent's pretty full,' Kat went on. 'Lots of chatter, the chinking of glasses. They're definitely not expecting visitors. The two guards were the only ones about outside. Everyone else is in the tent.'

'Right,' said Luke. 'Watches. We meet at the beach in exactly thirty minutes – on my mark.' He paused, then, 'Three, two, one . . . mark.'

Everyone clicked their watches.

Johnny turned to Natalya. 'Claymores,' he said.

Ethan watched as she crouched down to allow Johnny access to the bergen on her back. He could see how it saved time doing it this way, and meant she was able to react swiftly if something happened, without having to pull the bergen back on if they had to bolt.

Johnny took what he needed and turned to Ethan. 'Ready to go play?'

* * *

Together they ran quickly through the thick woodland, making for the path to the beach.

Ethan noticed that Johnny was weaving across the ground, dodging bushes, being careful to make no sound. Ethan did his best to step where Johnny stepped; he didn't want to make mistakes, not now. Jumping from a plane was one thing; getting shot at was another matter entirely.

Odd shadows loomed ahead and Johnny slowed. Ethan peered through the trees and saw the helicopters.

'Other than skydiving, a helicopter is the only way to fly,' Johnny muttered, then set off again, weaving left and right.

The woodland eventually thinned, and Ethan could just make out the sound of the sea in the distance.

Johnny had stopped. 'We're here. There's the path.'

Ethan looked and saw it stretching ahead – carved out of the cliff itself, at times dipping in under an overhang. It certainly wasn't for the faint-hearted. He could hear waves slipping over pebbles somewhere far below.

Johnny led the way along the path, but stopped again a few minutes later.

'What's wrong?' asked Ethan. 'Did you hear something?'

'No,' said Johnny. 'Just wait here, OK?' And without another word, he disappeared, heading back in the direction of the helicopters.

Finding himself alone, Ethan quickly checked the land-scape. The path didn't exactly lend itself to playing hide-and-seek, but just a few metres on he spotted what looked like a landslide partly covering the track. He decided he'd be better off hiding in the shadows than standing out on a narrow cliff path, so he jogged on down to the landslide and made himself as invisible as possible.

For the first few minutes he focused on what he and Johnny had to do when they got to the beach. He was looking forward to seeing what the canoes were like and how a mine was laid – though he hoped he wouldn't get to see one in action. But then, as the minutes ticked by, Ethan started to wonder what Johnny was up to – going off on his own had never been a part of the plan..What was he supposed to do if something went wrong and Johnny didn't come back?

But just then he heard something further up the track. Ethan peered out from his hiding place, fully expecting to see Johnny heading his way. But it wasn't Johnny: two men suddenly emerged from the shadows above him – and he had nowhere to go, nowhere at all.

29

They came slowly down the path. Ethan pressed himself into the cliff face, stretched out his arms, tried to become a part of the rock. Even so, he knew the landslide wouldn't hide him if the guys came much closer.

And if Johnny came back, he'd walk right into them, and then they'd really be in the shit.

Ethan could hear his heart racing. It felt like it was trying to smack its way out of his chest. The blood was drumming in his ears – he was surprised the two x-rays couldn't hear it. But he forced himself to focus on what was going on. Panicking would do nothing, he knew that. What he had to do was think of a solution.

The two men stopped, and Ethan saw a light flash as one

lit a cigarette, passed it to his mate, then lit one more. And in that brief moment of brightness he spotted their weapons. He didn't care what sort of weapons they were, just that things were now more than serious – one slip-up and he was dead.

The cigarette smoke caught on the wind, drifted down past Ethan. He could smell it, taste it. He nearly coughed, but managed to stop himself.

Then they just stood there, talking, only metres away from him. Their voices were clear, but he couldn't understand what they were saying; whatever language they were using, it certainly wasn't English. One of the men put his cigarette out, then nodded down the path.

Ethan realized they were going to continue on down to the beach, and the only way for them to do that was past him – in which case he'd be discovered for sure. He remembered how important it was for the team to remain unseen on this mission. Now was not the time to pick a fight with two armed men on a narrow cliff path. He had to do something else.

One of the men started off towards him, but the other stopped him, handed him another cigarette and a small hipflask. They both laughed.

Ethan knew this was his last chance – either he made a move now, or he waited to be discovered. He glanced around. The path disappeared into darkness, and he wondered about slipping on towards the beach himself, but then he remembered Johnny. OK, so the idiotic, egotistical bastard had left him in the lurch, but that was no reason for him to go and do the same. He had to get out of here, make his way past the x-rays, and warn Johnny they were there – before he came running back down the path and got them both killed.

Ethan sized up the situation. There was no way he could slip past the men. The track was barely wide enough for two people, never mind another trying to hide in the shadows. So what the hell was he going to do?

He let his head fall back as he tried to think – and saw the cliff face rising above him. It was jagged and rough. It was *climbable*!

He had to climb; it was the only way.

Ethan slipped further down the path, further into the darkness, so that the men wouldn't hear him. Eventually he could no longer see them, so he turned to face the rock, found some hand-holds, and started up.

The rock was cold and cut into his hands, but at least the holds were large and easy. It wasn't long before he was well off the path, but a glance upwards made him realize just how dangerous a position he was now in. The cliff stretched on up into the dark and he had no idea if the climbing got harder. Still, he had little choice but to press on. He kept climbing, trying to ignore the heavy bergen on his back, which threatened to drag him backwards off the cliff-face.

Adrenaline was surging through him, but so was fear. The HAHO jump had been fine, but this? It felt mildly insane. Ethan had never done much climbing before – having to do it soundlessly, in case he got shot at, sure focused the mind. At the same time, he was aware of the minutes slipping by: surely Johnny would be back any minute. He had to move faster, reach the clifftop and get back round to the start of the path so that he could head Johnny off and stop everything from going tits up.

But then he heard the voices of the two x-rays directly below him. He stopped, hugged the cliff, didn't move. If he dislodged a stone onto the men below, he knew he was dead. They wouldn't wait for him to climb down; they'd just shoot him off the cliff.

Then his left foot slipped.

Ethan caught himself before he fell, but the sound of his foot scraping against the rock seemed loud enough to wake the dead.

For a few moments he stayed where he was, a shadow on the rock, hoping to God that the two men below had moved on far enough not to have noticed the noise. He strained his ears to hear their voices, and was relieved that they sounded more distant now.

Ethan knew there was no more time to lose. He started climbing again, powering upwards as fast as he could go – foot . . . hand . . . foot . . . hand . . .

He felt no fear now, only determination. Just because the men had headed down to the beach didn't mean they wouldn't be coming back up again in a few minutes' time.

At last Ethan could see the top of the cliff. A little further and then he was pulling himself up over the edge and onto the flat ground. He didn't give himself a moment to think about what he'd just done or get his breath back; instead he jumped up and ran as quickly and quietly as possible to the top of the path.

He was only a few metres from it when he saw movement up ahead. It was just a blur, a shadow moving quickly through other shadows, but he instantly recognized Johnny. Ethan knew that unless he stopped him now, Johnny would be racing down the path, totally unaware of the two x-rays below. So he did the only thing he could.

He jumped, the weight of the bergen on his back adding momentum.

For the split second that he was in the air, Ethan felt like every sense was heightened. He could hear the waves crashing on the beach below. He could taste the tang of the sea in the air around him, even smell the damp rock he'd been climbing.

Then he crashed into Johnny – hard, tumbling him backwards into a hellishly prickly bush. Before Johnny had a chance to struggle or shout, Ethan wrapped himself round him, slapped his hand over his mouth and pulled him deeper into the bush.

Johnny struggled, but Ethan had him fast.

'It's me,' he hissed. 'Where the hell have you been?'

He felt Johnny relax and immediately let his friend go.

'I had something to do,' said Johnny. 'What's up?'

'Two x-rays on the path,' replied Ethan, and he knew he sounded pissed off. 'I had to do something to stop you running into them and getting us both killed. You shouldn't have left me.'

Johnny looked at Ethan, surprise in his eyes. 'You were OK, weren't you? You're alive!'

'Not the point,' said Ethan. 'We work as a team, remember? This isn't the goddamn Johnny Show.'

Johnny nodded. 'Point taken. So what were you doing on top of the cliff?'

'The x-rays came after you went,' said Ethan. 'I had to climb over them to reach you.'

251

'So they're still down there now?'

Ethan nodded.

Johnny looked thoughtful. 'OK,' he said. 'You've seen them. You've got a better idea of the situation than I have. What are our options?'

'They're armed,' said Ethan, the images as clear as day in his mind, 'so we don't want to take them on. I think we need a diversion – something to draw them away so that we can get down to the beach.'

'Like what?' asked Johnny.

As if in answer to his question, an explosion ripped through the air, lighting up the night around them as flames and shockwaves blasted across the island.

'That'll do,' said Ethan, and he could feel himself smiling.

30

A second shockwave hit them as another explosion followed the first. Ethan had never heard anything like it in his life. He could smell burning in the air, his ears were ringing, and he could feel his teeth tingling, as if the shockwaves were jarring every last part of him.

'What the hell are they using?' he hissed. 'Are the explosions supposed to be that big?'

'Sam wants a diversion, that's what he gets,' said Johnny.

Ethan heard the sound of running feet. 'Down!' he hissed, and pulled Johnny further into the bush.

The two x-rays shot up from the cliff path, racing towards the explosion.

'You really have to stop hugging me,' said Johnny as Ethan

let go of him again. 'I've told you before, you're not my type.'

'And you've really got to start taking this seriously,' Ethan replied. 'I can't be arsed with getting killed tonight.' He looked around. 'The path's clear. Let's go!'

Without giving Johnny a chance to argue, he bolted from the bush, dragging his friend with him. He gave a quick glance up towards where the explosions had come from. He could hear people running around in panic, screaming at each other.

Another explosion lit up the night, followed by the sound of gunfire.

'Come on!' shouted Ethan.

They took off down the path.

'You climbed up that?' said Johnny, glancing up at the cliff face rising above them. 'You're more of an idiot than I thought!'

'You didn't give me much choice,' said Ethan as they raced onto the beach. The crunching of the pebbles and sand underfoot sounded like they were running over Rice Krispies.

Ethan took off his bergen, dropped it to the ground and opened it. He pulled out two large square packages and handed them to Johnny. Then he glanced at the sea. It was dark and oily and he could see the white crests of waves falling into each other. The sky was a thick canvas of black, speckled with stars and flecked with cloud, the moon high. *Out there*, he thought, *is a submarine coming to lift me off this island. Is any of this really happening?*

But there was no time to think about that now. Ethan turned to see Johnny opening one of the packages.

'These are the canoes,' he said. 'Rip that one open, will you?'

Ethan knelt down and tore open the other package. He pulled out what looked like a bundle of tightly packed, rubberized canvas. 'Please don't tell me we have to blow these up ourselves,' said Ethan.

Johnny laughed. 'Automatic inflation,' he said. 'Like a life raft. They're up in seconds. Pull that tab there.'

Ethan looked where Johnny pointed and saw a yellow strap. He pulled it hard and the canoe ballooned in front of him as air rippled through it.

'Cool, eh?' said Johnny. 'Now put these together.'

He handed Ethan a pouch and opened another himself.

'Paddles,' he said. 'They clip together like tent poles. See?' He held up a finished paddle.

'You look so proud.' Ethan watched his friend clip together the remaining poles from the pouch to form a second paddle.

'It's the little things that keep me happy,' said Johnny; then he stood up and pulled something from his own bergen. 'I'm going to secure the area,' he said.

'Are they the Claymores?' Ethan asked, having clipped together the poles in his own pouch to make two further paddles.

'Yes. Nasty mix of explosive and ball bearings. If anyone comes in as we're escaping, they'll trigger them. Just be sure to look the other way if they go off. It's not a pretty sight.'

'Thanks for the advice,' said Ethan, hoping he wouldn't get to see one of the things in action.

Johnny ran off across the beach, keeping as low as he could. He set the Claymores and was back in a couple of minutes. Ethan wondered how he made everything look so easy, but as he came back, pebbles and sand exploded in a line across the canoes.

'Down!' Johnny screamed, and jumped on Ethan, throwing him to the ground.

Only then did Ethan hear the gunfire. 'Someone's shooting at us!' he yelled.

'Just keep your head down!' Johnny shouted back.

Another strafe of bullets zipped past, and Johnny rolled Ethan and himself out of the way just in time.

Ethan could smell the tang of the bullets smashing pebbles as the crack of gunfire ripped the air apart. He could hear the rounds thumping into the sand – and feel them too, the shockwaves from the impact making the ground ripple like it was alive underneath him.

'Too bloody close,' screamed Johnny. 'Less than a metre away to feel it like that. Keep fucking moving! We need to get back up that path. This exit is totally screwed!'

Ethan saw him glance up and down the beach to see where the shooting was coming from. The sea was behind them, the path somewhere in front.

'Follow me,' said Johnny. 'Go where I go. I know where the Claymores are; you don't. Got it?'

Ethan nodded and they crawled forward towards the path. He was soon able to make it out, carved into the cliff face. He willed himself on; forced himself not to think about the bullets flying above him or of the hidden mines somewhere on the beach.

Then more rounds came in. Johnny looked at Ethan and pointed left down the beach. 'Two x-rays coming from over there,' he yelled.

Ethan chanced a look and saw two men running towards them. One of them fired again, this time missing by a mile, thankfully.

'Get your head down,' shouted Johnny, grabbing Ethan and pushing him face-down in the sand, 'or there'll be nothing left of it but pink mist!'

As Ethan ducked, he heard one of the Claymore mines explode off to their left between them and the approaching x-rays. For a second it was like sheet lightning and the beach blasted into light; then the blaze was gone and they were back in moonlit darkness.

The sound was deafening, and Ethan looked up to see the bodies of their attackers falling through the air. He knew they were dead before they hit the ground. They hadn't even had a chance to scream.

They pushed on. The path was only metres away now. Then came more shooting, this time from the right, and Ethan could see another two men charging towards them, yelling, firing.

He looked at Johnny, who reached into his pack and pulled out two grey canisters. He gave one to Ethan. 'Pull the pin and throw it towards them!' he shouted.

Ethan did exactly as he was told, and they both lobbed the canisters over.

There were two explosions, and the two men disappeared in a cloud of thick white smoke.

'Move it!' yelled Johnny, and Ethan chased after him as he heard more firing from behind.

They reached the bottom of the path and just kept on running. Somehow Ethan's legs kept pumping hard

– he didn't know where the energy was coming from.

The cliff exploded around them as bullets ricocheted above their heads, sending out sharp splinters of rock. But Ethan didn't feel a thing – he was focused on getting to the top of the path. He'd never run so fast in his life.

As they emerged at the clifftop, another explosion sounded from behind them on the beach. Ethan guessed what it was. 'Another Claymore?'

Johnny nodded. 'Horribly effective, I'm afraid.' Then he squeezed the communicator round his neck. 'Guys! Can you hear me?'

Ethan heard the voices of Luke, Kat and Natalya reply with a simple 'Yes'.

'Beach is shagged,' said Johnny. 'Meet at the watchtower in five.'

Ethan looked at him. 'We're BASE jumping?'

Johnny grinned. 'Fun, this, isn't it?'

31

Ethan wasn't given a chance to argue: Johnny simply sprinted off, and he had to try and keep up.

They followed a wide arc around the ruins to the watch-tower behind. Another explosion tore the air, and the light from it brought the castle into sharp focus. Ethan could see that the diversion was having the desired effect. Whoever had stolen the disk was now convinced they were under attack. Ethan could see that the way the explosions had been laid gave the impression that someone was firing explosive rounds at the ruins from the other side of the island – and getting progressively closer as they homed in on their target. X-rays were milling about, firing wildly in the direction they believed the explosions were coming from. They had no idea that they were just charges going off at set intervals.

The air was filled with the smell of burning and cordite and the sound of weapons' fire and shouting. Ethan hoped the diversion had given Sam enough time to do what he had to do.

Then, as the flat ground disappeared and the ruins loomed up on their left, a man wearing an expensive leather jacket and carrying a weapon ran out through a gap in the walls and barged straight into Johnny. They both went down.

Ethan watched them tumble to the ground, rolling away from the ruins and towards the bushes that led to the cliffs. He heard the man's gun clatter on some rocks and hoped that he'd dropped it, but then saw that he'd managed to keep hold of it despite the fall. The man scrambled to his feet, raised the weapon and took aim at Johnny.

Instinct kicked in and Ethan launched himself, feet first, at the man's hand. Whether it was the sensible thing to do or not, he didn't care; if he didn't do something, he knew Johnny would be dead.

He heard bones smash as his foot connected with the man's hand and sent the gun spinning off into the dark. There was a shrill scream. Ethan's unexpected attack had given Johnny enough time to get to his feet and launch an attack of his own. But the man was quick, dodging to the right and catching Johnny, throwing him over and onto his back. Johnny cried out, briefly winded, and Ethan went in again with his other boot, this time to the man's stomach. The guy doubled over and retched – just as something smacked into the side of his head with a dull thud. He fell backwards and hit the ground.

Ethan stared down at him, ready for another attack, but he wasn't moving; blood was pooling beneath his head, leaking into the grass.

Johnny was on his feet again, looking quickly left and right. 'Move it,' he said, and grabbed Ethan's arm to pull him on.

'What happened?' asked Ethan.

'Stray bullet,' said Johnny. 'He was probably shot accidentally by one of his mates. But we have to get out of here. We don't want to get caught in the crossfire either.'

'It wasn't a stray,' said a voice from the ruins, and both Ethan and Johnny turned to see a large, familiar figure emerge from the darkness.

'Sam,' said Johnny.

Ethan spotted the machine gun in Sam's hands. He even recognized what it was: an MP5 – as used by the SAS. Sam looked terrifying. Like the rest of the team, he was head to toe in black, his face streaked with grey and white camouflage, like bits of the night had snagged on him. His knuckles were bloodied. He was also wearing a small back-pack that Ethan recognized as a BASE rig. He'd come prepared for every eventuality.

'No time for pleasantries,' he said. 'We need to get to the watchtower now. Move it!'

Ethan felt Sam grab his shoulder and drag him away from the body. 'Come on, Eth,' he said. 'Nothing you can do for him. Let's go.'

Ethan forced his legs to move and fell into step behind Johnny. They ran round the castle ruins and soon reached the watchtower. Luke, Natalya and Kat were waiting for them.

'What happened?' asked Luke.

'Must be another way to the beach,' said Johnny. 'Path was clear – we sorted the boats – then we were being shot at. Claymore took care of two x-rays. Two more chased us up the path. Then they ran into another Claymore. What about you?'

Luke made to speak, but then another explosion slammed across the island. Ethan was stunned by the sound of this one; it was the biggest of the night so far and thundered around them, the initial blast followed by a rumble of other smaller explosions. Everyone in the team ducked, half expecting to be covered in debris.

'What the hell was that?' asked Kat.

'Wasn't one of mine,' Luke told her.

'It wouldn't be,' said Johnny.

Everyone turned.

'Let's just say that they won't be able to leave the island in a hurry,' Johnny said smugly.

'The helicopters!' said Ethan. '*That's* where you went!'

Johnny nodded. 'I took the P4 and some detonators from Nat just in case an opportunity presented itself. And the helicopters were a pretty big opportunity. Couldn't resist it.'

The explosions continued to rattle on as the helicopters slowly disintegrated, ribbons of fire leaping into the air like dancers at a night-time rave.

'Right,' said Sam. 'Time to go. Johnny? Luke?'

Ethan watched as Johnny and Luke slipped off their bergens and opened them, pulling out the BASE rigs and life-jackets and handing them to the rest of the team. As Ethan took his, he saw Sam pull a lifejacket of his own from a pouch on his belt.

'The lifejackets will inflate on impact with the water,' said Sam. 'Each one has a beacon. When you hit the water, get out of your rig, locate the rest of the team and get into a circle. Luke, contact the sub and tell them what's happening. They need to know we're coming from the cliff, not the beach.' He turned back to the others. 'Ready?'

Ethan pulled on his rig and lifejacket. He double-checked every clip, holding the drogue chute in his hand. The last time he'd worn a canopy this small was when he'd flown a Raider. He remembered then how Johnny had described them – fast and scary. Much like what I'm doing now, he thought.

'Let me,' said Kat, and checked him over. 'It's not as difficult as it looks,' she told him. 'And these cliffs are way higher than the antenna Johnny and I jumped from. You'll be fine.'

'That makes me feel so much better,' said Ethan with a nod, face deadly serious. He didn't know whether to believe her or not. But it didn't matter; he had no choice. If he didn't jump from the cliff, he was dead. It was a no-brainer.

He turned, saw Sam looking at him.

'So, Ethan, you ready for your first BASE jump?'

Ethan was about to answer when shots rang out, cutting him off. He turned, spotted a group of men charging towards them from the castle.

'Move it!' yelled Sam.

Johnny looked at Ethan. 'Life's too short not to!' he said, turned and charged towards the cliff edge. He disappeared without a sound, then a loud whoop and the crack of the canopy opening told Ethan he was fine.

Kat went next, quickly followed by Luke and Natalya.

Ethan heard each canopy grab air as they threw out their drogue chutes.

'It's a piece of piss,' said Sam, looking at him. 'Just run like hell, jump as far as you can, and throw out your drogue chute. Now go!'

Ethan remembered what Johnny had told him when he'd watched him and Kat do their BASE jump. He visualized it, did his best to recall what he'd seen through the binos as Kat had leaped into nothing. Suddenly shots peppered the ground near his feet. He didn't think any more; he ran.

Then he was at the cliff edge and jumping into the darkness, chucking his drogue chute out as hard as he could. He expected to feel it grab air instantly, pull out his main canopy.

It didn't.

It threw him head over arse. And now he was piling towards whatever rocks lay below him, head-first. This was nothing like a skydive.

He tumbled, tried to stabilize, but it didn't feel right. He was falling too slowly. It felt like he'd fallen off a diving board. When the hell was he going to pick up enough speed to allow his drogue to grab air and pull out his main canopy?

Panic burst in Ethan's skull. He forced himself to ignore it. He could hear the windrush getting faster – he was picking up speed.

But the increased speed still wasn't enough: he still wasn't stable.

Shit . . .

He ran through everything he'd done, from clipping the rig on, to jumping far enough from the cliff, to throwing out the chute. He'd done it to the letter. No detail missed. Not a god-damned thing.

I'm dead . . .

Then the canopy blasted open above him. He looked up, checked everything, steered himself away from the cliff. For a split second he forgot what he was doing and pulled a steering toggle too hard. He nearly turned himself back into the cliff. But his reactions were so sharp now that he pulled away in time. Moments later, he had the canopy under control and was zipping through the dark, the cold sea air clammy on his skin, leaving salt on his lips.

Above him, Ethan heard Sam's canopy grab air. It was soon followed by the sound of gunfire from the clifftop. But there was nothing he could do about that now; he just had to get into the ocean and hope the sub found them all.

Ahead he spotted the rest of the team. The night was dying now and light was spilling over the horizon, making the sea visible below.

Another sound chugged into the air, and Ethan spotted the tiny dot of a boat heading out from the island. It was still a fair distance away, but the men were shooting anyway. They had obviously seen the team jump from the clifftop and were now heading directly for them.

More gunfire cracked through the air. Ethan could see that the boat was zigzagging across the water, and he guessed it was searching for them. He realized they couldn't be seen – not yet anyway. But that didn't stop him feeling helpless. Like the rest of the team, he had no choice but to keep on gliding until he touched down in the sea. Then he had to hope that the x-rays in the boat wouldn't be able to find them before the sub arrived – and that the ones on the cliff couldn't see them well enough to pick them off like fat geese.

Ethan heard a splash, quickly followed by three more. That meant that the only ones left in the air were him and Sam.

The boat was clearer now, no longer a dot, and he could make out two men in it. They had stopped zigzagging and were heading straight for the point where Ethan had heard the team drop into the water; they must have heard them too. They were on a collision course.

Without hesitation, Ethan pulled hard on his steering lines, altered course. He knew there was no point just piling into the water with the rest of the team. The men in the boat would be on them in a moment, and then they'd all be dead. He had to intercept the boat before it reached them. If he could get to it first and put it out of action, they'd have a chance of surviving till the sub arrived. It would be a gamble; he'd have to time it just right, come in fast enough to slam into the two x-rays and take them out of the equation. Perhaps it wouldn't work. Perhaps they'd see him coming in and shoot him, but he figured it was better to die trying than to wait in the sea like a sitting duck. His friends were depending on him. That was all that mattered.

He gritted his teeth, focused on the boat, increased his speed, and felt the acceleration push him down into his rig. He could see that one man was armed and firing ahead, but the bouncing of the boat on the waves was sending his aim all over the place, and in spite of the crazy thing Ethan was about to do – or perhaps because of it – this brought a smile to his face.

Besides, flying at night across open water made him feel like he was a part of the wind itself. The slightest change and he could react to it immediately, feeling everything through the canopy and steering lines. He was flying instinctively now, everything was second nature, the canopy as much a part of him as his own body. That was enough to make anyone smile.

The boat was just ahead of him. He was coming in from the side – and he was low, real low. Swooping. He could see the waves below him. The x-rays hadn't spotted him, not yet. One was driving, one firing, his rounds spraying across the water.

Ethan drew closer, lower, the sea only metres away. Then the man with the gun turned to reload his weapon – and spotted Ethan. Their eyes locked. They both knew one of them was going to come out of this badly. It was all a matter of timing.

Ethan pulled his feet up, played with the steering lines to pick up any extra speed he could from the wind. He had a split second to adjust his course and get himself on target. He realized he was too low; the sea was so close now he could practically tiptoe across the waves.

The man in the boat pulled out his magazine, snapped a new one into place.

Ethan sensed the wind through the steering lines, pulled the tiniest bit, and flicked himself up just enough to skim over the edge of the boat.

The man raised the gun, but Ethan's boots slammed into his head just as he pulled the trigger. Ethan heard the bullets zip past him and felt the man's head give way under his feet.

There was a sickening crunch and the guy was thrown back-wards off the boat and into the sea.

Ethan didn't have time to think about what he'd done; the sea rose up and he was in it, the cold of the water pulling the air from his lungs. Then the lifesaver exploded, and his head popped up above the waves. As quickly as he could, he ripped off his rig.

'Ethan!'

He looked up, salt stinging his eyes, and saw Johnny swimming over.

'You OK?'

Ethan nodded.

'That was unbelievable!' said Johnny. 'How the hell did you ride in so accurately? Swoop of the fucking century, mate! Unreal!'

Ethan said nothing, still unable to speak after the shock of hitting the cold water.

More shots rang out. Ethan turned to see Sam coming in. The one remaining man on the boat looked up, but Sam already had him in his sights. He opened fire and sent the guy tumbling over his seat to hang over the side of the boat like a marionette with its strings cut.

Then Sam was in the water.

'What about the bloke I hit?' said Ethan. 'Where is he?'

Johnny pointed out to sea. 'Fish food,' he said. 'With the speed you were doing, you probably broke his neck. Are you sure you're OK?'

Ethan nodded, unable to find his voice, then saw Sam pull himself out of the water and into the boat. Sam tipped the body into the sea. 'May as well make use of the boat and get out of the water till the sub arrives,' he shouted.

Ethan and Johnny swam over, and Sam helped them out of the water – then picked up Luke, Kat and Natalya.

'Well done, Ethan,' said Sam, sitting down in the boat. 'You probably just saved all our lives. That was quite something.'

Ethan didn't say anything; couldn't. All he could think about was the bloke he'd smashed into.

The bloke he'd killed.

He hadn't intended to kill him. He'd just acted instinctively to save the lives of his friends. But the sobering fact of the man's death chilled him more than the sea. Ethan didn't know what to feel except cold and numb.

A hand fell on his shoulder. 'Sam's right. You saved everyone's lives,' said Johnny. 'If you hadn't done what you did, we'd all be dead. Even you. Remember that. It was him or everyone else.'

'But I killed him,' said Ethan, the thought making him feel sick. He put his head over the side of the boat and threw up.

Sam came up behind him. 'You had no choice – you know that, don't you?'

Ethan nodded.

'There's no such thing as a good death, but sometimes, when your hand is forced, tough decisions have to be made. And you made the right one.'

'If I'd known I was going to end up killing someone . . .' said Ethan, but his voice drifted away. He didn't know what to say.

'Our aim is always to leave as clean as we go in,' said Sam. 'We're not about charging in, guns blazing. To be frank, this went tits up. But you, Ethan . . . well, you saved it from becoming a total screw-up. You should be proud. Not happy, but proud. It's different.'

Ethan looked at him. The man talked sense and he didn't piss around trying to make you feel better just for the sake of it. He liked that. 'I just hope something like that never happens again,' he said.

'We all do,' said Sam. 'But we also need to be ready in case it does.'

Luke looked over at Ethan. 'They'd have probably run us down first before shooting us. Either way, we wouldn't have stood a chance. You did the right thing.'

'You think so?'

'Know so,' said Sam. 'Feeling better?'

Ethan nodded.

Sam turned and pushed the throttle forward, taking them further out to sea.

Ahead, Ethan could see something breaking through the surface of the waves: a large grey shape pushing through the water like a whale.

The sub.

32

Inside the sub it was warm and dry. Ethan couldn't believe the size of the thing: it was like a small town. The captain had welcomed them on board as though they were about to set off on a cruise, all smiles and how-do-you-dos. They were taken to dry off, and given a change of clothes. Kat and Natalya had their own cabin to change in, but now all the team members were back together, drinking steaming hot mugs of sweet tea.

Ethan was still in a state of shock. The whole experience had been so extreme that he just didn't know how to deal with it. It had been the most insane day of his life.

'You did well,' Sam told him. 'All of you did.'

'So the mission was a success then?' asked Ethan.

Sam nodded. 'Totally.'

'What about a debrief?' asked Luke.

'We'll do that after,' said Sam, sipping his tea.

'After what?' asked Ethan.

Sam grinned. 'The competition.'

'You serious?' said Kat.

'Never more so,' Sam replied. 'We need you there, or people will start asking why you disappeared en route to France.'

'But we're in a sub,' said Ethan. 'At sea. How can we get to the competition now?'

'It's all arranged with the captain,' said Sam. 'We're headed for a naval base just a few miles up the coast. You'll be picked up there and then driven to the competition. You should arrive at about the same time as your luggage. You'll be in good time.'

To Ethan it felt like days had passed since they had left the airport, but he realized that, in reality, it was just a matter of hours – the most intense hours of his entire life. He thought back over it all with excitement and regret. He had no idea if he'd ever get over what had happened to the man on the boat, or if he really wanted to. It was the kind of thing that stayed with you. In that short time he'd done a lot of stuff that he'd never forget – a lot of stuff he would never have thought he could do. But he'd survived it all, and that was saying something. And now he had to get his head round the skydiving competition. The mission was over.

'One more thing,' said Sam. 'You need a team name. Can't have you turning up at a skydiving competition without one, can we? Any ideas?'

Before anyone else had a chance to speak, Ethan said, 'What about "The Raiders"?'

Everyone looked at him.

'Fast and scary, like the canopy,' he said. 'Makes sense to me, anyway.'

'Nice one, Eth,' said Johnny, and everyone nodded.

Even Sam approved.

Ethan was gazing up into a blue sky, holding a pair of binos to his eyes. The mission felt like a distant memory – well, most of it did. Now he'd had a sleep and a meal, and it was mid afternoon. He'd just heard the faint drop in the engine revs of the plane high above the airfield where the skydiving competition was taking place. A second later, he caught sight of someone zipping through the air. He focused the binos, zoomed in, seeing the figure clearly now. He was flying through the air, feet attached to a small surfboard. The figure flipped upside down, started to spin like a corkscrew. Then he was into a somersault, then another. Just watching it gave Ethan an adrenaline rush, made him want to be up there himself.

He kept his binos focused on the skydiver as his canopy burst into life above him. He knew what that felt like, to be riding ahead of the wind, everything so quiet. At last the skydiver swooped into the DZ, zipping past spectators. People cheered and applauded as he completed a perfect landing.

Ethan put down the binos and watched as Johnny pulled off his skydiving helmet, bundled up his canopy and jogged over.

'Nailed it,' he said, grinning. 'So, you going to stick with us then?'

Ethan frowned thoughtfully. In fact, he'd been thinking of nothing else for the past twenty-four hours. It was a big 'jump', he thought, going from being part of a skydiving team to being part of a very different kind of team – one that went on secret missions, did HAHO jumps, used explosives. And saw people being killed. He hadn't expected the killing bit, and he still found it hard to get past. But what did he expect? The work the team did was dangerous. It came with risks. But they were trained for it. They had Sam and Gabe. And now, at the end of the most insane summer Ethan had ever experienced, he had been asked to join them. His options were simple: he either walked away now, back to his normal life and all that it could – or couldn't – offer. Or he sealed the deal and joined the team.

He smiled. He had a feeling it was going to be the easiest decision he'd ever made. Still, it was a big one . . . .

'Don't go all silent on me,' said Johnny. 'I fear the silence. And you must be smiling for a reason. If you don't say something soon, some awful bollocks is going to come out of my mouth and we'll both regret it, trust me.'

Ethan looked back up into the sky. More skydivers were coming in. He was itching for a jump himself.

'You're dangerous people to know,' he said. 'That was some serious shit we went through. I wasn't exactly prepared for it.'

'Isn't that half the fun, though?' said Johnny. 'Not knowing what's round the corner and dealing with it when it turns out to be a ten-foot gorilla, desperate to chew your face off?'

'Your jokes really are crap,' said Ethan. 'We were almost killed.'

They were both silent for a moment, thinking about that.

'I keep getting flashbacks,' he went on. 'To those x-rays who walked into the Claymores on the beach. That guy we were fighting when Sam appeared and shot him. That other guy I kicked off the boat . . .'

'They knew what they were getting into,' said Johnny. 'Run around with a gun trying to kill people and bad things happen. Besides, if we hadn't helped Sam, who knows where that disk would be now, or just how the information on it might have been used? For all we know, we've saved thousands of lives.'

'Still,' said Ethan, 'it's difficult to get it out of my head.'

'I know, Eth,' Johnny said. 'But you can't just focus on that. You also have to realize that you're brilliant. You've got an instinct for this stuff, a knack of doing the right thing regardless of what's going on. You don't get flustered, you don't panic and you're a natural in the air. This is what you were born to do. Don't you feel it? You're what we need. But *we* are also what *you* need.'

Ethan looked at Johnny. Deep down, he knew that what his friend was saying was true. He was right for the team. And the team was right for him. He wasn't just good; when it came to skydiving, dealing with danger, staying calm despite everything going to shit around him, he was a natural. He couldn't explain why. He just was. And being on the team made him feel alive and useful and *valuable* in a way that nothing else in his life ever had.

Johnny said, 'That swoop you did over the boat – it was

unbelievable. And if you'd missed, I'd probably be dead. We wouldn't be having this conversation. Look,' he went on, 'I'm not going to force you into this. No one is. As always, it's down to you, your decision.'

'I know,' said Ethan.

'But what I will say is that we all want you on the team, including Sam. And that's a big deal.'

For a few moments neither of them said anything.

'Well?' said Johnny at last.

'You said you wouldn't force it.'

'I lied.' Johnny let his trademark grin spread across his face. 'What do you say?'

In spite of everything, Ethan couldn't stop grinning back. 'I'm in,' he said, as he'd known he would. Then his grin became a wide smile. 'Life's too short not to.'